THE
NIGHT
COUNTRY

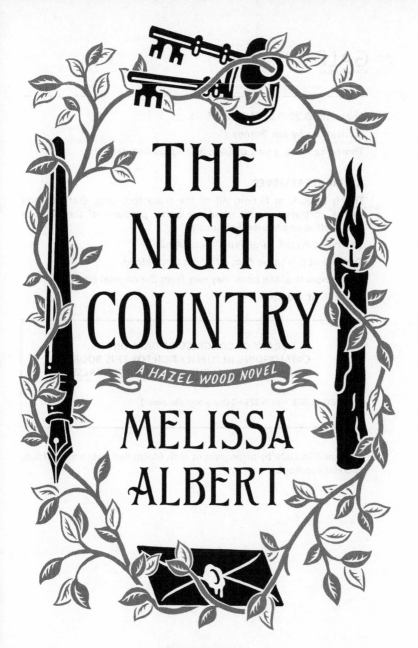

THE
NIGHT
COUNTRY

A HAZEL WOOD NOVEL

MELISSA
ALBERT

THORNDIKE PRESS
A part of Gale, a Cengage Company

GALE
A Cengage Company

Copyright © 2019 by Melissa Albert.

Illustrations by Jim Tierney.

Thorndike Press, a part of Gale, a Cengage Company.

Thorndike Press® Large Print Young Adult

The text of this Large Print edition is unabridged.

Other aspects of the book may vary from the original edition.

Set in 16 pt. Plantin.

LIBRARY OF CONGRESS CIP DATA ON FILE.
CATALOGUING IN PUBLICATION FOR THIS BOOK
IS AVAILABLE FROM THE LIBRARY OF CONGRESS

ISBN-13: 978-1-4328-7238-0 (hardcover alk. paper)

Published in 2020 by arrangement with Macmillan Publishing Group, LLC/Flatiron Books

Printed in Mexico
Print Number: 01   Print Year: 2020

To Michael and Miles,
my one and onlies

I love the company of wolves.

— Angela Carter

~ 1 ~

I was eighteen years old, give or take a fairy-tale century, when I had my first kiss.

I was in my senior year at a school in Brooklyn, where I'd enrolled not long after two twisted-up years in the Hinterland. I craved normal, I craved routine. I had, to be honest, this image of myself wearing a leaf-colored sweater and studying in a wood-paneled library, which was embarrassing to think about later, when I was reading *The Heart Is a Lonely Hunter* beneath our underfunded high school's flickering fluorescents. The only thing that made it all bearable was Sophia Snow.

Maybe *bearable* isn't the right word. She was the only thing that made it *interesting.* Unnerving is another way to put it.

Sophia was an ex-Story like me, another Hinterland reject. Wide eyes and a knotty ballerina build and black hair that moved against itself like water weeds. She had one of those hologram faces, different from every angle, the kind you want to stare at till you've uncovered all its secrets. And by the time you've figured out you never will, she's stolen your wallet from your pocket and your watch off your wrist.

Boys liked Sophia. Not just boys, but it was them she'd meet out, on shitty non-dates that mainly involved drinking and walking around. For a while I'd let her drag me along, because there was a period when I felt like nothing that was of Earth could hurt me. It made me brave, but it also meant I was just a couple clicks shy of feeling numb, *inhuman,* and I wanted to fight that feeling away.

There was this night when we were down by the water. Across the way we could see the geometric glitter of the Financial District, and I was staring at all the little pinprick windows, reminding myself that every light might have a person under it, and every person had a story, and the city was full of people whose lives were nothing like mine. It was supposed to make me feel less alone, I guess, but instead I was thinking that none of those people, not one, could understand what I was, or what I'd seen, or where I came from. The only ones who could, Sophia among them, were broken. Some of them had broken like glass, sharp and glittering, but some had cracked into dusty pieces that the city swept up and away. I was a little bit drunk on warm spiked Coke, wondering which kind I'd turn out to be, and feeling so sorry for myself I should've been ashamed.

One of Sophia's boys — there were three of them that night, two she might've liked plus a hanger-on — sat down next to me. He was one of the main ones, decently hot, with two lines shaved through his eyebrow. That meant something, I thought, but I could never remember what.

We sat for a minute in silence.

"You know, I watch you sometimes."

That didn't deserve a response, so I said nothing.

"You're quiet, but I like that. You've got a lot of soul, right?" He smiled at himself as he said it, in that way guys say those fake-sensitive things they think will make a girl's clothes come flying off. Just because I hadn't been kissed yet didn't mean I hadn't heard some lines.

"What makes you think that?"

"You're so little," he said cryptically. He'd clearly come to the end of his material. "But I can just tell, you've really got a lot of *soul*."

"To be honest, I don't know if I've even got a soul." I said it to the skyline. "If a soul is what makes you human, then I probably don't. Unless a soul is something you can *grow,* like, after the fact. And I don't think it is. So. No soul. Just to explain why your pickup line's not working on me."

It was the truest thing I'd said to any-

12

body in a long time, and the most I'd said all night. I thought he might stand up and walk away, or get confused and call me a bitch. Instead, he smiled.

"God, you are so fuckin' weird," he said. Then he kissed me.

It wasn't that simple. First I stiffened, then I ducked my head and turned away. Finally I scrambled back and tried to stand, because he wasn't taking my high-beam hint.

"Hold on, hold on," he said, laughing. He put an arm around my waist, and he was so strong he made holding me in place feel casual. I wasn't scared exactly, but I couldn't get away from him, either. His mouth tasted like Coke and garlic, and it was gummy with dead skin.

The part of me that could have killed him for this, once upon a time — that could have turned his blood to ice with a touch — fizzed in my chest. The Hinterland in me: it had dried up and drained, it was nearly gone. Maybe it lived where my soul would've lodged, if I'd been truly human. Now I wasn't either, exactly — Hinterland, human — and the way his face was shoved against mine made it hard to breathe.

Then all at once I was panting, and he was screaming, and the places where his skin had mashed against mine were damp with cooling sweat. It took a scrambled second to make sense of what I was seeing: Sophia had dragged him off me by his hair, then thrown him to the ground. She kicked him twice, efficient and well placed, while his friends yelled *oh, shit!* and did nothing to help him. The whole time she kept a lit cigarette in her mouth, like dealing with him wasn't worth throwing it away.

Finally she pressed a dirty low-top to his neck. She must've been pressing down pretty hard, because he was rasping out all sorts of stuff but you couldn't really hear it. When he tried to pull her down by the leg, she stepped back and kicked him again, then leaned far over to look into his face.

"You're gonna die before you're thirty," she said, blowing smoke in his eyes. She didn't say it meanly, just matter-of-fact. "In an accident. Quick, at least. If that makes it better."

His friends were helping him up by then, calling Sophia crazy and worse, but taking care not to get too close.

"What?" the boy kept saying, his face stained with fear. "What are you talking about? Why would you say that to me?"

She didn't answer, just watched them scramble and take off, yelling ugly stuff over their shoulders.

When they were gone, she turned to me.

"Was that asshole your first kiss?"

Maybe. Kind of. At least in this version of my life. It was too much to get into, so I just nodded.

She kneeled next to me, put her hands on my shoulders, and pressed her mouth to mine. It tasted like smoke and sugar, and under it a tickling electric-green current that must've been the last trace of the Hinterland, or whatever magic it was that allowed her, still, to look at people and know things she shouldn't. Like when and how they would die.

"There," she said, pulling back. "Forget that boy. That was your first kiss."

That's what I like to think of when I

think of Sophia Snow. That small, sympathetic proof that not everything the Hinterlanders did was meant to cause damage. But they didn't belong in this world, and that was the truth. The cracks they made were small, but cracks can bring a city down.

And if they didn't belong here, I didn't either. We were predators set loose in a world not made to withstand us. Until the summer we became prey.

~2~

The day after Hansa the Traveler died, I was sitting in a humid auditorium in Brooklyn, suffocating inside a polyester gown.

Sophia had enrolled in high school alongside me, but she hadn't made it to graduation day. She'd barely lasted a month. The rumors around what finally got her kicked out were conflicting: Petty theft. Less petty vandalism. Affair with a teacher. Her terrifying confidence, the product of an ancient brain and a smoldering death wish shoved inside the casing of a teenage girl.

That was the main one, I think, but they were all some version of true. I might've left with her but for Ella. My mother, incandescent with pride that her daughter was getting a high school degree. I'd squeaked my way to passing, did a couple of phys ed makeups, and picked up a starchy blue graduation gown from the front office that swished like a prom dress and fit like a habit.

It was an oppressively hot Sunday in June when I crossed the stage toward the principal and his stack of fake diplomas, because the real things came by mail. I had the oddest swell of feeling as I approached him: pride. I'd done it. I'd done *something.* Clawed my way free of a fairy-tale loop, put my head down, and achieved a thing that was never meant for me. I squinted out across the auditorium, looking for Ella in her black party dress and unseasonal lace-up boots.

I found her near the back, fingers in her mouth to whistle. I lifted my hand to blow a kiss, then saw the woman sitting just behind her. Close enough to reach out and touch.

The woman's hair was as bloody bright as a redcap's hat, and her eyes were hidden by the smoky circles of street vendor shades. She smiled when she saw me looking, leaning forward till her chin nearly grazed my mother's shoulder. Then she put up a finger and crooked it. *C'mere.*

The air of the auditorium swelled a little as the two halves of my life met and repelled like inverted magnets. I stumbled heading back to my seat, feet suddenly stupid. I craned around once I'd sat but couldn't see over the ocean of graduation caps.

The woman was Hinterland. Her name was Daphne, and she was the reason I'd been steering clear of the other ex-Stories for months.

Applause brought me out of my head. The ceremony was over, and my classmates were laughing and shouting like we'd done something real. For a second there, I'd agreed with them.

I sped to the lobby as soon as I was free, looking for Ella. I found her beaming at me from behind a bouquet of blue hibiscus.

"Hey, you," she said, as I grabbed her and hugged her hard.

"Hey. Are you okay?"

"Am I *okay*? I'm amazing."

She pulled back but didn't let go. Even though I'd grown my hair out and dyed it darker, we still looked nothing alike. It's funny the things you can ignore when you don't want to see them.

"So what do we do now?" Her voice was almost giddy. "I'm in a dress, you're in a — what do you have on under that robe?"

"Eh. It's laundry week."

She made a face. "Whatever that means, *I* am in a dress and I don't want to waste it. Pick somewhere fancy, we'll get lunch. We'll get ice cream!"

I should've done it. I should've slapped on a smile and let my mom take me out for sundaes to celebrate the day neither of us thought would ever come. But I couldn't. Because Daphne was here. She'd come close enough to touch. And needing to know what she wanted from me was a splinter beneath my skin.

"Tomorrow?" I said abruptly, scanning the room over her shoulder. When her

20

face fell, I kept talking. "I've got to work today. I forgot to tell you. So, tomorrow?"

"Okay." She pasted a smile over the expression that let me know she smelled my bullshit, and brought me in for another hug.

"Thanks for coming," I mumbled.

She gave me a little shake. "I'm your *mother*. Don't thank me for being here. Just come home after work, okay? We'll get the good takeout tonight."

She cupped my face, her hands cool. Then crisply she turned away, sweeping off through the crowd without looking back. That was a new thing, too: when she sensed herself clinging, she'd cut it off quick. It left me feeling bereft every time, wishing I'd hugged her longer. Wishing I hadn't lied, and we were on our way to a fancy lunch. But I had, and we weren't, so once she was gone I made my way to the exit, too.

I thought Daphne would be waiting for me, but I didn't see her. Families dotted the pavement, siblings batting at each other and moms wearing summer lipstick and dads in khaki pants looking

21

at their phones. I wound around them like a wraith. When I passed a trash can, I peeled off my gown and dropped it in. The sky was soft and low, in a way that made you feel like you were inside when you were out. And there was this feeling in the air, this *waiting* feeling. Like the square of city I stood on was a mouse, and a cat's paw hovered just above it.

Things were different now, I reminded myself. Our lives had changed. If they hadn't, I might've called the feeling by another name: bad luck coming.

Here's a story I don't like to tell.

It started on an ugly day last spring, frigid and murderously bright. I walked into a Hinterland meeting late, my fresh-washed hair frozen into pieces. When I first discovered the weekly gatherings of displaced ex-Stories, on the second floor of a psychic's shop on Avenue A, I thought I'd been saved — from the loneliness of singularity. From being the oddest creature I knew. And the meetings *did* save me. But they messed me up, too. Kept me from trying too hard, I guess, to be normal. To stop being so damned

22

easy on myself, because who could expect much from a girl created to live in a fairy tale, attempting now to fashion an unmagical life?

I was used to mixing with the same junk drawer of ex-Story oddballs. Even the ones I couldn't stand were comforting as old wallpaper, drinking instant coffee and kvetching about something or other week after week. But that day a woman I'd never seen was standing at the front of the room. She had the hard, painted-on beauty of an Egon Schiele portrait: dark-lipped and paper-pale, with perfect heroine hair that flowed and bent down her back in flat red colorblock. She was sitting on a high stool with her knees pulled up, sleeves pushed to her elbows, talking. Her talk turned the room's drowsy air into something crackling.

"We're infiltrators here," she was saying. "And we always will be."

It was about eighty degrees hotter inside than out, and I was sweating through my layers, trying to shuck my coat while balancing a full coffee cup. But the fervor in her words stopped me cold.

"This world is a gray place. A place of small and scattered lives. Disordered. Ugly. Chaotic." She brought a fist down on her knee. "But us? We *blaze*. We blaze against it like red ribbon."

Her voice was a drug. Dense as fog, rubbing its back against your ears like a cat. Everyone in the place was angling closer, warming their hands by her ferocity. Even me: I hated to think about it later, but she tugged at something in me, too.

She'd looked at someone sitting by her feet, a boy I'd never heard speak. His head was always down and his lips were always moving, noiseless. I suspected most of his mind was still lodged inside his broken tale.

"What were you?" she asked him. "In the Hinterland, what were you?"

I couldn't see the boy's face, but I could see the panic in his rising shoulders. "I was a prince. Conjured by a witch of dandelions and blood, to fool a princess." He darted a look around. "Sometimes I can feel the Hinterland sun on me again. Hear the insects whispering in the dirt. I

24

don't understand why I'm still a boy."

The woman had looked at him with such ferocity. "You're not. You are *magic,* through and through. We all are. Be proud of that."

She'd looked past him then, right at me.

"We aren't like the creatures who were made in this world. We aren't meant to *debase* ourselves with them. To live a human life is to forget who we are. To forget who we are is to be an enemy to ourselves. To each other."

"You," she said, pointing at a man in a frumpy hand-knit sweater. "Stand up."

He rose slowly, shaky in his frost-stained boots, and my heart dropped.

Because the thing was, these meetings weren't just for ex-Stories. They were for anyone still drifting after leaving the Hinterland behind. People from *this* world, who'd found their own doorways in and out again, different from us but bonded to us all the same. The man in the snowflake sweater was one of them. Not Hinterland, but human.

"I'm not trying to . . ." he stammered, "I'm not here to . . ."

25

"Shhhh." The woman pressed a finger to her lipsticked mouth, then smiled behind it. "You walk a very narrow path. And the woods are full of wolves. And the wolves have sharp teeth. And we've had no one to bite for a very, very long time."

She closed her eyes. "I want to live in a world of wolves. When I open my eyes, I won't see a single lamb."

Snowflake Sweater grabbed his coat and fled. A pair of teen girls in black lipstick followed, holding hands, and a man with dreadlocks hidden under a shapeless hat. An old woman in wire-rims shuffled out after them, slow enough to make her point.

I felt half of myself leave with them. The half of me that opened my eyes to my mother's face when I woke from bad dreams. That burrowed all the way into the heart of fairyland to find my way back to her, when the Hinterland tried to take her away. But I didn't move. I waited to see what would happen next.

When they were gone, the woman

opened her eyes with a baby-doll click. She smiled, a flash of needle teeth.

"Hello, wolves."

The meeting had broken up pretty quickly after that, everyone still buzzing with a bent energy. I hated the way they looked so jacked and cocky, like they'd just won some kind of war. I tried to sneak out without talking to anyone, but the new woman caught me by the stairs.

"You're Alice, right?"

She was even more startling up close. Her eyes were the silver-blue of shallow water, like the Spinner's had been. More than one ex-Story had those eyes.

"Nice show," I told her. "Very dramatic. You make all that wolf shit up on the spot?"

She wrinkled her nose a little, like we were just teasing each other. "I've heard about you. The girl with the ice. The one who broke us free."

She said it so slyly I couldn't tell how she meant it. I'd been the first one out of the Hinterland, yeah. The one, I'd learned, whose escape left a snag in the weave, allowing the other Stories to crawl out after me. Not that they thanked me for it.

"That's right. You're welcome." I made to elbow past her.

"Is it true what I heard, that you live with some woman?"

I paused. Some of the hypnotic hum had gone out of her voice; I realized she could turn it on and off.

"In Brooklyn, right — cute place on the second story? I like it. I like the blue curtains on your woman's bedroom window."

I grabbed her arm. Half to hold her there, and half to steady myself. "What are you getting at?"

She looked at my hand, then up at my eyes.

"It's all gone, isn't it? The ice?" The wicked lightness had left her voice. She looked at me with something like disgust, speaking loud enough that all the stragglers could hear it.

"I said I didn't want to see any lambs here."

Her name, I later learned, was Daphne.

She was the very last Hinterlander to come through. The one who tightened the ranks and broke all attempts at assimilation against the rocks. Within weeks, according to Sophia, she had all of them on a string. Even Soph, I think. Though she wouldn't tell me much.

I didn't stick around for it. Till graduation I hadn't seen Daphne again in the flesh, but she visited me sometimes in dreams. There was a night I woke up panting, my chest feeling crushed and tight, like the devil was sitting on it. I swear I saw her standing by the bed, streetlight catching on her pointed teeth and red hair. But when I turned on the lamp there was nothing there.

Daphne's threats were a good thing in the end: they made me do what I should've done ages ago. I gave the Hinterland up for good, and set about making my life an entirely human one.

It was half past eleven on a Sunday. If Daphne wasn't waiting for me, I knew where to find her: packed into the muggy air of the psychic's shop, along with Sophia and the rest of them. It was meeting day.

Something in my stomach twanged as I approached the building for the first time in months. It was shabby brick and a foggy glass door, with a palmist's sign above it and a staircase just behind. But all I could see as I walked up was Daphne. Leaning against the brick with her legs crossed, her eyes hidden by the smoky circles of street-vendor shades. When she saw me coming she gestured at me to hurry up.

"Hey, you," she said in that smoky, bullshit voice. "It's been a minute."

I approached slowly, stopped a few squares of sidewalk away. "What do you want?"

"I want to make amends," she said. "I think you got the wrong idea about me."

"I'm pretty sure I got the right one. Tell me what you actually want."

"That was a nice ceremony. Is Ella real proud?"

That dark thing that lived below my sternum stirred. "Get my mother's name out of your mouth. If you want something, want to talk to me, want *anything* from me, you don't mention her again.

30

You don't go *near* her again. Ever. Got it?"

Quick as a whip, she grabbed my hand. Squeezed it once, then dropped it. Checking, I think. I shouldn't have cared what she thought, but for a minute I wished I was what I used to be: full of ice to my fingernails, and ready to bury her in it.

"If you were *my* daughter," she said, "here's what I'd teach you first: never let 'em know how to hit you where it hurts."

I felt my cheeks going hot. "Fuck's sake, you've *won*. You warned me off. I stayed away. Why are you still bothering with me?"

She lifted her sunglasses, trapping me in the twin tractor beams of her eyes. "Oh, sweetie. What makes you think watching out for you is any bother?"

A man walking by us slowed, turning so he could keep staring at Daphne as he went. She kept her shades up, smiled at him sweetly, and popped off her top veneers, revealing a double-row of filed-down shark teeth.

"Mother of God!" the man yelped, half stumbling over a stoop, then sprinting away.

31

She used a pinky to push the veneers delicately into place, turning her attention back on me. "Let me start again. I'm not trying to make an enemy of you. I want you here because Hinterland blood is precious, more now than ever. Despite what you might think, you're still a part of us. And I need you *here* for us, the way we're here for you."

I stared at her. Half the creatures gathered up those stairs would knife me for a hot dog. "Where is this coming from? Why now?"

"There've been some deaths lately."

"Some . . . deaths?" She said it like you'd say, *Some rain*.

"Three since the beginning of spring."

"Who died? How did they —"

"Killed. The Prince of the Wood first. Then Abigail."

The prince I'd known a little. Aggressively handsome, with hair like a pony's mane and a brick of urgently white teeth. Abigail, though. I felt shitty that I couldn't even put a face to the name.

"And a third was killed last night: Hansa the Traveler."

I startled. I'd met Hansa in the Hinterland. I knew she was in New York, but the last I'd heard she was living with two older ex-Stories, attending a charter school on the Lower East Side. The news shocked me into forgetting who I was talking to. "But Hansa's a *kid*. And she's actually got — she had a chance. Who would hurt Hansa?"

"What does being a kid have to do with it?"

"It's horrible," I said quietly. Hansa had been a little girl when I met her in the Halfway Wood. The moon's granddaughter. "What happened? How did they die?"

Shadows moved beneath the blue of Daphne's eyes. Looking at them too long felt like staring into infested water. "Death is death."

"What does *that* mean?"

She ignored me, turning toward the door, imperious. "Now you know. And now we've made peace. Come on, come be with your people."

I peered through the glass at the staircase behind it, water-stained and disappearing into the shadows of the second floor. With a longing as palpable as thirst, I did not want to go up there.

"Thanks for telling me. But I can't right now. I've gotta work." I tried out the lie for the second time that day.

"No, you don't." She opened the door. "Your last shift was Thursday, and you work again tomorrow. But you don't work today."

I couldn't say what my face looked like when she turned around to smile at me.

"I take care of my people, even the prodigal ones. Don't worry about a thing, princess. I've always got eyes on you."

~3~

I followed her upstairs, because what else could I do?

Run. Hide. The thoughts were listless.

There is nowhere I am free from them.

The words came unbidden, a hard spike of realization that set my blood to humming. Nauseous with nerves, I walked into the tea-scented air of the psychic's shop.

I'd learned quickly who to avoid back when I was coming here each week. The scary ones weren't the ones covered in ink to their eyes, or flipping a knife over their knuckles like they were in a bad prison movie. They were that kind-eyed man in the well-cut suit, the faintest tint of blue in his cropped black beard. That boy with the hard-baked smile, no taller than me. The steel-haired woman who whispered that she had a telephone line open to the Spinner, who was going to let us back in any day.

My heart squeezed when I saw Sophia sitting cross-legged on a window seat in the back, next to a guy with the prettiest lips I'd ever seen. I'd been kind of a shit friend since spring: giving up the Hinterland meant pulling away from her, too. Being here after months away felt the same, but different. The air was lightly electrified, bodies shifting like cattle before a storm. Heads dipped, mouths pressed close to ears to whisper.

They were looking at me. Flatly, or with suspicion. I didn't think I was imagining it. When I reached Sophia, she did a double take.

"What the hell are you doing here?" she muttered.

I blinked, surprised. "Hi to you, too."

Her eyes stayed hard, but she linked an arm through mine.

"What's with everyone?" I asked, low. "What did I do?"

"Most things have nothing to do with you."

After talking to Daphne I was uneasy; now my skin was starting to crawl. "You heard about the deaths?"

"Later." She spat the word like a bullet.

I wasn't going to get anything else out of her. I looked to the front of the room, where a fortyish guy had taken the floor. I guess Hansa had been the first order of business; the rest of the meeting would play out like they always did, like any support group meeting anywhere.

The man up front was a stranger, but I could tell at a glance he was one of the scary ones. He was the exact size and shape of a nightmare: the man in the alley, the body crouched over yours in the dark. It was hot up here but he wore a dirty stocking cap anyway, and too-big overalls.

"That's how I ended up here again," he was saying. "Another woman — it's always a damned woman. It becomes hard to hide it, too. Every time one of them makes me do it, it's move on, start again. I want to live somewhere small, somewhere I can be alone. Like it was back home. Just me, and a woman when I want one. But they're different here, everything's different here, and every time I have to hide it."

I looked around the room. Most everyone had their backs to me now, watching him, and the faces I could see held their secrets.

"So I thought I'd come back," he went on. "To a place where no one notices no one. The women here are even worse, but they're easier to get rid of when you're through. Less to take care of. I don't even have to leave, I can stay in one place."

I could've misread his words, if I'd wanted to. But I was a Hinterland woman listening to a Hinterland man. I understood that he'd hurt women, and would continue to hurt them if he could. When I looked at Daphne her face was easy. Still. She could've been listening to anything.

"I'm glad to be back," he said, shifting

in his overalls and slicing his face into an ugly grin. "They're pretty here, I'll give them that. And it feels like a bit of home, in this room."

Nobody clapped, or said anything, but he whipped off his hat anyway, giving a little bow. As he leaned over, dirty red hair flopped over his forehead.

And I tasted again, with perfect clarity, the rot of his mouth in the Hinterland. The taste of death and hate and the rancid leavings of his last meal.

I knew this man, because his tale had been my own.

"Alice-Three-Times," the tale had been called. Again and again I'd lived through it in the Hinterland, a place that ran on the telling of tales. It was written down decades ago by my mother's mother, Althea Proserpine, and bound within the pages of a book: *Tales from the Hinterland.* I'd been the princess in the story, this man the suitor who'd won me. To be his wife, or his servant, or worse. In the tale, I killed him before we got far enough to find out, tipping ice into his veins with a kiss. I didn't know any more than that, because someone had made it his mission to free me from the story.

But in *this* world, outside the broken borders of the place that bonded me and this violent man, I ran. Crouching down so he wouldn't see me, I shoved through the crowd of my kin. Past Daphne, who looked at me sharp, then pounding down the steps to the street.

The low gray sky had finally broken. Clouds slopped loose of each other like soaked-through paper, letting in a steady rain. I kept running when I hit the side-walk. Maybe the raindrops should've felt cleansing, but they were warm as tongues, warm as blood. I stopped under a bodega's green awning and tried to pull myself together.

I'd *fought* for this life. Normal. Boring. All the days proceeding in an orderly fashion. I'd been imprisoned fighting for it, broken my mother's heart on my way to it, ripped through cosmic walls to win it. I hated all of them for reminding me how flimsy my normal could be: Daphne. That awful man. Whoever had killed poor Hansa.

What if it was the man from my tale who'd done it? It seemed possible. I'd only met one figure from my story in this world before: the man's younger, better brother. Once when I was six years old, and he coaxed me into a stolen car, and again when I was seventeen. But I hadn't seen him since. Not all of us had left the Hinterland after my broken tale tipped over like a domino, knocking the rest of the world askew. After I got out — after someone long gone helped break me out — the tales fell apart faster than the Spinner could spin them. There was a time I'd thought the Hinterland was gone completely, but I learned that it was still out there, still bleeding, like a slashed-up magical apple dripping its juice. Only its doors were now closed.

I stood beside a cooler of watermelon halves stuck like oysters in ice, smelling rain and exhaust and cut tulips. I closed my eyes just long enough to trace the memory of his face: the boy who helped me break free.

When this place felt too hot and bright, too busy too angry too iced with electric lights, I thought of Ellery Finch, traveling through other worlds. Finding them behind hidden doors, under acorn caps, inside steamer trunks. It was nice in there, inside this daydream. I used to never let myself think of him, but lately I figured, what's the harm? It's better than a meditation app.

When I was calm again, when I'd hardened my skin against the trio of deaths, against the man's words and the violence inside them, I started walking. When I was sure nobody from the meeting had followed me, I got on the subway.

And I wondered. I wondered what it said about me now that I'd run from the man in the meeting, when in the Hinterland, I'd killed him.

~4~

Ella wasn't home when I let myself in. Our AC was broken and she kept insisting she could fix it, which meant there was a scatter of tools by the overturned window unit and the air was so hot it practically wobbled. I stood in front of the fridge in rain-soaked clothes and ate a slice of leftover pizza, fanning the freezer door back and forth. I'd moved on to gelato out of the tub when something made me stop: from the back of the apartment, a quiet creak. The singular sound of a foot placed carefully on old floorboards.

I put the ice cream down. Behind me, the fridge strained and settled. Outside, a mockingbird imitated a cell phone. And from the back of the apartment came another creak.

My breath switched from automatic to manual. I walked down the hall, peering into the quiet rooms. Mine, Ella's, our bathroom the size of a crow's nest.

"Hello?"

My voice dropped like a pebble into the quiet, and I knew I was alone. A shaken-up idiot in an empty apartment, hallucinating the thing I was always waiting for: the return of bad luck.

In the bathroom I washed my face, splashing water into my eyes, my mouth, swishing the ice cream off my tongue. My heart was still banging like an offbeat drum. When I came up dripping I saw a face in the mirror behind me.

I saw the blue and white and black of it, the pale smear of teeth. I stopped breathing, and didn't breathe again till I had them pinned to the bathroom wall, my hands pressed like butterfly wings over their throat.

Ella's throat. Her blue eyes and black hair. Skin pearling up with sun freckles. It happened so fast she didn't look shocked till I'd already pulled away.

We stared at each other. I heard a dog barking through the open windows, and a child's cut-glass scream.

"I snuck up," she said, a little breathless. "I startled you."

We nodded in unison, like a pair of metronomes. "Sorry," I said, then coughed and tried again. "I'm sorry. I didn't know who it was."

She reversed her way out of the bathroom, like she didn't want to turn her back on me. "You're home early. You didn't have to work after all?"

It took me a second to remember, to understand. "I didn't," I said. "I got it wrong."

We waded through dinner, through small talk of graduation and Ella's coworkers at her nonprofit gig, eating to the sound of one of our old car tapes. I'd gotten her a vintage cassette deck for her birthday so she could play the music she loved to listen to on the road: PJ Harvey and Sleater-Kinney and Bikini Kill, and bands with names like paint colors — Smog, Pavement, Gabardine. We stayed at the table long enough to pretend the thing in the bathroom hadn't happened. She'd put my graduation flowers in an empty pickle jar. I kissed her cheek and made a big thing about carrying them to my room.

I tried to lose myself in the solitary mysteries of *A Wild Sheep Chase,* but my eyes kept going to the door. To the window. Around midnight I heard Ella's radio go quiet. At one I finally got up, giving in to the itch running under my skin.

I moved through the house like a thief. Ella was breathing easy in her bed, and the front door locks held. Nobody hid behind the shower curtain, or in the shadows of the couch. Hansa was still dead somewhere, and the awful man from my tale wasn't, because no world ever balanced itself just right.

In the kitchen I brewed coffee by the city's borrowed lights, sweetened it with honey and cooled it with milk, then dropped in ice. June came in through the windows, slinky and edged with a gasoline tang. There was a mimosa tree in the yard; when I pressed my forehead to the screen I could see breeze pouring itself through the blossoms.

In my fairy tale I'd been a black-eyed princess, unloved. My hands were filled with a killing cold, my touch was death. When I left the Hinterland I took the barest chip of it with me. But I'd let that last little bit melt away.

I didn't want to mourn the loss of the thing that made me wicked, but hearing about three ex-Stories being killed made me feel disarmed without it. My head was full of formless black thoughts I couldn't allow to settle. I didn't want to think about things I couldn't have, that I shouldn't want.

I took the coffee back to my room. In the minutes I'd been gone, the room had filled up with the scorched-earth scent of unfiltered cigarettes. I unlatched the barred window that let onto our fire escape and stuck out my head.

"Those things'll kill you," I said.

Sophia took a last drag and stubbed the butt out on her shoe. "Funny."

47

She dropped into my room, then did what she always did: started to case it, like a criminal or a cop. Ran a finger over the spines of my books, took a sip of my coffee. Moved over to the dresser and picked things up, inspecting them one by one. Dr Pepper lip gloss. A bloom of blue hibiscus. The rosette my mother had made from the dirty silk of the dress I'd worn home from the Hinterland. I didn't know what she'd done with the rest of it.

"Can't sleep?"

I shook my head, though she wasn't looking. She'd always had a knack for showing up when I was restless. Or maybe she showed up even when I wasn't, and I slept right through it.

"So," she said, inspecting herself in the mirror bolted to my closet door. "You ran away."

"Oh, screw you," I said, and buried my face in my pillow. I felt the bed dip as she sat down beside me, then poked me between the shoulder blades till I turned.

"I'm not giving you shit, I swear. I just want to know why."

Why had I? What had I felt seeing him

again, remembering how it felt to be bound together inside our tale? Disgust, fear, those were easy. Anger, too. But there was something else: a serrated sort of curiosity. It was bad enough I couldn't make myself feel nothing, I didn't want to feel *that*.

"I killed him," I said to the ceiling. "I've killed him a hundred times. Wouldn't you have run?"

She stared at me till I looked back, her eyes two distant planets. "You killed him because he deserved it. I bet he deserves it here, too."

I studied her, a tickling, terrible thought blooming. "Soph. You know . . . you understand that it's permanent here, right? When you're dead, you're dead."

"Of course I know that," she said, suddenly savage. "Alice, why'd you have to come back around *today*? Of all days."

"What do you mean? What's wrong with today?" She didn't answer. "Ask Daphne why today. She's the one who dragged me there."

"*Dragged* you. Kicking and screaming, right?"

49

"What's that supposed to mean?"

"It means stop pretending you don't have a choice." Her voice was hard. "Because of all of us, you're the only one who does. To be part of us, or not. So. Coming back today, does that mean you made your choice?"

"Jesus, I showed up to one meeting."

"The way Daphne runs things now, it's not . . . Alice, you don't come and go."

"*Daphne*. She doesn't really want me there. She checked — I think she checked today to see if I could still do it. You know. To see if I still had the ice." I laughed a little, around the urge to cry.

Sophia didn't laugh with me. "Do you?"

"What? No. You know I don't."

She studied me for a moment without speaking. "Here's what I don't get about you," she said. "In your tale, you had all the power. You were a monster in the Hinterland. Why now are you pretending to be a mouse?"

She didn't say *monster* like I'd say *monster.* She said it with reverence, like it was a title. Like she was saying *queen.*

"I'm not a mouse." I looked down at my hands and remembered the sight of them flexing over my mother's throat. The exhilaration of it, that came before the shame.

"I'm not," I repeated, "a *mouse.*"

"Good," she said. "Because you can't afford to be. Something very bad is going on."

"I know about the murders. Daphne told me."

"She didn't tell you everything."

Her pause had dark things in it. Things with teeth.

"They weren't just killed. There's something else."

My shoulders went high. Whatever she said next, I wasn't going to like it.

"Whoever killed them, they took something away. Like, a *part.*" She breathed out hard and lit another cigarette. She wasn't supposed to smoke in here, but I didn't stop her. "They took the prince's left hand. Abigail, they took her right. And they took Hansa's left foot."

My toes curled in, automatic.

"Where'd you hear that?" I was whispering now. "Does everyone know?"

"I don't know who knows. Robin told me, he didn't say where he got it from."

I didn't ask, but she passed her cigarette to me anyway. It'd been ages since I'd had one, and the nicotine hit my blood like sickness. I smoked it down to my fingertips, thinking, trying not to think. I looked out the window, searching for the white sailing ship of the moon. But the sky was thick with cloud cover, and the moon was just a rock here anyway.

"You've been gone," Sophia said. "You've been trying to walk away. And I get it. I do. You've got more in this world than the rest of us, and that's nice. But there's something starting here. So either you're out of this, all the way, or you're in it. And if you're in, it's time to remember who and what you are. Or you might not survive it."

I would feel guilty later. Later, I would think of my mother lying defenseless down the hall, and my window swung foolishly open to let in Sophia, the night, and whatever else might come. But right then, I looked into her flat, beautiful eyes.

"What am I?"

"First tell me you're sure. Be *sure*."

I wasn't sure. About anything. But I nodded my head.

"You are not a victim, or a damsel. Or a girl who runs." She gripped my hands. "You're Alice-Three-Times."

"I don't remember how to be that way." I squeezed back. "I forgot. I *had* to."

Her smile came out like a sickle moon, all edge. "I'll help you remember."

~5~

Since leaving school, Sophia had stopped messing with New York boys. I understood now that being human, being *with* humans, was something she'd tried on like clothes. They'd never fit her right. Now she had a sort of boyfriend among the ex-Stories. Or he might've just been who she called when I wasn't answering her texts.

Robin lived in a low-ceilinged Crown Heights apartment with a business school dropout named Eric, a rock-thick bro who thought his roommate was weird because he was from Iceland. They slept in twin beds shoved into a single room, so they could give their second bedroom over to a growing operation.

It was nearly three in the morning when Sophia let us in. Eric was slumped in front of their flat-screen playing a first-person shooter game, pit stains yellowing his Pussy Riot T-shirt.

"Ladies," he said, pausing the game. That was a sign of great respect in Eric's world.

Sophia inspected the desiccated pile of pizza crusts on the coffee table. "Where's Robin?"

"You know. Messing around back there." He darted a look at me and unpaused the game. "Tell him I ate his pizza."

I think Sophia liked Robin because he never slept, either. We found him crouched in the back bedroom, fiddling with something I couldn't see. Plants slumbered beneath the singed halo of grow lights, lined up in tidy green rows.

"Ilsa!" he said when he saw Sophia. He always used her Hinterland name, and she always corrected him.

"Sophia." She nudged him with the toe of her shoe. "Alice is here, too."

He unfolded from the ground, all six and a half wiry feet of him. Everything he felt beamed directly out of his face, and right now he was watching me with an uncharacteristic wariness. "You're all right?"

"I'm good. You?"

"I'm well." His jaw was tight. "Better than some. Aren't I breathing?"

"Robin." Sophia voice snapped like a rubber band.

It's hard to stare down a beanstalk, but I tried it. "Do we have a problem?"

He shook his head, turning away. The way he did it hurt a little. I'd always thought he liked me.

Sophia ran a careful finger over a plant with spade-shaped leaves. "What's wrong with this guy?"

Robin's eloquent face darkened. "Not just that one." He swept a hand over his sleeping garden. "All of them."

I leaned in, throat thickening in the mossy air. The plants were limp. Dropping dead leaves. Some were speckled gray and white, some were as brown as my mother's underfed rosemary bush. These were the plants Robin dried, ground, baked, and steeped, to be smoked, inhaled, eaten, or drunk — Hinterland plants, every one. He'd harvested them in a seam of trees that used to be in the Halfway Wood, where the door the ex-Stories escaped through once stood. I'd never tried any of them, but I'd heard what they could do to your body, to your head.

"Poor things," Sophia murmured, her face almost tender. "What happened?"

"I don't know. I've tried everything, but each day more succumb to it. I cannot turn them from dying."

He still lapsed, sometimes, into talking like an extra in *Game of Thrones.* At least he came by it honestly.

Sophia crumpled a leaf into powder. "So get some more."

"There aren't any more. The ones in the woods, those are dying, too."

"Strange," Sophia murmured, and stood. "Tell me you've at least got something for Alice."

"Alice." The way he said it was halfway to a curse. "What does Alice need?"

The question pricked the wrong places of me. "Nothing from you. Soph, let's go."

She ignored me. "Something that'll help her remember what it was like. What it *felt* like, in the Hinterland."

"It seems to me she's the last one who needs it."

"What are you talking about?" I said. At the same time, Sophia reached way up and slapped him, midway between a joke and a knockout.

"Cut it out," she said sharply. "If you want me coming back at all, stop being a shit."

After a long moment he bowed to me slightly, looking harassed. "Fine. I've been rude." His eyes slid over to Sophia. "I've got something that'll make it up to you."

We sat on Robin's stoop in the quiet of the city in the middle of the night. Street-light trapped itself inside the old Popov bottle in his hands, half filled with a viscous green liquid.

He tilted it. "The plants I used for this

grew everywhere back home. They didn't feed on sun. This works better under starlight."

"What happens when I drink it?"

He grinned, looking like the devil he might've been in the Hinterland. "Only one way to know."

I didn't love altered states. I'd already lived in one. The most I went for now was the fuzz of one drink, the clarifying burr of caffeine. But I'd already run from the Hinterland once today. I wasn't about to do it again.

I took the bottle. Sophia was gimlet-eyed, her hands under her thighs like she was trying to restrain them. The liquor smelled like the hills in *The Sound of Music* and shimmered over my tongue. It was bubbles in my bloodstream, helium in my head. "Damn," I whispered.

Robin laughed, took the bottle and drank. He'd loosened up after Sophia slapped him. We passed it around, sitting on the steps, the liquid flashing through me like lights over water.

"Good to feel alive," Sophia said, tilting her head way back. "While we still can."

"Don't," said Robin, low.

The drink went coppery on my tongue. "She had parents, didn't she?" I said abruptly. "Hansa?"

Sophia shrugged. "She had some people she lived with. I guess they were raising her."

"Right. That's parents. Do they go to meetings? Has anyone talked to them?"

"It's bad luck to speak of sad things when you drink," Robin said.

I opened my mouth to respond, and gasped.

I think we all felt it at once, the moment the magic hit our systems. Whatever they felt, for me it was a cold uprush, a scouring wind that came from below my heart. I squeezed my eyes shut, and opened them on a new world.

Brooklyn was still bath-warm and hazy, still concrete and iron and slabs of brown- and red- and cream-colored stone. It was still perched in that formless, deadly deep part of the night. But it was *more.* The trees stood out in 4D, some extra dimension making them denser, vivid, more articulate. Everything was as stark-edged as a Man Ray photograph, but it was flattened, too, its depth of field all out of whack. The waving buds of a magnolia tree and the town car idling half a block down looked as close to me as Sophia. The world seemed infinitely touchable, manipulable, the street a night-lit realm we could swim through like water.

Robin held up a palm like he was weighing the air, and began to sing.

Red bird black bird
Damselfly bee
Weave a gown as fine as silk
To cover me

A few seconds passed, then a trio of starlings swept over the roof of the adjacent apartment building, making a beeline for Robin. I ducked as they executed a dizzy circle around our heads, looking as surprised as birds can look, before flying up and shooting off in three directions.

"Holy shit!" I said.

"Lazy damned birds." Sophia leaned back on her elbows. "No dress."

Robin's face was dreamy and sharp at

61

once. "I'll weave one for you myself, my love. If you will it, I'll give you anything you want."

"But never the thing I need." She put a hand to his face, fingers gently crooked, so they made five fine lines down his cheek as she stroked. "I promise you, one day you'll love someone who can be won with dresses."

Ignoring his expression, she turned to me. She'd lit a cigarette and was tangling her fingers in the smoke as it drifted, shaping it into ribbons and daggers and icicles. I blinked and they were gone. She stuck the cigarette in Robin's mouth, then dug with both hands inside her gigantic street-stall purse, heavy with half-drunk bottles of juice and books I'd given her and makeup shoplifted from the Duane Reade. After a minute, she unearthed a liquid eyeliner pen.

"Sit still," she said, holding it up.

"Why?"

"Shh." She crouched in front of me, knees on the concrete steps, smelling of tobacco and coffee and shoplifted soap. Her brows winged out like a silent film star's, and her eyes tilted toward the golden side of brown. Rays of ochre and whiskey and sand, with nothing behind them. Even when I loved her best, I was chilled by the impenetrable flats of her eyes.

The liner licked over my cheeks. Robin watched us, and said nothing. After a few minutes she capped the pen, blowing lightly on my skin. "There," she murmured. "That's perfect."

She pulled out a little heart-shaped hand mirror, held it up. I heard my breath halt and restart.

Vines. She'd painted my face with vines, in an intricate, swirling freehand.

"Sophia. Are these . . . these are . . ."

"Power." She spoke into my ear. "That fear you felt when you ran away from that man today? That's the power you're giving away. But we could make this world fear *us*, Alice. We could make them so afraid."

She'd painted my face with the twining tattoos of the Briar King. He was the one who'd let himself into my stepdad's apartment and stolen Ella away from me when I was seventeen. He might've been dead, or he might've been anywhere. There was a time when my nightmares wore his face. I'd told her all of this. Sophia *knew* this.

As I tilted my head from side to side, my mirror self moved a half beat behind me. I was remembering something. Something I'd spent all my months back in New York pushing down and away.

It hadn't always felt bad to be a monster.

The girl in the mirror was smirking at me. Vines swirled around her eyes like the mask of a robber bridegroom. Beside her, Soph's gold eyes glittered. We looked right together, like this. We looked like a pair of avenging — well. Not angels.

"I know where he lives," she whispered.

"Who?"

She stood up. She knew I was bluffing.

The path that forked at my feet was dark and bright. I could walk on with Ella, down the road my diploma had started to pave. Or I could stumble off it, into the briars. Sophia waited for me there, among the thorns and the dark.

"Alice," she said, and held out her hand. *Be sure.*

I took it.

~6~

Being drunk on the stuff Robin gave us made Brooklyn into a floating place, a green-resined dreamscape. We walked past sleeping brownstones, under the rustling canopies of old trees. My fingertips sparked as I ran them over the peeling skin of a plane tree, and I remembered living in a world where the trees had faces, where they dreamed their sap-slow dreams.

A group of men drinking from brown paper bags was walking toward us. They were hard-eyed and thick and they swelled when they saw us, their step turning to swagger. Until they came close enough to really *see* us, and shrank under our sight. And I felt, for once, like I might actually look on the outside how I felt on the inside. My blood ran keen and high, too close to the surface of my skin; I felt so *alive* I knew I must be a magnet for death.

Then the moon's cold eye caught mine, and I remembered Hansa was cold, too. Thinking of her, of Abigail, of the prince, brought me to the surface of my drunken dream. Where, I wondered, did dead Hinterlanders go now? Were they lost completely? Or were they taken back, to wander, maimed, around some living underworld?

The man from my tale lived in a shitty little house that grew out of trash-strewn weeds, stuck to the end of an industrial block. We'd walked by the open doors of factory-sized buildings to get here, past men in Carhartts working too late, or too early. By the time we reached it I was a kettle set to boiling. A held-in breath, a cresting wave. I wanted to exhale, to crash, to do something reckless. Sophia was in full-on manic mode, her eyes shining like dollar coins.

"Let's ring the doorbell," she said, giddy. "Let's put a rock through the fuckin' glass!"

As a wingman, she was a mixed bag.

"Shh," I hissed, watching his windows. He lived in the garden apartment, where blue TV light played over closed blinds. The house was detached, and it was easy enough to walk around toward the back, climb over the splintery mess of his fence, and drop into the backyard's itchy overgrowth.

We didn't talk about a plan. If we had, I'd have had to admit I was really here, breathless in the metal-scented dark, on the edge of doing something I didn't want to put words to. I wasn't sure *what* we were going to do.

Better just to let yourself into the unlocked screened porch. Find the cracked-open window. Fit your fingers under its lip, wince as it screeches, and pull till it's open just wide enough to admit two girls.

I climbed in first. Adrenaline made it hard to see, my vision popping with anxious flashbulb flowers. The room was dark, tinged with the secretive stink of an animal's warren. It knocked some of the glitter from my head.

First I saw the bed, mounded with blankets. Then I saw the sliding stack of magazines against the wall, a hoard of breasts and lips and heat, like he was a time traveler who didn't know there was porn on the internet. Everything was low to the ground: bed, magazines, drifts of soiled clothes. And just there, lit by an errant fall of porch light: the red coil of a hair tie, the kind of thing Ella left scattered around the house, a fistful of them in every purse she owned.

A hand on my arm sent lightning up my spine, but it was just Sophia, nodding toward the door. It hung slightly open. Over the submarine chug of my heart, I could hear the rhythms of a game show. Delicately we picked our way across the room. The hall was short, running past the open door of a filthy bathroom and what must have been a linen closet, and opening to the right into an unlit kitchen.

We had clean sightlines on the back of his head. It was bobbing faintly, like he was listening to music we couldn't hear. The sight stalled me out. Winnowed my mind from my body. I floated over myself, watching the girl with the steady step and the messy hair walk down that hallway. I almost wanted to stop her, but it was too late. I witnessed the sudden stillness of the man as he heard her, then swung around, face frozen with surprise. It curdled into something worse when he saw who'd come for him.

Then I snapped back into my body, standing alone in front of him for the first time since I'd left the Hinterland.

"Hey, asshole," I said. "Remember me?"

"You." He sounded unsurprised. Pleased, even. "My little bride."

"Never your bride."

"But here you are. Come back to finish our story the right way?" He grinned, his gaze skirting around my face, not quite catching it. "I think we'll skip the wedding."

It was different, seeing him up close. This wasn't heady or daring, it was something else. I ran his words at the meeting through my fingers, sicker in the remembering. I tasted his mouth on mine, felt his hands on me. And the words came out of me like water from a well I thought had run dry.

"Look at me," I told him. "Look at your destruction."

His eyes went incredulous, and he started to laugh. Behind him, Sophia stepped lightly out of the kitchen.

"Listen to you!" he said. "You still think you live in a story."

I rose up on my toes, light as air, dense as lead. "You still think you live in a world where girls will lie down for you and show you their throats."

He rocketed up from the couch, moving faster than a man that size should be able to move, grabbing the hair at my nape and yanking my head back.

He had a smashed-flat nose and skin that looked grated. One of his eyes hung a little different than the other, like he was hating you out of two different faces. His face was a history book about violence, and his breath smelled like cooked meat and bad hygiene.

"Now this feels familiar," he said.

"Yes, it does."

I darted forward, took his lip between my teeth, and *pulled.*

It split like fabric, like pulp, like a blood balloon. He cried out, but he didn't let go of me.

"You *bitch.*" He spat red, laughing. "You don't win in this one, honey. The Spinner can't save you now. Oh, I'm so glad you found me."

His blood was thick and corn-syrup sweet and it should've disgusted me. But its flavor got into my head, mixing with the liquor there, making me dizzy and hungry and very, very cold. My eyes ached with it and my blood leaped so high I couldn't tell if it was with rage or joy.

"What's this?" he said, looking over my head. "We're making it a party now?"

Sophia held a butcher's knife in her hand. I guessed she had found it in the kitchen. Her face was blank and she was twisting the knife's point on her fingertip.

His grip on me tightened. "You brought a friend, did you? Do I get to call one, too?" He looked at me full on, still laughing.

Then his face went hard, the humor dropping away. He shoved me, sent me reeling back into the wall.

"What's that?" His voice wavered, his hands rising. "You didn't tell me you could still do *that*."

I moved closer. I moved *fast*. It felt like chips of time were being chiseled away, and I was shaking off the bits I didn't need.

When Sophia looked at me, her mouth went slack. "Alice," she breathed. "Your *eyes*."

The man looked back and forth between us, from Sophia with her knife to me with nothing but my two hands. That was all I'd needed in our tale.

"Look at me," I said. My head was a howling sea cave and my voice wasn't my own. "Don't worry about her. Don't worry about anything but me.

"Now lie down and show me your throat."

~7~

I blinked.

I closed my eyes and light shifted over my lids, moonlight and lamplight and the delineated scatter of stars fading out as the sun dragged itself over the skyline. Streetlights buzzing, blinking out, headlights white and the yellow flicker of the subway. I knew something, wanted to hold on to something, but it was like clinging to a flashlight's beam. Another blink, and it was gone.

I opened my eyes on early morning coming through my bedroom window.

A zip line of nightmare slid through me, retreating to its hidden place. For a moment, my head was an empty room. Then the night rushed in.

Drinking at Robin's. Walking to Red Hook. Slithering in through the brother's window. The claustrophobic apartment, the sweet awful rip of his lip. His scorn turning to fear, and Sophia looking at me. *Alice. Your eyes.*

There was a weight bearing down on me, making it hard to breathe, and I thought it was panic till my fingers followed the feeling up, to my neck.

Something was there, wound around my throat, hard and warm and too tight to see. I kicked free of the sheets, tumbled out of bed and ran down the hall. The bathroom mirror reflected the cold hollows of my eyes. The faded eyeliner vines.

And a necklace of fat red rubies circling my throat.

I'd bitten the man from my tale. I thought I'd done worse than that, but there was a void in my memories, its borders tidy as an egg's. His blood made rusty swirls around my lips. It was a slaughterhouse flavor on my tongue. And where the worst of the blood had been, where it ran down my chin and settled in a brutal collar, lay this circle of stones.

They gripped my neck like a row of ticks. I scratched, frantic, feeling my way to the back. There was a hook under my hair; I unclasped it. The necklace slipped off, coiling over my hands, rubbing red on my skin. I flung it into the sink and turned the water on. The stones bled and ran under its stream, melting away like paste, till there was nothing left of it but the pattern of its claws and catches imprinted in my skin.

I thought it was a cry, bubbling up in me, but it was laughter. A low sound, boiled thick as campfire coffee.

This was magic, and it wasn't benign. It was a world I wanted to forget and a night I couldn't remember, and a dark gift left to strangle me. The Hinterland was tugging at me, blowing its breath in my face, wrapping its fingers around my throat. My laugh cut off clean.

Be sure, Sophia had told me.

I said I didn't want to see any lambs.
Daphne.

"What did you do?" I asked the girl in the mirror.

She looked back at me. She showed her bloody teeth.

I stripped off my clothes and climbed into the shower. The water started out tepid and shifted by degrees to just this side of scalding. When my skin, at least, was clean, I dried off with one of the scratchy towels Ella stole from the pool at the Y, hard decisive strokes that burned. The vines were washed away. The blood, the liquorish sweat, the night.

"It's okay," I whispered. I combed my hair back, put on ChapStick. No eyeliner, my face scrubbed. Fresh clothes, old sneakers, my stomach a mess but I ate toast and jam anyway, washing each bite down with a flood of cold tea.

No missed calls from Sophia. I pulled up the internet and considered it for a moment. A quick news search: *red hook.*

I put the phone away. My ChapStick had come off on my toast. I went to the bathroom to put on more, staring at my soft eyes, the eyes of a damsel, circling the stick round and round till my lips were waxy. Then I jerked away sharp from the mirror because —

No *because.* No need to think too hard. If you poke around too long in the dark, you've only got yourself to blame for what you find. I had a feeling in my chest, a persistent asthmatic ache I couldn't quite rub away. A walk would help. It was early yet, so early Ella was still sleeping. I didn't have to be at work for hours.

I checked my phone again. No texts. I looked toward Ella's closed door. Typed and deleted, typed and deleted.

Out getting coffee, I said finally. Have a good day.

The sidewalk ran with morning commuters holding cups and phones and briefcases, flowing around me like water breaking itself on a rock. A terrier recoiled from my feet, growling through its teeth. Its owner looked up to apologize, then said nothing, his jaw tightening as he sped away.

I walked for a while without really seeing where I was going. Some uneasy frequency hummed off my skin. Men playing dominoes under awnings looked up warily as I approached, an old woman pushing a shopping cart veered into the gutter to avoid me. When sirens shrilled a block away, my hands went sweaty, my mouth dry.

Two police cars hurtled around the corner, passed me.

When they were gone I could breathe again.

The ache in my chest was climbing, it was a weight in my throat. When I realized I would throw up if I kept walking I dropped onto a stoop and texted Sophia. My fingertips trembled over the screen.

What happened last night?

Her reply came almost instantly.

Wait you don't remember

I waited for a follow-up. Waited, waited, unshed tears making rainbows over my sight.

Nothing to worry about, she said finally. Really. Talk later

The sounds of the city crashed in on

me. Birdsong and morning traffic and children screaming for the sheer joy of having lungs. I wanted to scream, too. For about half a minute all was bright, and the sun on my face felt like a benediction. Then the wicked math came back.

Three murders. Two hands. One foot.

Under the industrious light of seven a.m. I felt suddenly exposed. I imagined how I must look from behind: the flapper tangle of my grown-out hair, my sparrow-weight bones, everything about me crushable or ripe to be sliced. I was awash in adrenaline and relief and a jittery fear, and I didn't want to go home. But I was too edgy to stay out here. I figured there was one place I could hide.

Months ago, when we first moved back to New York, I made a pilgrimage to the coffee shop where I'd worked before leaving town. It was gone, a children's shoe store sprung up in its wake. More remnants of my old life absorbed into the whirlpool of the city. For a while I'd worked at a co-op, but I wasn't really the cooperative kind.

I stumbled into my new job by chance,

or luck, or fate. On a wandering evening last winter, I hid out from a snowstorm in a bookshop on Sullivan Street, narrow as a corridor and lit the color of coffee milk by old bulbs. The guy behind the counter had a chin-strap beard and little wire-rims, and was yelling into an ancient flip phone.

I'd pretended to look at books as I listened to him dress down some guy named Alan.

"It's not about their quality, *Alan*," he kept saying. "It's about coming through with *what you promised*."

I pulled an old hardback off the shelf, tea-brown pages and a cover illustration the colors of a heraldic flag. *Creatures of the Earth and Air: A Compendium.* I flipped gently through it as the man behind the counter became sarcastic.

"God forbid you waste *your* time coming to *me*," he said. "I'm sure it's a full-time job burning through your *trust fund*."

I was trying not to laugh when the book I held fell open to a place where something was stuck between its pages.

My breath caught. I didn't take lightly

things found in the pages of a book. But this was just a playing card. A jack of spades, its back the classic red Maiden design. I flipped it over and back, not noticing the bookseller had hung up till he was standing next to me.

"Found that in a book?" he asked, taking the card.

"This one." I held up *Creatures.*

"Huh." He bent over the playing card, then made a triumphant sound. "There. Look at that."

I looked close. The Maiden held up her flowers, and fork-tailed women chilled in the card's four corners.

"Her." He pointed at the mermaid in the upper left. Where the others' hands reached toward flowers, hers extended toward a spinning wheel. Stylized, but unmistakable. You wouldn't notice it unless you were looking.

"What does it mean?"

He looked gratified by my curiosity. "It means it's from a marked deck."

"Like, marked by a gambler?"

"Or a magician. It's an odd marking,

though, doesn't really correspond to the suit or number. I tell you, I find the strangest things in books."

I'd followed him to the front of the shop, where he brought a cigar box out from under the counter and slipped the card inside. "Like what? What else have you found in a book?"

"Well . . ." He looked around, like the walls might have ears, and reopened the cigar box, faced toward him so I couldn't see its contents. "Things like this."

He showed me a pressed blue flower as big as my fist, its stamens flattened in all directions like a fireworks spray. A cookie fortune that read, simply, "Woe betide you." A neatly clipped page of personal ads dated September 1, 1970, from a paper called the *East Village Chronicler.*

"Funny stuff, right?"

It was. I liked it, the thought that you could find harmless, interesting things tucked inside books. A reminder that the world contained mysteries that didn't have to write over the entire narrative of your life.

"Once I found a Polaroid in an old

book," I said, watching his face for a re-action. "A collection of fairy tales. The weird thing was, it was a Polaroid of *me*."

"Holy crap," he said, his eyes bright with respect. It didn't seem to occur to him that I might be lying. I wasn't, but I could've been.

"Are you guys hiring?" I asked him.

He'd run a palm over his beard, in a way that made it clear he was proud of it. "We might be. If you like odd hours, I think we are."

That's how I started working at a cramped used and antiquarian book-store, where the odd hours warning was for real. Beard guy's name was Edgar, he owned the place, and he never sent my schedule more than a week in advance. My shifts ranged from two hours to ten, and sometimes when I got there the shop was closed without warning. It was the buyers who bought rare books by mail that kept the lights on, not the random college kids popping in to browse and walking away with a five-dollar used copy of *Howl*.

The oppressive heat had picked back

up after yesterday's rainstorm, and I was sweating through my T-shirt by the time I hit the shop. It wouldn't open for a couple of hours yet, but luckily Edgar was a terrible judge of character: I had keys.

My heart settled as I walked in, breathing coffee and paper and sunburnt dust. Like all good bookshops, Edgar's was a pocket universe, where time moved slow as clouds. Mainly I read on the clock, or listened to him enumerate his various grievances with the world, or drank coffee in the surreal quiet till my fingers started to quake.

Edgar and I had a running contest going since the day I'd first come in: whoever found the weirdest thing in a used book wins. Since discovering the marked card that first day, I'd found an extremely formal typed breakup letter, a photo-booth strip featuring a man posing with a pineapple, and a business card for a "Noncorporeal Matchmaker" based out of South Florida (and called her; the number was out of service). Edgar was currently ahead, with the flattened toupee he'd found in a copy of *Pamela.*

Today was the day I would win our contest for good, though Edgar would never know it.

I circled the store when I got in, checking the spaces between shelves, my head full of rubies and blood. I plugged my phone into the bookshop speaker and listened to *Pink Moon* on repeat, prodding at the missing memories of the night before like a rotten tooth. When Edgar opened the front door a couple of hours later, he made it a few steps into the shop before he saw me, and screamed.

"What is wrong with you?" he shouted, ripping out his earbuds. "Do you live here now?"

"Sorry," I mumbled. God bless Edgar, he had no follow-up questions.

By ten a.m. we were sharing a bag of Swedish licorice in companionable silence, and I was feeling halfway normal. By eleven the bookstore was busyish, my nerves winding tighter with every jingle of the bell. It didn't feel right, that one city, one life, could hold all these things: A rush of shoppers carrying clever tote bags. A night in Red Hook colored by liquor and blood. And three dead ex-

Stories, pieces of them spirited away. Finally, during a lull, I sidled to the front and turned the sign to CLOSED, flipping the lock shut.

Just for an hour, I reasoned. Then I'd go buy Edgar a compensatory coffee. He was too lost in his book to notice anyway.

For some reason the carpet was squishiest between English Literature and World Mythologies, so I sat there and pulled down *Persuasion.* I'd been reading it on shifts for the past week, and sank back into it now like cool water, letting my fevered brain trapdoor into Austen's amiable world. I started out distracted, but soon I was reading headlong because I was getting to the sexy part, where Captain Wentworth writes Anne the letter.

I can listen no longer in silence, it began. I'd read it a hundred times, sometimes out loud to Ella on the road. *I must speak to you by such means as are within my reach.*

I sped through the pages toward the letter. Anne had her conversation with Harville, Wentworth stood stricken at the other end of the room. He scribbled something on paper, rushed from the room, then returned to press the letter into her hand. I swallowed my last half inch of coffee, gritty with undissolved sugar, as Anne opened it and began to read.

I am lost and stupid and doing this all wrong, it began. *Maybe you'll never read this.*

I sat straight. Reread the words, not Austen's. They stayed the same, in bleary black text on a page that smelled like paste and old houses.

I am lost and stupid and doing this all wrong. Maybe you'll never read this. If it reaches you, the magic worked. And if the magic works, that must mean we'll meet again. I think we'll meet again. I think we're meant to. I don't know what I think any-more.

Have you forgiven me, for not coming back? Do you think of me out here, banging around the stars? Sometimes the image of you hits me so hard and sudden I believe the only explanation is you're thinking of me at that exact moment, too. But I might be kidding myself. Maybe you'll never read this. Or maybe when you do, you won't let yourself believe in impossible things.

But I don't think so, because you are one of those impossible things. When you left, I was lost. But I think I'm finding my way back now. Will we meet again? Some days I think yes, others, no. You'll never read this, will you? I've said it three times now, it must be true. I don't know how to end this. How do I end this? Maybe I just stop

~8~

There was no signature. The letter ended, Anne swooned. I paged forward, my fingers clumsy. Wentworth got his girl, and she got her captain. I paged back — the detestable Mary Musgrove, poor Captain Benwick, Louisa falling from the wall. All of it unchanged, except for the letter.

All my anxious thoughts gave way under a wave of wonderment. The world went bigger and smaller at once, closing in on the page and expanding around me into a place of impossibilities.

Where had we gotten this book? It was

old, though in perfect condition, and the letter — the wrong, new, not–Captain Wentworth's letter — matched the type in the rest of it. The page fit snugly into the binding. If I asked Edgar about it, he'd grow suspicious — he had a Spidey sense for weird, it was why I liked him. But I had the silliest, headiest feeling anyway: that I knew who wrote this. That it was meant for *me.*

I troubleshot the notion, trying to keep my head clear. It could be an extremely unlikely printer's error. A very old joke. A newer joke, neatly done. Or it could be — could it be? — a letter written to me.

I'd found stranger things in a book.

Someone battered the front door with the heel of their hand. The floor creaked as Edgar wandered toward it.

"Why are they — wait a minute. Alice, did you lock the door?"

I crouched between shelves, listening to him let someone in. Before he could come find me, I shoved the Austen under my shirt, into the waist of my cutoffs.

"I'm buying you a coffee!" I announced, springing to standing.

"Yah!" Edgar pressed a hand to his heart. A grad student–looking dude stood behind him, browsing the overstock table. "Did you lock the door, then *hide? Why,* Alice?"

"I need more coffee. I'll get you one, too. I'll be back in ten, okay?" I was barely listening to my own words, I just had to get *out.*

The heat and noise and bright insult of the sun were a shock after the shop's quiet. It was coming on five and he was everywhere.

There, on the corner, leaning over a bucket of bodega flowers to fish out a fistful of daisies. Jumping onto the bed of a truck, the back of his T-shirt thin with sweat. Headphones over his ears, holding a blue-and-white paper cup, gaze gliding over me as he walked by. All of them, for a moment, were Ellery Finch.

The air felt thin, the sun felt close, the sidewalk gave under my high-tops like it was made of rubber. The guy behind the counter of the coffee shop was him, too, staring back as I stared too long, before shaking myself and ordering something cold. And decaf. My blood was already buzzing.

That boy, the one who'd saved me, then let me go. In my memory he was soft and hard and shining. Eyes a carbonated color and smile with secrets in it, good ones and bad.

You are one of those impossible things.

I didn't remember walking back to the shop, but I got there somehow. A couple my age were prowling the shelves when I walked in, and Edgar was looking at me expectantly.

"Oh." I brought a hand to my face. "No. I forgot your coffee. Want me to . . . ?" I gestured at the door.

He rolled his eyes. "Forget it. Just . . . go talk to a customer."

I stashed my bag, the Austen shoved to the bottom of it, beneath the counter, and went to give the couple some extremely cursory service. They left with books anyway, and Edgar was appeased.

He headed out soon after they did, leaving me to close. I read the letter a dozen times, slow then fast. I read the chapter leading up to it, trying to recapture the feeling of finding it for the first time. I read it all at once and in pieces. It never wobbled, or turned back into Austen's words, and every time it sent fire through my veins.

By nine I was doing laps of the shop. All of yesterday's angst and terror and confusion had burned off like fog. The world felt limitless, its bright spaces brighter. I craved high skies and open sidewalks and to run flat out till I couldn't breathe. Finally it was closing time. I counted out the drawer, locked the door behind me, and headed to the train.

Persuasion was nested under my arm like a talisman. But untethered from the shop, I became less certain. The sticky press of anxiety settled itself back around my shoulders, like it had been waiting all day for me to be alone. I wanted to be sure. I wanted to *know*. So I didn't take the subway down, back to Brooklyn. I took it up, toward him.

The train was full of teenagers with good shoes and too much confidence. I wanted to put sunglasses on to block out their light. I'd felt younger than them once, and older than them now, but we'd never really been the same age. I didn't know what age I was. I wedged in between a dude pointedly reading a scuffed copy of *Siddhartha* and an Orthodox woman bowing her head over a child, the subway light bouncing greenly off the smooth brown wings of her hair. At Eighty-Sixth Street I climbed out and into our old life on the Upper East Side.

We'd lived here when Ella was married, when I briefly attended private school. I was afraid now of seeing someone from my past, but nobody I knew showed their face among the scatter of summer-dressed women and men in suits, the tourists with their heartbreaking, shower-damp hair. The summer light had held on tight, but now it was finally gone. I walked to Central Park first, skirting its edge till I was across the street from his old building's front door.

It had been a while since I'd come here. In the early days I kept my head down, but now I didn't bother. I looked so different. I'd grown an inch, my hair was darker and grazed my neck.

The building looked like it always did: imposing and implacable. There was no sign that a boy had lived here once, with his books and his wishes and his questing heart, and that he was gone now, farther than you could reach with money or longing.

What would Finch think of me now? He'd given so much to save me from my own monstrousness. What would he think if he saw me wading back in? I wasn't sure what I'd expected, coming here, but all I got was the empty feeling of calling down a cut line. There was no secret knowledge waiting for me, no final chapter. For a minute I'd felt sure of something at last — sure of *him*. But staring at the building's indifferent face, my certainty drained away. He was distant. He was gone. And the letter in the book was just words on a page.

And three of the Hinterland were dead.

And this morning I'd brushed blood off my teeth.

It was late and I had better reasons than the hour to hurry back home, but the park was an appealing patchwork of dark and light, and I just felt so damned low. Finch and I had walked here together once.

Well, we'd *run.* From the sight of fairy-tale horror unfolding on the sidewalk, our very first glimpse of the Hinterland. Back before I understood what I was running from was me.

Now I walked its paths alone, breathing the sweet and toxic city air. Along the water a while, then down toward the lawn. Couples kissed on benches, or poked at their phones. A little girl too young to be alone watched me from atop a rocky embankment. When a jogger zipped past, I whipped around without thinking, to see who was chasing them.

There was music coming from somewhere. Silvery champagne-glass music, combing itself into the breeze. I followed it a long while, expecting at any moment to come upon a late-night wedding party, a dance floor lined with lights. But I never could trace it to its source.

It was so late now it was early, the park long since closed. My body felt heavy, full of too many things, more than I could possibly contain. A little grief gnawed at me, and fear I held off with one arm, and my brain kept circling back to the question of what I'd really done last night, what Sophia called *nothing to worry about.* I tried to float over it all, but the crash was coming. I wanted to be home before it happened.

I made my way back to the subway. It was late, the train to Brooklyn took forever to come. When it did, the car was almost empty. A few stragglers spread out among seats: a teenage boy playing hip-hop on his phone, a man in scrubs, and a woman with an old-fashioned pram, sleeping with her head against the window. The pram was pink and lace-trimmed and way too big to be hauling down the subway steps. There was a woven blanket inside it, but I couldn't see the baby.

Everyone looked sickly under the lights. I closed my eyes and listened to tinny cell phone hip-hop flicker and pulse. The guy in scrubs was watching me, I was sure of it, but every time I checked, he'd just looked away. The air smelled vaguely of weed and French fries.

We were rolling slowly between stations when I heard a noise coming from the pram. Something like a huff, something like a whine.

I looked at the mother again. She was in her early twenties, her closed lids frosty with shadow. Her hands were hidden in hoodie pockets and there was a collapsed purse on the seat next to her, its top spilling over. Nothing about her said *Hinterland,* but. But. The train inched along, the kind of slow friction-less roll that feels like falling. Then the sound repeated itself. Doubled up, a *huff huff whine.*

We were underground and suddenly I felt it, the weight of pavement and dirt and city pressing down. I stood. The guy in scrubs looked at me again, and this time I caught him. The mother was still sleeping, one of her feet propped up on the pram's front wheel.

I moved closer, making like I was look-ing at the map behind her head. My brain spat awful images at me as I edged toward the pram, *hair and tooth and bone and blood,* all of it wiped away when I got near enough to see inside.

A baby lay in a cocoon of blanket, snuf-fling its odd animal breaths. It was so new it looked uncooked, its face as sweet and secret as something found inside a seashell. I exhaled hard, starting to back away, but my nearness had woken its mother. She blinked up at me like I was inside her house, standing over her bed. Like I was the nightmare.

"I'm sorry," I said.

She opened her mouth to say something back, and the lights went out.

All the way out, all of them. No safety lights, no lights in the tunnel. The car stopped moving. The music had cut out, too.

The dark weighed more than the light. A three-point constellation came out, almost in unison: phone lights, illuminating nothing. They were bright, but they didn't bend the dark.

"Dude." The man in scrubs. "I can't see shit. What's wrong with the lights?"

Instinct kept me from taking out my phone. Made me move away from the mother and child. I burrowed through the blackness, toward the door at the far end of the car, feeling my way from pole to pole. The skunky scent of cheap weed was heightening, sharpening, becoming an impossible breeze. It ghosted through the closed car, touching my face with cold fingers.

Behind me, on the far end of the train, the door to the next car slid open.

"Is that the conductor?" someone said hopefully.

The door banged shut. The silence that followed stretched so long I started to hallucinate other sounds: scratching. My blood pumping triple time. Something outside the windows, beating itself against the black.

Whoever had let themselves in started walking. The dark heightened the sound of their shoes trudging over the floor. As they passed the baby, it let out a cry, hopeless and thin. The walker paused.

"Shh," the mother said, urgent. "Baby, *shhhh*."

"Who's hiding there?" said the hip-hop kid, his voice high and younger than I thought it'd be. "Yeah, asshole, I'm talking to you."

I think he was trying to draw them away from the baby. But when the steps resumed, moving toward him, he sucked in a breath and went quiet.

The step was a steady *shush shush,* mocking and slow. It moved past the boy, past the man in scrubs, and on toward me.

When I reached the door at the end of the car, the latch wouldn't turn. The baby had hushed, the car was filled with frightened breathing and the slide of someone's shoes. I was scared, too, but the fear was changing: chilling, hardening, making my fingers flex and my head fill up with a cold white hum.

The person stopped an arm's length away. The locked door was at my back and my vision was pulsing, fracturing the dark into purples and reds. They were so close we could've touched.

"Who's there?" I said.

They took a breath, and sang in a whisper.

Little mouse
Scratch scratch
Hasten to your home
Lock and latch, do up the catch
And pray that you're alone

Little spider
Twitch twitch
Run to seal the gate
Weave and sew, stitch stitch
Pray it's not too late

Something about that whisper tugged at me, distant but familiar. The words they spoke were a Hinterland rhyme. I knew by the way it played over my tendons like a rosined bow. The tide of the place was lapping at me already; the rhyme drew it over my head. The cold in me was a frozen wave climbing. As the rhymer reached for me, the wave broke.

Their hands were fast and certain. But I slipped around and behind them; I slithered like smoke. Then I was on them. Running my fingers over their body, searching for skin. I felt the rough drag of cotton and the rasp of knit — they were wearing something over their face, like a balaclava — before plunging my fingers into the slit over their mouth.

Their teeth were sharpened pearls and their breath felt like nothing. I could feel my eyes clotting black, my mouth filling up with ice, but this time my head stayed clear. I wasn't going to forget this: breathing in the subway's stale air, transmuting it into cold. Into death. I held it in my mouth like a marble, trying to twist their face toward mine. They gave a noiseless shudder and bit down. I grunted and ripped my hand free, feeling their teeth dig bloody grooves. I jerked a knee into their gut and they folded over, spinning in my grip like a fish. A flash of heat lightning skittered down my side and I screamed: their nails, hard as glass.

The air smelled like a fairy tale, glitter and green things and blood. The person's nothing breath was in my ear, with a catch in it that made me think they were laughing. I yanked them down by the shirt and pressed my arm to their covered throat. I hovered over them, my mouth all ripe with ice, and *now* they were quiet.

I lunged down to press my mouth to theirs. When we touched, the air between us puckered with static. I recoiled just long enough for them to dart forward and bite me.

They caught the edge of my chin and bit all the way through. I felt warmth before

I felt pain, banging my head against an empty subway seat as I fell back clutching my face.

The air was still. It didn't smell like magic anymore, it smelled like a stalled-out subway car laced with blood. The person stood up, and I braced myself. But I must've made them think twice. They walked the few steps to the nearest doors, peeled them open with a straining mechanical clang, and dropped to the tracks below. I heard the wood-and-metal thump of their falling. The doors shrugged shut, and they were gone.

A few swollen moments. Then the lights came on, their milky yellow glow revealing the wreckage that had been made of me. Holding my head, pressing the hem of my T-shirt to my chin, I stood.

The other passengers stared with open mouths. At my arms, an ombré of whites to my elbows, and my eyes, I was certain, a galactic black. Blood dripped from my bitten hand, my bitten face, the mess over my ribs. The guy in scrubs was peeking down at his phone, its camera angled discreetly toward me. He stiffened as I stalked over and slapped it out of his hand, stomped its screen twice, and kicked it down the car.

"What are you?" asked the teen boy, his voice reverent. "Are you a supervillain?"

The adrenaline and the ice would recede. Soon I'd be shaking. Soon I wouldn't be able to stand. "Yeah," I said. "I'm a supervillain. Now gimme your phones. On the floor, slide 'em over. And you." I said it to the mother. "I need your sweatshirt."

Her face was stone as she shrugged it off, throwing it after her phone so it pooled at my feet. Pulling it over my head made my scratched side throb. New blood soaked into the waist of my jeans as I crouched to gather their surrendered phones. "Sunglasses. Somebody here has sunglasses." I snapped my fingers. "You want me to get them out for you?"

The boy took a pair from his pocket and slung them at me, wincing when they hit my chest. "Sorry. You can keep those."

I caught them, shoving them on and tugging the hoodie's sleeves over one hand, using the other to put pressure on my bleeding chin. A seat hit me behind the knees and I collapsed into it, feeling the first tremor roll through me, the aftereffect of shock and ice and magic. But my thoughts were edged finely as frost.

I'd almost become the fourth Hinterlander to die. Whoever had tried to kill me, they were Hinterland, too.

~9~

At least someone in the car had a god who listened. The guy in scrubs had been praying with his eyes closed for only a few minutes when the train started to move again. The mother was crying, though her baby was quiet. When we reached the next station, they all watched rabbit-eyed as I walked off, their phones stuffed into the front pocket of my stolen sweatshirt.

I felt like I should turn around and say something scary to them as the doors closed. But my mouth still tasted like freezer-burned death and all the places

I was hurt were running together, pain pumping through me like central air. I let the moment go.

I stood at the very edge of the platform and let three trains pass by, woofing my hair back and sliding their doors open to show me their insides. Half of me was sure the lights would turn off, and the figure would come back to net me with fairy-tale rhymes in the dark.

Little spider
Twitch twitch . . .

I shook my head sharply and spat onto the tracks.

They must've had a knife tucked somewhere. They wouldn't have come after me with only their teeth and nails. When I imagined that knife going in between my ribs, sliding down my arms to unpeel me, I could only think of pressure and a sudden, sheeting heat. What piece would they have taken from me? My hand. Ice-white and malevolent, curled in like a Hand of Glory. Or my eye, a plucked marble turned black from end to end.

Right foot, said a sensible part of my brain. To make a matched set with Hansa's left.

Finally anxiety chased me onto a car nearly filled with what appeared to be a single, sprawling tourist family, all of them upsettingly bright-eyed. They looked at me in my hoodie and my sunglasses and my bitten face. The smallest one, too little to be awake at this hour and swinging in dizzy circles around the pole, froze in place when she saw me, making a sound like an injured dog.

I gave her a thumbs-up and sat between a big man in bigger shorts and an alarmed-looking grandpa holding a walking stick. I wondered what stories they were telling themselves about me.

Coke addict, I decided. Clipped her chin falling down in a bathroom.

They wouldn't be far off. The Hinterland had crept toward me like a waking dream, crashed in like a wave, and receded. I was left adrenalized and salt-starred. Remembering, completely, what it was like to feel *power.* Not the kind you got drunk on and forgot by morning, but the real thing.

109

I was sick with it, shivering, busted up in three different ways. And I was high on it, clinging as it left me, feeling the delirious ache of its retreat. I ran over everything that had happened in the dark. The Hinterland rhyme, the smoothness of the skin around the rhymer's mouth, the nothing feel of their breath. That voice. I couldn't shake the feeling that I knew it.

The sky was warming to gray when I finally climbed out of the subway. When I peeked at my fingertips, they were warming too, an almost acceptable shade of pale. I bought a bottle of water at a bodega and splashed the blood off my face and hands, but didn't dare peel my T-shirt away from the mess over my ribs. My gouged-up side was a burn and an ache and a hideous numbness, like it couldn't decide what kind of awful it wanted to feel. My vision went prismatic as the corner of some asshole's duffel bag strafed my rib cage as I walked down Bowery.

I wasn't heading home yet. The place I was going to was one I'd only heard about, and never wanted to visit. I didn't want to go there now. It was a narrow brick build-

110

ing on a windy stretch of Lower Manhattan, its front laced up with flaking iron balconies. Letters crawled down its side: an H, then an EL, the missing OT between them punched out like front teeth. Of course everyone who lived there called it Hell.

Which was fitting, because all of them were Hinterland. It wasn't clear what state the hotel had been in when they got there, how its rooms were turned over to them one by one, but they'd made it their squat in the end. I pictured bellhops stuffed in closets, old ladies who'd spent half a century in their rent-controlled rooms shoved out into the streets.

It wasn't quite five in the morning. The sidewalk in front of the hotel was empty, spangled with broken glass. Across the street, a man with a green juice in one hand and a yoga mat in the other powered by, like a messenger from another planet.

I watched him disappear, then pushed through the tarnished gold and smeared glass of the revolving doors.

It was three steps down into a sunken

lobby, but it felt much deeper. There was a subterranean taste to the air, of must and hidden water. The room was lit by a flotilla of lamps on low tables, their stained-glass shades shining like fish.

On a semicircle of long velvet couches, seven sisters reclined like fussy, card-playing cats, their hair the color of old pewter against their dark brown skin. I knew them a little. They liked to tell everyone they'd been princesses, but that wasn't what I'd heard. They always wore thin satin gloves that stopped just above their wrists, in hard-candy colors. On one girl it would've been odd. On seven, it was creepy.

The guy behind the desk sat perfectly straight, hands folded in front of him and fleshy mouth resting in a vulpine half-smile. He was asleep. I brought my hand down hard on the little desktop bell and watched his eyes shutter open. They were cloudy, pupilless, yellow as a cat's. Then he blinked, belched, and stretched all at once. By the time his eyes fixed on me they were sandy, the same basic color as his skin and hair. In his tacky taupe suit, he was a study in monochrome.

His gaze slid from my torn chin to my fingers. He snuffled at the air, lifting his chin, and looked at the place where my sweatshirt hid the worst of the blood. "Interesting night?"

I didn't take the bait. "Is Daphne around?"

"Who's asking?"

"You're not in the mob, Felix," I snapped. "The sun's barely up, I know she's here. What's her room number?"

"You don't know the hours she keeps," he said starchily, and jerked his head toward the elevator. "Ninth floor, room nine oh three. Knock before you open the door."

"I know how doors work."

As I crossed the lobby, one of the sisters gave me a languid wave. At least I thought it was a wave. Those girls would look half asleep running out of a burning building.

The elevator was barely big enough for one, and smelled like an apartment where a chain smoker had made cabbage soup every day for a year without ever cracking a window. To distract myself from the pain in my side I focused on the pain in my chin, then switched to my hand, and around again. On the ninth floor I stepped out into a hallway with the flat look of a trompe l'oeil, like a badly painted set. The door to room 903 was beat up even worse than the rest, its paint scuffed and scored. There was an old bullet hole just below the lock.

I knocked with my uninjured hand. When Daphne finally opened the door I stepped back before I could stop myself. I'd never seen her without her lipstick on. Bare, her mouth was the same color as her skin. Her red hair and long red robe flickered around her like flame over bone, and her skin breathed a multitude of sins. I was grateful she was wearing her veneers.

"Morning," she said, leaning into the doorframe and looking at my chin. "Take a fall?"

"Something like that," I said. "Actually, you don't have any Band-Aids or anything, do you? Or some painkiller?"

She turned without answering, and I followed her in. Her room had a baroque little sitting area and a tiny kitchenette by the windows. Through half-open French doors I saw a tumbled bed, a pair of long legs sticking out of white sheets. Daphne shut the doors when she saw me looking.

"You came all the way here just to get patched up? I thought your mama would want to do that for you." She put a sugary venom into the word *mama.*

I put my hands up. I wasn't taking her bait, either. "You don't have to do anything. I'm just here to talk."

"What about?"

"I got attacked by someone on the train. I'm pretty sure they were trying to kill me."

I told her all of it, and it was like I was telling the story to myself, too. I don't think I fully believed it had happened till I said it out loud. Halfway through I had to sit down, a hand over one eye, my vision glittering with the beginnings of a migraine.

She kept her mouth shut till the end, fiddling with a matchbook and staring at a point over my shoulder. "Say the rhyme again," she said.

I did. It was circling in me like a restless dog.

"They were trying to kill you." Her voice was dangerous. "You're *sure* of that."

I thought about it. They'd been reaching for me, hadn't they? I came at them, but they'd reached first. "Yeah. I'm sure."

She was angry. I couldn't say how I knew it, she was perfectly composed. But her anger made the hair rise on my arms. It made the air thicken.

Then she leaned back, legs flashing beneath her robe as she crossed them. "So why'd you come to me?" She laughed at my expression, the sound of it catching like rock sugar in her throat. "What? I know you don't like me. I thought I'd be the last one you'd ask for help."

"I'm not asking you for help, I'm telling you because they listen to you. It didn't end with Hansa, they need to know that. You have to *tell* them."

"I have to, do I?" She eyed me. "You're paler than I am. How much blood did you lose? Look, I'll play nurse if you keep it a secret."

116

There was something surreal about watching her gather up a grubby first-aid kit and a cup of hot water and a wad of brown coffee shop napkins. She gestured at me to peel back the T-shirt from my side, which hurt about as much as getting scratched. The mass of napkins softened to sludge as she blotted.

"I don't think you need stitches, but you got opened up pretty good. It might close quicker with a drop of glue. You want me to send someone down to the store?"

"Hell, no." I was staring through tears at the ceiling. "I'm not a birdhouse, I've got skin."

"Suit yourself." She painted livid stripes of Mercurochrome across my ribs, each feeling like the rough scrape of a cat's tongue. Even in this crummy light, her hair looked like treasure. Her hands were blunter, more capable than I'd figured they'd be. Slowly, almost resentfully, I could feel myself blooming in her direction.

"I heard what happened in Red Hook," she said, not looking at me.

I let a few breaths go by. So she knew what I'd done, while I still didn't.

"What'd you hear?"

"That you're not the nice little girl you've been pretending to be." She assessed me, top to bottom. "What I'm wondering is, why now? After all these months of good behavior?"

It took me a minute to decide what kind of honest I should be. "Because he deserved to be scared. Because nobody else was going to."

"So it was a good deed?" She put away the disinfectant and started unwrapping a stack of Band-Aids. "I guess I can't blame you for trying to play out your tale."

I dug my nails into my palms. In my tale, he ended up dead. "I don't really know my tale."

"Really? Your mother doesn't want you to know, is that it?"

She'd already brought Ella up twice. I didn't like that. "My mother . . ."

I paused. My mother what? *My mother survived the Hazel Wood. She survived Althea Proserpine. My mother's not scared of you.*

Saying it felt too close to a dare. "My mother's got nothing to do with it."

Her long fingers pressed a Band-Aid over my side, then another. "You're afraid of knowing, then."

But that wasn't it, either. Not anymore. Finch had told me half my tale — the tale of Alice-Three-Times — in a diner on Seventy-Ninth Street. His hands around a coffee cup, the whole place leaning in. He loved those stories. His love was a halo. If I was going to hear the end of mine, I wanted him to be the one to tell it. And if that was never gonna happen, I could live without knowing.

But I wasn't about to give her all that.

"How about you?" I said instead. "What's your tale?" Sophia and I had speculated on that before. I thought step-mother. Daphne thought queen.

"One day you might earn the answer to that. But not today." Daphne tilted her head, looked at my bandaged side, and gave it a slap. The pain of it filled my eyes and sent me speechless.

"You're all patched up, princess. I'll send you the bill."

There was more I wanted to ask, more I needed to say, but I couldn't find it around the pain. *Someone tried to* kill *me,* I wanted to shout, but she already knew that.

I was halfway out the door when she said my name. Just the shortened, human part of it.

The sun was higher now, filling the window behind her and making her features indistinct. "You don't know your tale," she said, "but I do. You don't know what you did in Red Hook, but *I* do. You bit him. You bit a chunk of him clean off. Then you pressed those icy hands to his skin and you nearly killed him."

Her robe trailed behind her as she moved closer, revealing the spidery sprawl of her limbs. "You didn't know you could do that here, did you? I bet you didn't. Hiding out with that woman you call your mother, playing house. I bet you thought you were human all the way through."

She took another step forward and I stepped back and I no longer had a handle on the game we were playing. "You bit him and you tried to kill him and your

120

friend had to pull you off. You can thank her for that. And don't worry about retribution, I got that indiscreet fucker out of town. For that, you can thank *me*."

~10~

Eleven missed calls from Ella, starting just after midnight. Four voicemails, a screen full of texts.

It was half past six a.m. when I got home, and she was waiting at the kitchen table. A mug of coffee by her left hand, a filled ashtray and sprawled-out copy of *Magic for Beginners* at her right, like a goddess with her attributes. She'd never smoked in this apartment before. The scent of coffee and cigarettes in a dim kitchen sent me down a wormhole to the past.

She took me in. My chin and the way I

hid my hand and the gait that favored my injured side. The unfamiliar sweatshirt, still bagging in front with a pair of stolen cell phones. Her eyes went big, and I waited for her to cry out, to ask what happened, but she said nothing.

"I thought you quit," I said finally, nodding at the ashtray.

"Did you?" She took her time tapping out another cigarette before she spoke again. "I think it's time we have some honesty between us, don't you?"

I had four steps. From the doorway to the chair across from her, four steps to decide what I'd tell her and what I couldn't, and how that would play with what I'd already said, and it just wasn't enough. I stayed standing.

Finally her voice revealed a quiver. "So this is what I rate? You stay out all night, don't even text, come home looking like a goddamned cage fighter, and now you won't even sit down and talk to me?"

There were words that would undo this, that would heal what I'd cracked, but I didn't know them. I shook my head, willing her to understand.

She mirrored me, mockingly. "What? What are you doing? What aren't you saying? Where have you *been?*" She put a hand to her head.

"I chose you," she whispered. "All those years ago. You were a lonely little thing tucked into a basket, and I knew just by looking at you that nobody loved you. I held you. And I took you. I watched you grow. I watched your eyes go clear. Go brown, like mine. You were . . ." She shook her head. "Your hands were like starfish. The top of your head smelled like dried apricots. Oh, my cranky girl."

Somewhere in her, Ella knew. She knew I could've stayed in the Hinterland two years ago, knew I'd thought about doing it, if only for a moment. It was love that made her hold on to me, but it was something else, too. She'd shaped her life around giving me mine. Sometimes that sacrifice was a gift that bit. A rose with thorns.

"I chose you first," she said, like she'd read my thoughts. "But you chose me back. You got free of it, you came home to me. I'm not an idiot, I know what's

124

happening here. Why are you letting it right back in?"

She turned realer and realer as I walked, finally crossing the kitchen to stand beside her, in sweats and an old T-shirt and hair more gray by the day. Her spiky beauty was going soft. I could see the end of her days as a warrior. I could see the day coming when she couldn't stand another fight with me. *For* me. Love rose up like a noose and circled my throat.

I bent over and wrapped my arms around her, pressing my nose into the space where her neck became her shoulder. It smelled of rosemary and iron, like a ward against fairies.

"I love you." I said it quietly, right up into her skin, but she heard me anyway. After a moment, her arms lifted to hug me back. Her hair stuck to my cut face and my side tugged against the Band-Aids but I was afraid of what might happen if I pulled away.

"I never wanted to spend my life in New York anyway," she said.

I shot up. Her face was defiant. I'd seen that expression before.

125

"What's that supposed to mean?"

"We'll go somewhere beautiful."

Oh, shit, I'd heard that *voice* before. That exact promise.

"We could live on a farm. We've still got money left over from the Hazel Wood sale, enough to live on while we wait to sell this place. We could live in a place with red rocks, where you can see the Milky Way. We could finally get a dog."

I breathed in and out before I answered. "We can't keep doing this. Promising me rocks and dogs — it's not enough for us to keep doing this."

She lifted her chin, looked me in the aching eyes. "I once promised you a whole world. Did I not make good on that promise?"

"I can't move again," I said. "I can't."

Because my life here wasn't just blood and violence and secrets I didn't want to keep. It was walking over the bridge with Sophia at two a.m. It was hiding a deck of vintage playing cards in the books on Edgar's shelves, little unsigned notes to fifty-two buyers. It was having the world's best Danish on Church Street and the world's worst coffee on Cortelyou and seeing the divot in my bedroom wall from all the times I'd opened the door too hard, a divot that was *mine,* in a room that was mine, in a city that belonged to no one but at least you could borrow it, in pieces, and pretend it loved you back.

"So what do we do? Just go on like this? On and on like *this?*" She stalked over to the junk drawer, where rubber-banded takeout menus bred like rabbits. Yanked it open, pulled out a shiny-covered something and held it up.

It was a college brochure. Two sweatered people laughed together over their books, a manicured lawn glowing green around them. She pushed the bottom edge of it hard into my chest.

"Look at this." She was half laughing, but her face was wet. "I look at these things all the time when you're not home. I hide them like they're porn. It's not even — you don't have to go to college if you don't want to. I just want you to act like you're *here,* act like you'll *be* here, start putting down some roots with me." She cupped my face in her hands. "Or not with me. Whatever you need. Alice. My god, what more needs to happen for you to stay away from them?"

I put my hand over hers and slid it gently from my face. Then I stepped back.

"Mama." She stood up straighter when I said the word. I hadn't said it in years. "What more needs to happen for you to understand that I *am* them?"

Smoke played like ghosts over the ceiling. The morning light was a lie. And my mother was a forlorn figure in a room where she lived with a girl who was only a figment, really.

~11~

She wouldn't let me touch her. Her hand or her cheek or the ends of her black hair. My mother pressed herself small against the counter so I couldn't reach her. Finally I left the kitchen, stumbling down the hall to my room.

I was parched and starving. I had to pee, and pain sawed at me all over. But after twenty-four hours without it, sleep took me down.

I woke up shaking.

I was hot, then cold, then both at once. The midday light through the blinds was heavy, pouring over me in scalding stripes. I was too weak to roll away.

"Mom," I said. But the apartment was empty. I could feel it.

Infection. My attacker's nails that had sliced over me, there must've been something on them. It took three tries to pull up my shirt. My ribs looked like shit, the Band-Aids puffed with blood, but the skin around them seemed okay.

My shoulder itched. I scratched through my T-shirt, then under the fabric, finally dragging it over my head. A Hinterland flower was tattooed up my arm, and it itched. The tattoo was years old, it didn't make sense. The itching deepened to a burn.

I lay down for just a minute, closed my eyes. When I opened them, the light had changed. Time had come unstuck, hours passing without my seeing them go.

Something was wrong with me. It wasn't just my injuries, I was *sick.* I thought of ice water gliding down my throat, soaked into a compress laid across my head. I pictured my phone where I'd left it, with my keys by the door. Tears slid over my temples.

It got worse every hour. By early evening I was twisting under the sheets, watching leaf shadows play on the walls. I had to close my eyes and turn away when they became little faces, winking at me.

When my mother finally walked in, I thought she was a hallucination, too. Her face was stricken, her hand on my forehead cool.

"What is this?" she said. "You're burning up. *You.*"

I'd never been sick. Never, not once. I'd sprained an ankle, gotten a concussion, been hungover, had headaches, broken a rib once, vomited from bad shrimp tacos, and gouged the absolute shit out of my chin on a coffee table, but I'd never even had a cold. Ella crouched beside me.

"Do we need to go to the emergency room?"

She sounded so young. She had no script for this. Everything she'd dealt with, raising me alone, almost losing me, she'd never had to figure out a sick kid. "No, I'm —" I pushed up a few inches, tasting something in the back of my throat. Something bilious and thin. "I need water. And something to throw up in."

She brought what I'd asked for, plus a sleeve of crackers and a skimpy sampling from our medicine cabinet. Her steady hands propped me up with pillows, fed me water and crackers and aspirin, and touched a hydrogen peroxide–soaked cotton ball to my chin. I thought of Daphne patching up my ribs, then giving them a slap. The image broke as Ella climbed into bed with me and took my hand.

"Christ. Your head's on fire, but your hands are *freezing.*"

I had a sudden terror that my eyes would go black. But I was too tired to do anything about it, too weak even to walk to the bathroom; when I thought I might actually wet the bed, my mom had to help me down the hall.

Back in bed, the cold warring in me finally won out over the heat. Ella wrapped me in a robe and buried me in blankets dug out of summer storage. Her voice was drawn up tight.

"If you're not better soon we're going to the hospital."

It can't get worse than this, I kept thinking. *This is as bad as it'll get.* But I was always wrong.

I drifted off eventually, me under the covers and Ella on top, holding the lump that was my hand below. The long white road between waking and sleep stretched like taffy. My bed and my mother and the walls of my room melted into trees and castle walls and a courtyard spinning with snow.

It was the Hinterland, trying to break through. I wavered there, on the precipice of dreaming, and I fought it. But I was weak, and I staggered, and I fell.

When I stood up, I stood on a curve of sand, lapped at by dark water. Behind me huddled a line of shivering trees. The sky was so low I could touch it, like there was no air here that *wasn't* sky.

I was in the Hinterland. Not a dream of it, but the thing itself. It was altered: the land felt wilder. Unlatched. There was a looseness to it and a saturation too, the trees too close to the sea too close to

133

the sky, like someone had grabbed up a fistful of the Spinner's dark country and *squeezed.* The trees were bedded in a roiling black mist and stars crowded overhead, so beautiful and bright I forgot to be afraid. I was alone, watching the stars watching me.

Then one of them *trembled.*

It stepped out of its constellation. In the big, soft, humming silence, the star pitched itself into the sea. It was a fizzing ball of sodium white that became a girl as it drew nearer, with streaming hair and the noble, blunt-cut face of a figurehead. It slipped silently into the water, shining briefly below the surface before its light went out.

Others followed. One by one, then whole constellations, drawing courage from one another's plunge. The air thickened with plummeting stars like sparks thrown off a downed power line, till my sight sang purple and white.

After the last star fell, the moon hung like a lonely searchlight. I wondered if she knew that her granddaughter, Hansa, was dead. I wondered if she mourned her.

I watched as she lowered herself through the dark.

She was an old woman in her perch in the sky, a maiden crossing the horizon line, and a child when she touched the surface of the sea. She glowed beneath the water for a long time, lighting it the dreamy mermaid green of a motel pool.

I stood on the beach and watched her wane, feeling the shift of sand under my feet and smelling the sulfur of the fallen stars.

When the moon went out, there was nothing left but sand and water and empty sky. The trees whipped up wilder and the sea slid higher, moonless and misguided, till its cold fingers locked around my ankles, my knees, my hips. I heard a sound like splintering and a faraway singing, so high it made my scalp prickle, so low it made my knees bow, then the endless rushing of water falling over the edge of the world.

I could hear someone crying, someone moaning, someone writhing in their sleep. I knew it was me, that Earthbound version of me, but I couldn't reach her.

The water was to my chest now, to my throat, and I was lifted.

Something was being taken from me. I didn't know what it was, but I knew it was precious. I was back on the precipice: here, in a Hinterland running together like finger paints, and there, in Brooklyn, the press of my mother's arms holding me together.

For a moment both worlds held me in their grip, one of them dying but both of them strong, and I was wrung like a rag between them. At every joint and join I came apart and I thought that was the end of me, but I reconnected with an electric *pop,* and when I screamed, I screamed in both worlds. And though I couldn't hear it, I knew every Hinterlander on Earth screamed with me.

Then that world let go, dropping me back on my bed, in the city, with my mother's face over mine, terrified and smeared with tears.

"Alice, hold on. Alice, I'm here. I'm here. I'm here."

She said it like she was speaking every promise over a rosary bead, till she understood that I was looking back, that I was awake again, returned from wherever I'd been taken. My eyes burned with falling stars and my skin puckered with the chill of a dying land beneath an emptied sky.

"It's dead." I gripped her hands so tightly she winced. "The Hinterland is dead."

~12~

Everyone felt it.

Sophia and Daphne and Robin and the rest of them. All the fallen kings and eldest sons and cruel queens and maidens cast in colors of ebony and copper, blood and salt. Everyone knew it in their bones when the world we'd abandoned left us for good.

I didn't know that yet when I woke up, sweat-soaked and thirstier than I'd ever been. Ella lay on the floor beside my bed, watching *The Good Place* on her laptop with the sound on low.

138

I watched her for a minute before she noticed I was awake. Her mouth turned down, hair sweaty at the temples. She'd pulled off all her rings, her hands looked undressed.

I wondered if Finch had felt it, wherever he was. Probably not. He was born here, he was of the Earth. I guess he'd feel it if his was the world that drowned its stars and spun out into particles.

"Mom," I said, my voice a rasp.

She looked at me quickly, and smiled.

My phone was thick with texts from Sophia. The oldest just said my name.

Alice

Are you feeling this

Text me back

Text me back

Text me back

CALL ME

Then one from a number I didn't recognize.

Sophia's apartment tonight at 10. We're having a wake.

It was from Daphne. It had to be. Drawing all of us to one place: me, her, Sophia, the rest. The figure from the subway might be there, too. Maybe they'd bring their rhyme and a hidden knife. Maybe they'd want to finish what they started.

I texted back.

Do you think that's a good idea?

She never replied. When I called Sophia, her phone was dead, which wasn't unusual but worried me all the same. I told myself I might not go, that I *shouldn't* go, but I knew I would. I had to. I had to grieve for the Hinterland.

After a day spent lying low, drinking chicken broth and watching TV and picking at Thai takeout, I put on black jeans and black high-tops and a black T-shirt. I tried a Zelda Fitzgerald thing with my hair and a New Wave thing with my eyeliner, and I got both of them halfway right. I tucked a pocketknife into my jeans.

When I told Ella about the wake, she nodded, then turned away. We were still being delicate with each other, unsure where we stood after our fight. My sickness had drawn us into a tentative détente.

I stared out the window on the cab ride up, seeing nothing. When I closed my eyes I saw the faces of the stars, the moon in her declining phases. The Hinterland was dead. Hansa, the Prince, and Abigail were dead. I could've been dead, too. My brain sputtered, trying to forge a connection among those pieces. It was there, it had to be. But I couldn't see it. When we got to Sophia's, the driver had to tell me twice.

She lived in Lower Manhattan in a seedy old building you could tell had once been gorgeous. At some point it had been gutted, mostly rebuilt, then abandoned. It reminded me of those half-finished development projects you find sometimes off the highway. Ella and I used to pull over to explore them: cracked black streets petering to nothing, lonely cul-de-sacs, empty houses looking like they'd been dropped by a neat-fingered tornado.

I let myself in — the street door lock was broken — and climbed to the seventh floor.

The apartment where Sophia lived with five other ex-Stories had good bones, but that was about it. Construction dust clung to the corners, and patches of exposed drywall freckled the rooms. It was a temporary place, loose and rotten. Usually it was empty as an ice rink, but tonight it was haunted by forlorn figures. The long windows were bare and moonlight poured through, casting everyone in silver. Pockets of candles lined the sills and clustered like mushrooms on the ground; if we ended the night not dead in a fire, that'd be ten points for Slytherin.

There were more of us here than I thought still existed. Meetings were usually twenty, twenty-five of us, tops. But there had to be forty Hinterlanders in this room, with more arriving. I felt like a rat lifting its head to watch a tide of other rats running from a storm drain, and shuddering.

The murderer could've been anyone. That reedy boy, all deep dimples and curls to his shoulders, stone-cold putting away vodka like a sailor. That woman with the crown of blue-black hair, who looked like a consumptive Snow White and glared at me before I could turn away. Had it been her whispering to me in the dark?

There were cliques here and there —

packs of siblings, some pairs — but mainly we were a roomful of loners, unmixed. I saw the three brothers who lived in the pin-neat room next to Sophia's lined up against the wall drinking beer, T-shirts tucked in and pale hair pasted to their paler skulls. They looked like inbred royal cousins, perishing in the corner of some dusty Flemish painting. Genevieve was there, sitting alone on a windowsill drinking from a bottle of Stoli, her ridiculous Ren Faire sleeves almost dipping into a clutch of candles. Across the room, the Hinterland's creepiest kid, Jenny, perched on a stool wearing a ruffled dress, eyes ticking back and forth to see who was noticing her.

Even among the loners, I felt out of place. The eyes that met mine were cold, or slid away too fast. I nodded at a few whom I knew, whom I'd talked with sometimes when I was a part of things, and two of them looked right past me. The third stared a moment before spitting through her teeth.

Well, fuck Daphne. Whatever she'd been telling them about me, it had clearly worked.

"Alice."

I turned and smiled, my first genuine smile of the night. My favorite of Sophia's roommates had an executioner's build and the hard hatchet face of a murderess. But Nora's looks lied. She talked with the prim rhythms of a grammar primer, was fascinated by Earthly religions, and was deeply shy. I liked her a lot.

"My condolences to you on our loss," she said. Her tone was dry.

"Same to you," I said carefully. The Spinner had unwound Nora's story a long time ago. While she wouldn't talk about it, anyone could look at her and know she'd been built for villainy. It made me hate the Spinner more, to think of Nora's gentle nature bottled inside a weapon.

"Look at that," she said, jerking her chin at something over my shoulder. "A bit full out for a funeral, isn't it?"

Daphne, her lips red, her eyes bedded in sparkling shadow. She wore a brief black dress that made her skin and hair look like something you'd display on velvet in a jewelry shop window. I felt the oddest stab of irresolution, seeing her again in her lipstick and glitter. It struck me that I spent more time than I should deciding whether and how I despised this woman.

"Has she told you yet?"

Nora frowned. "Told me what?"

"Not you, I mean *all* of you — has she told you what happened to me?"

"She tells us lots of things," she said evenly. "It's hard keeping track."

I glanced at her. "How did she hook us, do you think? How did it get to where she snaps her fingers and we all come running? It's not really what we are."

Nora had green eyes clear as spring water. Even in the tarnished glow of moonlight and candles I could see them darken. "What we were. What are we now, but the lost children of a dead world?"

That was a bit too much poetry, even for me. "What does that mean? We already left the Hinterland. So it's gone now — what does that change?"

Her eyebrows went up, like she'd been stung by my stupid. But it wasn't rhetorical, I was really asking.

"People in this world have a thing they call god," she said. "Or gods. Yes?"

"Sure. Yeah."

"And they do good acts and take care to justify their bad ones to please their god or gods."

"Right."

"There are some among us who began to think of the promise of a return to the Hinterland as a sort of promise of paradise. They thought of the Hinterland, or the Spinner, perhaps, as a god. With the Hinterland gone, what's left to serve as our god?"

She looked pointedly at Daphne, and my stomach went cold.

"You understand, I think, why I fear their acts will grow godless."

I looked around at my kin, the culled-down lot of us. They were capable of such cruelty, such strangeness. They had such a disregard for the rules of this world. Thinking of them gone truly amok — gone *godless* — made my palms prickle.

"Listen," I began. "Something happened to me last night on the train."

Just then the room's chatter dropped to a hush. Nora turned away.

Daphne stood on a rickety card table in the center of the room, holding up a glinting something. A cup, I thought. No — it was a knife. She waited till the room was silent. Till we could hardly breathe, waiting for her to speak. Then her words cracked the quiet.

"The Hinterland is lost," she said. "But we are not."

She stood there a moment, knife still held aloft. All the faces of the Hinterland's motherless children were turned toward her, painted in flickering light.

"The body is dead, but we are the blood."

She glared up at the knife, looking like a figure from some other world's tarot deck. Then she brought it down, slashing it across her fingertips. She held her hand straight out and let the blood fall down, let everyone see the tears streaming over her cheeks. And despite everything, I did believe her sorrow was real.

"I grieve our loss," she said. "I grieve with you. I *bleed* with you."

I could hear other people crying. Even Nora's face was intent. The man beside us lifted his hand to his mouth and bit the pad of his thumb till it bled, holding it up to Daphne in tribute. A woman copied him. Then another. A rangy guy in blue jeans took out his own knife, used it to cut open his thumb, and passed it.

I flexed my injured hand, bile rising. I had the irrational thought that the killer, if they were here, would be drawn to the blood. That the drifting iron perfume of it would bring them slinking out of the shadows, weapon raised.

An arm came around me, and I jumped.

"Come on," Sophia whispered. "Let's go hide in my room."

She'd told Daphne, I knew. About Red Hook, and what I'd done. She was the only one who could have. But she'd stopped me, too — from killing the man from my tale. On the edge of doing something irrevocable, she'd pulled me back.

There was a bottle of grape soda waiting for us on the fire escape, next to a handle of bottom-shelf gin and a pair of sooty coffee mugs. Sophia poured a slug of gin in our cups and diluted it with grape. We sat so the bars of the fire escape pressed into our thighs and our legs hung down over the city. It was muggy on the street, but up here the air was witchy and restless, stirring itself into our hair. I could breathe again, away from Daphne, and I wanted to talk about anything but the murders, and the subway, and Red Hook. I wanted to remember what it felt like when fear was just the backbeat to my life, not the only thing I could hear.

"Here's to being orphaned. Well and truly, at last." Sophia lifted her glass, took a gulp, and gagged. "Ugh. The next wake I spring for the good stuff. When this world goes up in flames, we'll drink champagne."

I stuck the tip of my tongue into my cup. "It tastes like unicorn piss." I felt hyped up and shaky and suddenly soaked in grief. Inside was the wake, and Daphne's batshit display, but it was out here, with my mercurial, untrustworthy best friend, that I felt I could actually mourn what we'd lost. My skin prickled as I looked down on rooftops and cars and the slow-moving crowns of strangers' heads. A whole world, *gone*. It didn't seem possible. Sophia was looking, too, though I couldn't guess her thoughts within a mile.

"Robin's heart is broken. He really thought we'd get back in someday. He really wanted us to." Her voice was heavy and light at once. "I always thought it would be me that broke his heart."

I lay my head on her shoulder. I would tell her what happened on the subway. Soon, I'd find the words.

"I saw you on the beach," she said into my hair. "I watched you watching the stars come down."

"What?" I pulled back to look at her.

She smiled a little and didn't respond. Then, "Shut up," she said, though I wasn't talking. "I need to do a thing I never do."

I turned to her and waited. And waited.

"I'm sorry," she said.

"You're *what*?"

"I know. Don't tell anyone."

"For what, though? For loitering outside my bedroom window? Being late for everything ever? Never paying for anything, even though you carry an old-man cash roll in your purse?"

"You think I'd apologize for that?" She looked genuinely offended. "I'm sorry about . . . about what happened. In Red Hook."

I arched my foot, let my shoe slip off my heel, daring it to drop to the street. "Which part of it?"

"I knew you just wanted to scare him. I knew you didn't want to kill him."

The cocktail in my stomach was turning to acid. "I didn't kill him. You stopped me."

"I thought you couldn't remember."

"Just *tell* me. Tell me that's what happened."

Her nod was shallow, her voice hoarse. "I didn't want to, though. I wanted to let you. Because I could almost see him." She looked at me, pleading. "He was so close, Alice, I could *smell* him. That burning red-dust smell."

"See who? Who was close?"

"Death."

She'd told me her tale when we first met, but we hadn't talked about it since. It was about a girl who faced off against Death, and the price she paid for it: her death was taken away. She, Sophia, became *deathless*. I don't think she slept, either; even that little death was withheld from her. I tried never to think about it, but now it was a knife of cold air sliding between us. Because how did someone live when they knew they'd never die? I guessed I was learning.

"You didn't, though," I said. "I mean, you did. You stopped me."

"Right." She slopped more cocktail into her cup, then stood abruptly. "But I've been thinking. What if things are different for me, now that the Hinterland is gone?

"What do you think?" She kicked off her shoes and put one narrow foot on the first rail of the fire escape, then the other. Her dress was a thin cotton sack. I could see her body inside it, outlined by the city's lights.

"I think you should sit down and drink with me."

152

"I thought I'd find him here one day," she said. "I thought I'd find Death and convince him. But he never came to any meetings." Her laugh was fringed with hysteria. She perched on the top rail of the fire escape, looking down at me.

"You still could." I pushed up onto my knees. "Maybe he's here tonight."

"Maybe he's the one who's been killing us. Maybe he's coming for me next." She kicked a leg over. Seven stories of open city sang beneath her foot, summer smudged and readying its hands to catch her. I had to look straight up to see her face. Her hair hung down and her eyes were empty tunnels and she looked like a corpse already.

"What if I don't want to wait anymore?"

As she kicked her other leg over, I surged up, locking my arms around her waist. At the same time we heard a thin, nerve-racking scream from inside the apartment. It sent us startling back onto the fire escape, my hip landing hard on metal and the lip of the windowsill catching my shoulder blade. My injured ribs hurt so bad I could only breathe in sickening sips.

Sophia stood, unsteady. "I think that was Jenny. What do you do to make *Jenny* scream like that?"

Her face was neutral, her posture straight. In the way she turned away, I could tell what just happened was going to be another thing we never talked about.

I wasn't scared just then. In the relief that followed Sophia's aborted flirtation with Death — or her successful attempt to fuck with me, I couldn't know for sure — a scream just seemed like a scream. We followed the rising buzz of voices, past Sophia's bedroom and toward the next window.

It opened onto a bathroom, big and old-fashioned and kept fastidiously clean by the brothers. Just below the window was a claw-foot tub lined with more lit candles, and dishes holding fat chunks of apothecary soap.

When I saw Genevieve lying in the tub my first thought was that she looked *frosted*. Her skin veined blue, her mouth hanging open, her legs folded to the side like a mermaid's tail. The skin around her lips was blackened and the whites of her eyes pocked with broken vessels.

Frozen. She'd been frozen from the inside out.

Jenny stood in the doorway, her face blank, like the scream had scoured the fear from her and left her empty. Hinterlanders pressed into the spaces around her, trying to get a better look. They didn't see Sophia and me, framed in the window like Lost Boys.

Then Daphne was there. Slipping into the bathroom and crouching beside the tub. She touched Genevieve's face with careful fingers. Slid them down.

I was cold. Colder even than I'd been when the Hinterland was dying. If I screamed now, I didn't know if I could stop. "What is she doing?" I whispered.

Sophia crouched beside me like a gargoyle. "Looking for the missing piece."

She was right. With Genevieve's body split between moonlight and dark, it was hard to tell. But Daphne's clever hands found it: Genevieve's right foot was gone, hacked off at the ankle.

My knees were wet. I looked down and saw that I was kneeling in blood. The

155

windowsill was black with it. Whoever had killed and cut Genevieve must've come out this way, the stump of her foot draining as they went. The world fell away and I saw —

Finch. At the edge of the Halfway Wood.

with his throat sliced and

I swallowed, brought a hand up to cover my eyes.

falling forward

onto dirt and grass and

"Death was just here," Sophia said in my ear, her voice almost dreamy. "He must've been *laughing* at me."

The figures in the doorway weren't looking at Genevieve anymore. They were looking at *me*. Even Daphne, mouth pressed thin and bloody hands steadying herself on the tub's high side.

"Alice-Three-Times," one of them hissed. Jenny's eyes bored into mine.

Grape and gin boiled in my stomach, clawed up my throat. I turned around and vomited through the bars of the fire escape.

~13~

When I could stand again, Sophia was gone. I rinsed my mouth with grape soda and splashed my hands with gin.

Ice. Genevieve had been killed with *ice.*

Who else could do it? I'd thought I was the only one. I'd thought, too, that the cold was a piece of me that was gone. But I'd summoned it in Red Hook, and again on the train. A thought skittered through my brain like a cockroach: that this murder was a message. Someone forging my signature on a girl's death. There'd been *four* deaths now. One was a warning, two a coincidence, and three completed the fairy-tale set. But four. Four was an open door. An invitation to more.

The lights were on, the rooms emptying out. I kept my head down, but the possum glint of eyes still pricked at me. Daphne called my name as I hurried to the door, and someone grabbed my arm — the upper part of it, over my T-shirt sleeve. I ripped it from their grip.

I wasn't walking right. I jerked over the pavement like a marionette, forgetting then remembering to put one foot in front of the other. I looked up at Sophia's fire escape, imagining her diving from it. Or pushed, by whoever had killed Genevieve, sliced off her foot.

Who else could kill with ice? Had the Prince and Abigail died this way, too? Had Hansa? I was sharply, suddenly certain that she had. I remembered the way Robin looked at me the day after she died. Sophia asking if I still had the cold in me.

At least she'd believed me when I told her I didn't. Then — Red Hook. Why would she believe me now? Why would anyone?

Who else could fucking do it?

I walked by habit to the subway entrance and stopped. The stairs descended, disappeared to the left, and I knew where they were going but I didn't *know,* and even though the danger was behind me it felt like it was ahead, too. I swam in it.

If I were a different kind of girl I'd call Ella right now. *Mom. Come get me.* I could almost taste the words. But I couldn't do that to her. She was more fragile since the two years she'd spent looking for me when I was lost in the Hinterland. The grief of almost losing me had hardened her, yeah, but it was the kind of hard that cracked.

So I took a few breaths. Hobbled away from the subway and toward the street. Got into the first cab that stopped. I waited out the driver's attempts at small talk, sitting in the back seat and soaking in the scent of car tree and old leather. By the time I got home I was okay. I was. I could walk without looking like a broken toy and I had just enough in me to make it to my room.

But I didn't go there. I went to my

mother's. I stood beside her bed like a kid who'd had a nightmare, till she shifted, groggy, and sat up.

"Alice?"

She was exhausted, too. Neither of us had slept much lately. One look at her weary, laugh-lined face and my armor melted and ran. I climbed in beside her and curled up there and cried. She wasn't much bigger than me but she wrapped me up. We rocked and she said soothing nothings. The words I said back started out too blurry to hear but resolved into this: *Don't ask me. Don't ask me. Please, don't ask me.*

I must've smelled like vomit and grape and blood. But she didn't ask me. She nudged me toward the shower and brought me fresh clothes, and there were clean sheets on my bed, too, the ones I'd sweated through peeled away.

I climbed in with a feeling of containment, caught up again in the tiny safety net my mother spun around me, that she'd always spun, with love and hope and lies of omission. As I stretched out long with my arms over my head and my wet hair dampening the pillow, my toes just grazed the edge of something tucked into the very bottom of my new-laid sheets.

The light was out and the room was quiet and it could've been anything down there, a sock or an errant bookmark, but its touch sent an electric current up to my thigh. I sat up fast. Flipped the sheets back, then kicked them the rest of the way. With my phone light I scanned the foot of the bed. The thing my toe had touched sat bright in its beam, benign as a sleeping snake.

A flower. Unrumpled, perfect. It had a corona of blue petals, clustered so tightly you couldn't see its heart. When it didn't immediately light up or blow up or emit a poisonous gas, I bent slowly forward to touch it.

Its petals were scentless. Papery. They were *made* of paper, the whole flower was. It was origami-light on my palm. After a bodiless, wondering moment, I tugged at a petal. It fell away with a soundless snap. One after another, they all did. The flower's heart was a saturated pink. One end of it came away, and I saw that it was a scroll of paper. There were words on the scroll, but I didn't let myself read them till I'd reached its very heart, where the first words were written.

Dear Alice, they said.

Dear Alice,

I didn't start my last letter this way, and one day I want to tell you why. I promised myself I'd only write to you once, but I remembered I hadn't even started that letter right — Dear Alice — and I told myself I could write to you just one more time. I might break that promise. I might write to you again. Would you forgive me if I do? I don't know if you'll ever read any of this. But I hope you do. I hope, I hope, I hope.

I pressed two hands to my chest, where my heart beat so fast it was fizzing. Because this time I knew. It was him, it had been him, it was him.

Him. Reaching across stars and through doors and over distances so unfathomable the idea of them made my skin shiver and sting.

It was Ellery Finch.

~14~

If you ever have the chance to bear witness to a dying world, don't.

Ellery Finch didn't know what he was doing when he cracked open the golden prison that held Alice Proserpine, Alice Crewe, Alice-Three-Times, and let her loose.

He learned quick.

Her departure from the Hinterland left a tear in the skin of his world. For a while there, saving her had been his life. His obsession, his penance. He'd watched her grow up from afar, sealed inside her tale.

With some help, he'd sprung her loose. Or he guessed it was Alice, in the end, who'd saved herself. But he'd started the thing.

It should have been enough. When he said goodbye to her she was wearing a heavy dress that could've been a McQueen and shoes that might've been spun from cobwebs and her eyes were a raw, desperate brown. The scent of her broken story hung around her still.

He watched her disappear over the Hinterland's tricky horizon line, riding away on a rusty red bicycle. When she was gone from sight, the very last tether between him and his old life, the one he'd lived on Earth, snapped. Their tale together was through.

He had his own life in the Hinterland. Of course he did. That world, the one he'd sacrificed decency and a hefty amount of blood to gain, was beautiful and befuddling, inexhaustible and heedless. Its trees told stories. Its grass was fed by them. Finch had never come so close to having a book hold him back. There were patches of sky where the stars moved like living fireworks, creeks where girls with corpse-colored skin and dirty hair sang like bullfrogs and watched him through hungry eyes. He had friends there, other refugees, who understood without asking that he had more scars than the ones you could see.

In the days after Alice left, he tried to remind himself why he'd stayed. He and his friends — Alain, a broadly built Swiss guy who worked at the tavern, and Lev, a laconic Venezuelan who ran an occasional smithy — went skinny-dipping in a pool behind a tumbledown castle, lining the shore with lanterns. They trekked through the constant early summer that reigned in the heart of the Hinterland, up across an afternoon of cold spring, over a fiery stripe of autumn, and into the hushed halls of a winter so enchanted and still, walking through the trees felt like church. They camped one night in a cove of glittering sand, where a white-furred stag took to the waters each night, and cried to the stars in the voice of a human soprano.

They'd had years to learn the movements of the Stories and steer clear. It should've been easy. But ten days after

Alice left, Finch woke up in his sleeping bag on the cove's cold sand, in the silvery, predawn hour, with a girl crouching beside him.

He didn't speak. Neither did she. She was younger than he was — twelve or thirteen, he'd guess — with dark blue eyes and a solemn little face. In one hand, she held a compass.

She was a Story. That enervating Story scent came off her, and her skin had the radiant tackiness of a makeup ad. She shouldn't be here. Shouldn't have noticed him, certainly shouldn't be hanging over him like she was waiting for him to speak. If his friends were awake, too, those cowards sure weren't showing it. Finally he became too nervous to stay quiet.

"Hi," he breathed.

"Hello." She had a scratchy little voice, like Peppermint Patty.

"Um. Did you . . . want something from me?"

She shrugged. Nothing to say, and no apparent intention of leaving. Finch had the most inappropriate flare of social anxiety.

"My name's Ellery. Finch." She didn't seem like she wanted to kill him, but still. Maybe it would be harder for her to do it if he had a name.

"My name's Hansa," she replied. "I'm meant to be somewhere else today. But I decided I didn't want to go." She looked a little bit proud of herself, a little bit astonished. "My grandmother will be mad at me, I suppose."

Hansa. Hansa the Traveler. The moon's granddaughter, heroine of one of Althea Proserpine's tales. Finch bit down hard on a helium panic.

"Where are you supposed to be?"

She shook off the question like she was shaking off a fly. "I don't want to talk about that," she said cryptically, and stood, the rising sun slicing sharply over her shoulder. "Well. Goodbye."

Now that she was actually going, Finch was oddly frantic for her to stay.

"Wait! Are you — I mean. This is weird, right?" He looked around, at the quiet sand and lightening sky and the corroded metal of the water. "That you're here? That you're —" *Free. Outside. Of your*

167

tale. He wanted to say it, but he didn't want to piss her off.

The little girl was already looking away, bored. "I've never swum in the sea before," she told him. Then she took off, legs scurrying toward the water like a sandpiper's.

Finch watched her for a minute, his jaw feeling slack yet tense, like he'd been clenching it all night.

Lev whistled from the sleeping bag behind him. "Look at that. Another one of the Spinner's birds flown free."

"Another?"

"Her, your Alice." He looked at Finch, the sun on his glasses making his eyes into silver circles. "I think you've started something."

Neither spoke for a moment, watching the unlatched Story splashing at the water's edge. Behind them, Alain was still asleep.

"I wonder." Lev's voice was quiet, amused. "If this *is* because of you, I wonder if the Spinner's mad. I wonder if she's the vengeful type. I'd bet she was, wouldn't you?"

She is, Finch could've told him. She'd shown her face to him — one of her faces — just once, back when he was trying to break Alice free. She'd been amused, flirtatious, and frightening by turns. He figured it was just a matter of time before she showed up again. That was one more reason he couldn't sleep.

Finch was pissed at Lev as they packed up their stuff. Pissed as they both agreed without talking not to say anything to Alain. Still pissed as they set off on foot toward home.

Alain was talking about some new invention he'd made, an amplification system Finch knew without knowing more was a bad idea. It didn't do to call too much attention to yourself here. They were walking through a quiet stretch of trees on the edge of a pretty town when Lev spoke up.

"Hansa lives there," he said.

Alain, interrupted, frowned. "Hansa who? From-the-story Hansa? Who cares?"

Lev just smiled like a goddamned sphinx. "We should walk through it. Nobody'll be awake yet, come on."

He was like that. Quiet and chill, then suddenly an anarchist, basically daring you not to have the guts.

For once Finch was a step ahead: he'd walked through that town before. He'd dared far stupider shit since landing in the Hinterland. Almost dying will do that to you. And besides, Althea had done it when she was collecting her tales. For a while he'd tried to follow in her footsteps, just to see if he could survive that, too.

"Let's go," was all he said, turning toward the town.

If Norman Rockwell ever illustrated a fairy-tale book, he'd have painted this town. A blue haze hung over it, like the steam that sometimes came up off the sea. The houses had thatched tops and candy-colored doors and secretive windows roosting in ivy. Finch could see a woman through one of them, running a brush through her heavy hair.

Alain was afraid, Finch could tell by the way he walked. Lev, though. That fucker was *cocky*.

They were coming up on a small yellow

cottage that seemed a little more solid than the rest, though Finch couldn't have explained why. Then he saw it: a blackness ran around the cottage's base. It looked ephemeral at first, a trick of your eyes or the light, the kind of thing you should be able to blink away. It resolved, as they came closer, into a thin layer of simmering mist. It made the house look like it was a countdown away from taking off.

"What is that?" Lev muttered. He looked at Finch, sly. "Must be Hansa's house."

He walked toward it in his enviable leather hiking boots. They were still in excellent shape, though he'd been in the Hinterland longer than Finch had. He bent over just beside the mist, hands on his knees. "Huh."

"Don't," Finch said sharply, as Lev nudged the mist with his boot.

He spoke the word to no one. In the moment between opening his mouth and speaking, the mist claimed Lev. It wicked him into itself like a sponge taking in water. Mischief managed.

■ ■ ■ ■

The Hinterland was a clock, perfectly weighted and balanced and spinning in time. The refugees lived tucked among the cogs, learning when to duck and what parts of their borrowed world to avoid.

Finch, it turned out, had fucked with that clock. Alice's removal wasn't smooth and surgical. It was a fist plunging into the guts of what the Spinner had made, and ripping out a handful of smoking pieces. The center could not hold.

After Lev disappeared, Finch got drunk. He and Alain, shaken, sick, run through with guilt — Finch's worse for having been halfway hoping something would happen to shake Lev's infuriating cool, but not something like *this* — holed up in the tavern. Lights off, doors locked, they sat at the bar in companionable horror and drank. There was no one to tell, no one to report this to, no next of kin to notify. There was just them, trying and failing to fathom what the hell had happened to their friend.

The shadows were long and Alain asleep when Finch had a hypothesis.

He'd spent hours in Alice's castle before her tale broke. Sneaking in through its many doors, circling its grounds. He'd moved among its footmen and hand-maids and cooks, all the nearly invisible figures that kept a fairy tale afloat.

He'd breached it first at night, and then, when he got a little braver, during the day. The whole place fizzed like a fishbowl full of magic, but it was only where Alice was, where the air got woozy, that it was dangerous. It was a weird and winding place, full of doors that wouldn't open, staircases that led nowhere, odd rooms that had no place in her tale. There was a courtyard at the castle's heart where it never stopped snowing, a nestled globe of permanent winter.

Even inside a nightmare, the Hinter-land could be beautiful.

Now he left Alain sleeping behind the bar and walked out into the alarmingly sweet evening air. He'd bicycled drunk before, more times than he cared to count. But the dizziness he felt wheel-ing away on his bike couldn't be blamed on intoxication. He pulled over, checked the bike's chain, squeezed the tires. The slight vertigo that made him list to the side, that pressed down on him funny from above, wasn't confined to biking: it was systemic. It was *atmospheric.* There was something off-kilter in the very air of the Hinterland.

He pushed the bike the rest of the way. Alice's castle should've been showing itself through the trees, slices of darker dark between branches. The white stone path broadened and still he didn't see it. He thought he might've gotten lost somehow, until he came to the familiar dip in the road, the half-circle of honeysuckle bushes, and the open plot of land on which the castle crouched.

On which it *had* crouched: the castle was gone. All of it. Gates and stables and mossy stone walls. Hidden rooms and corridors and all the other odd fancies of the Spinner. It wasn't burned to ash or left in ruins — it was *gone.* In its place was a low, swirling mist, an eye-aching emptiness that shimmered in places like lights on water.

It was the same blackness that had hooked its fingers around Hansa's cottage. But it had spread, and consumed.

Alice's tale had broken, and in its wake was annihilation; Hansa stepped off the path of her own story, and the destruction of it had just begun.

His hypothesis had proved correct.

In the deep dark middle of the night, he went back to Hansa's. For a long time he watched the place where Lev was lost. When nothing happened, he walked away, ten long steps. Then he turned and ran at the cottage, throwing himself over the blackness at its roots. Safe on the other side, he let himself in.

He walked through the cottage's quiet rooms, running his eyes over its beds and curtains, its dishes and chairs. Moving through one of the upper bedrooms, he paused. There, on a low table, sat a little spyglass made out of a rosy metal. For a long moment, he looked at it.

He took it. From the kitchen he took a wooden spoon with a ship's silhouette burned into its bowl. From a windowsill, a little mechanical fox that twitched its anime eyes and its three tails and made a whirring sound. He couldn't say why he did it, just that these particular objects made his fingers itch and he knew that soon enough they'd be lost, along with the cottage and whatever was left of Hansa's tale, to the spreading fog.

He dropped them into his old leather bag, jumped to safety, and ran all the way home.

~15~

I pulled out *Persuasion* and read the letter again. Then the second letter, the one that proved it. How had he done it? That mattered less than that he'd done it at all. Wherever Finch was, he was thinking of me. *Missing* me. My eyes were wet, my lips felt nervy under my touch. The air tasted heady and my whole life looked different under the spotlight of knowing this one incredible thing: he was reaching out for me.

I'd thumbed over the brief story of me and Ellery Finch so many times it was falling to pieces. The boy I'd used without telling myself I was using him. The boy who'd betrayed me, saved me, then abandoned me to this world, alone.

Not alone. I'd come home to Ella. He'd gone on, following the thread he'd tugged when he learned about the Hinterland, that led him on a journey to other places. *That boy has other worlds to explore,* I'd been told. *We're not always born to the right one.*

I'd asked myself the question a thousand times, and I asked it again now: Who was Ellery Finch? I hadn't paid enough attention when he was right beside me. The possibility that I might get another chance to find out glowed in me, electric.

I rolled onto my back and pulled up his sleeping Instagram. Mostly it was shots of street art and squares of sunlit water, pretentious quotes written on dirty windows and pictures of his friends, good-looking people with shining faces who made me feel jealous years too late. But there were a few of just him: lying in the curves of a snow angel, drinking beer on the ferry. Backlit on a rooftop, sun setting behind him.

Something else was keeping me up, filling me with a fine white fire, pushing away thoughts of silent attackers and blood in bathtubs and the death wish that followed my best friend around like her shadow.

Magic. That letter, written by a lost boy and delivered here by unseen hands, it was *magic.* There were other worlds out there, I'd almost forgotten that. And all enchantment hadn't died with the Hinterland. I had a feeling I hadn't had in a very long time: of possibility. Of the world, the *worlds,* as a vast place, where the cost of magic wasn't always so horribly high. Where it could take the shape of something simple and beautiful. Like a perfect paper flower.

I sat up in bed and called Sophia. She picked up on the third ring, and said nothing.

"You left me," I said. "On the fire escape."

More silence.

"It wasn't me. You know that, right?"

The connection was bad, her voice sounded far away. "I know you," she said.

I didn't know what that meant, or whether it was meant to be comforting. I guess I didn't care. "We need to talk. Meet me at the diner in half an hour."

It would've been a whole thing getting out if Ella was still awake. But she'd crashed on the couch, her feet slung up over the back and our old afghan thrown over her legs. I wanted to kiss her forehead, take the crack-spined copy of *Tender Morsels* off her chest. But if I tried that she'd pop out of sleep like a jack-in-the-box.

So I just watched her. Watched the dark mass itself over her head like the gathered detritus of her dreams. There was a time when I could've guessed at their contents, but that time had passed. I'd been holding myself back, letting her grow strange to me.

And tonight, I'd done something worse: I'd come home to her. Even after what happened on the subway, even after seeing Genevieve dead in the dark, I'd traced my steps back to Brooklyn. Not knowing who was watching me, whether they'd try one more time to hurt me, whether I was leading death to her door.

The annihilating anger that made me reckless in Red Hook, that saved my life on the train, was folded away. What I felt now was clinical and bright, more promise than threat.

I wasn't going to be a victim anymore. A monster, either. I was going to find the creature who'd turned me into both, in that subway car in the dark.

~16~

The breaking of "Hansa the Traveler" was an end, and it was a beginning. It was the start of Finch's new career: he was a scavenger. A thief. As the tales kept breaking and people started panicking and the roads and trees and even the tavern were crawling with recent ex-Stories, confused and enraged and stinking of burnt sugar and exploded flashbulbs, Finch was moving through the cracked landscapes they left behind. Before the tales and everything in them could turn into black holes, he walked their disintegrating halls.

From a fading farmhouse he took a blown glass rose and a child's leather boot. From the bottom of an abandoned coracle he took a bone fishing hook, a little tarnished mirror, and a handful of iridescent fish scales, big as his palm and diamond hard. In an overgrown pear grove he found a dancing slipper, worn through. It looked like one of the beat-up Capezios his junior high girlfriend used to wear with her jeans. Deep in the trees, from a murder cabin straight out of *The Evil Dead,* he took what looked like a ginger root, colored a deep, burnished maroon. But the thing felt so vile, even through the old leather of his bag, he ended up throwing it out his window in the middle of the night.

When I wake up there's gonna be an evil beanstalk out there, he thought, lying back in bed. *It's like I've never read a fairy tale.*

The beanstalk didn't show, but he still had things to worry about.

He was living with Janet and Ingrid in their cottage, which smelled like rosemary and soil and a tinge of the goat pen Ingrid was bad about wiping off her boots. It drove Janet nuts. They'd given him a home, helped make the Hinterland feel like a home, and now they were talking about leaving.

Everyone was, those days. The Stories were shaking loose and the sinkholes were getting worse and Lev was only the first death — the first disappearance. It was possible, Alain liked to say hopefully, that he was still alive. Maybe he'd slipped right back through to Earth. Maybe that was what everyone should do: show a little faith that the sinkholes worked like doors. It was a popular theory nobody ever tested on purpose.

No, their continued survival depended on the Spinner. They were waiting for her to step in, to rebuild her world, tale by tale. Surely the wound Finch had made in it wasn't mortal. Surely she'd show herself at last, and open a door. The ex-Stories had their own ways out of the Hinterland, but none of them seemed inclined to talk. The refugees were trapped together like rats on a splintering ship.

Everyone had a theory about the Spinner: that she was an ex-Story herself. That she was just another human, or had been, once upon a time. Someone swore she was the Empress Josephine. There was an old straight-edge dude who hung around the tavern sipping water, who claimed the Spinner used to send him to Earth for cases of gin, satin pajamas, paperbacks and chocolate bars and black tea. Finch believed it.

"She's not human, not Story, and not to be trifled with or depended upon," Janet said briskly. "We need a contingency plan."

But that was just talk. Even Janet couldn't muscle up an escape route where none existed.

People were starting to lose faith. There were town hall meetings almost daily, and patrols were set up around some of the bigger sinkholes. Janet did her best to impose a curfew. Still, people were lost. The Hinterland's refugees were wanderers by nature; Finch wasn't the only one pressing his luck, poking around the changing land.

Then came the night when they were packed into the tavern, sardine-tight and hiding out from a rare rainstorm. The weather had gone off since the Stories started to break. Alain was in the back checking on a batch of home brew when he gave a holler, and Finch *knew*.

It was a rounded little hobbit door set in a place that had been solid wall, the top of it coming to Finch's thigh. Janet looked at it with her hands on her hips.

"Let's not be hasty," she said.

"Hasty?" A man pushed to the front of the crowd, blond eyebrows scaling his bald head. Finch had known his type back in New York: he was the guy who composted and canvassed and spent his weekends gathering signatures for a petition to save an endangered beetle, then called the cops on kids being too loud on the sidewalk. "We're dying out here, and you're talking about don't be *hasty?*"

Janet sized him up. "Thank you, Leon. We can always count on you for the dissenting opinion. If you're volunteering to go first, please, be my guest."

Leon's eyebrows climbed even higher. "You'd like that, wouldn't you."

"I'd like it tremendously. I think most of us would."

Even Janet was getting ruffled these days.

But it was Alain who got to his knees and opened the door. Half the room gasped, and Leon ducked and covered.

All you could see through it was gray fog, like it opened straight into a cloud. Then a wind came through, a bracing, whistling thing that lapped the room and left them in silence.

"Perfume," Alain breathed. "Isobel's perfume."

Leon's face was red; he looked like he was hardly breathing. "Baby powder," he choked out. "And grilled cheese. Did you smell that?"

Everyone was murmuring now, their faces lit up or shut down, naming the promises that had blown through the door. Finch looked to Janet; she said nothing, but her face was stricken.

They were all wrong anyway. The wind had smelled like his mother's coconut oil, and the gingery spice mix she'd kept on the kitchen counter. It smelled like the lace of overdone waffles, the very last meal he'd eaten on Earth.

■ ■ ■ ■

Within a few hours, people started leaving through the door. Whatever was on the other side of it, they'd decided it was better than what lay through the sinkholes. Finch figured they were probably right.

But he remembered something he'd read once, about the door to the kingdom of Heaven being so low you had to enter it kneeling. This didn't feel like that. It felt like the Spinner being petty, making them crawl their asses out through a doggy door. The sheer *cuteness* of it felt sinister as fuck.

He was still waiting for her to show up and show him what she thought of idiot Earthlings who messed with the works. But if she blamed him for her falling-apart world, she hadn't said so. Some days he thought that was deliberate, that she knew it was worse for him this way: forever bracing for the hammer to come down. And some days he thought the worst thing she could do was to just let him leave. Maybe the door in the tavern wall would drop him in New York. He'd move back in with his dad and stepmom. Get his GED, let his dad pay his way into a good college. Ring a buzzer somewhere, wait for Alice to open the door.

Part of him *wanted* to go home, but none of him wanted it to be like this: raw, scarred, pared down. If he went back, he wanted to be like a king in exile returned. Someone who had *seen* things, and wasn't shit at processing them.

But as the days passed and the population dropped, he started to think it wouldn't happen that way. On a humid morning, with nowhere at all to be, Finch sat at a table in the tavern. It had lost its heart when Alain left the morning after the door first appeared, and had practically become a bus station since then. People walked through with their packs tied tight, alone or in pairs, said tearful goodbyes by the bar or slipped through without a word.

And always the place smelled like memories. Every time the door was opened, that antic wind sprang free, teeming with lost things. The sugar cloud of baked ice cream cone at the sundae shop a few blocks from his apartment on the Upper

East Side. The rubber-and-sweat scent of indoor basketball practice. His dad's clovey cologne. He marinated in the scents of home, watching people disappear forever into the back of the bar. While he did it, he toyed with the little metal fox he'd taken from Hansa's cottage.

There was a trick to it. He was sure there was. It had big eyes and three twitching tails, like those creepy vintage cat clocks, and it made a chittering sound in its throat. The points of its ears and tails were tipped in gold, but the rest of it was red metal. If you put your ear up to its belly, you could hear the faintest hum.

It took time for him to notice the girl watching him from another table. Early twenties, hair bleached out and tied back into Heidi braids, wearing three different shades of faded black. She had an unflappable vibe that reminded him of Janet. When Finch finally looked at her, she smiled brightly and stood, like being noticed was as good as an invitation.

"Hey," she said, sitting down across from him. "Come here often?"

Finch nodded at the weak joke and said nothing.

The girl pulled out a red glass bottle and set it between them. "I think we missed last call, so I brought my own. You want?"

He put down the fox. "Look, do I know you?"

"I doubt it. I just got into town."

Reluctantly, he was interested. "From where?"

"I've been on walkabout. Well, sail-about, I guess. I wanted to check out the islands, see what came after the edge of the sea."

Finch's heart twanged. He'd always planned to do that. "How far did you get? What did you find?"

Her voice fell into the easy cadence of a storyteller's. "I found a tale that played out on an island the size of this bar. I saw mermaids singing down storms and stir-ring them into the water. There's a square of sea that's *always* stormy, with a ship tossing inside it. There's a place where you can take a staircase down to the bottom of the sea and walk in a garden there, with the water just over your head." Her voice stalled out. "It was beautiful. But it wasn't home."

The way she said the word caught at him. Like *home* meant just one place to her, and she knew exactly where to find it. "Where's home?"

"It'll take more than one drink to get me to tell you that." She smiled, but he didn't think she was joking. "I came over here to ask you about that thing you're messing with. That —" She squinted. "What is it, a fox? Mind if I take a look?"

Finch took his hands off it, like, be my guest.

"Tale-made, right?"

He nodded grudgingly. It was the first time he'd heard the term.

"I thought so." She picked it up, inspected it. With a jerk, she yanked its central tail.

The fox gave a whirring shudder as she placed it in the center of the table. They watched it rearrange itself, the tails elongating, becoming two arms and a pair of molded-together legs, the eyes transforming, disconcertingly, into breasts, and a head sprouting from the body of the thing as it went from apple to hourglass.

It had become a metal woman, with a sly, foxy face.

Finch picked it up, held it to his ear to see if he could still hear the hum. "How did you know it could do that?"

"Better question is, what else can it do?" She flicked the thing onto its side. "Do you have any more like it?"

Finch thought of the glass rose, the fish scales, the rest of the cache he kept under his bed. "I might. Who's asking?"

The girl put out a hand. "Iolanthe. Happy to meet you."

He shook it, taking in her ice-haired prettiness, the shallow bowls of her clavicles and the unearthly planes of her face. He was starting to think she might come from someplace farther than New York.

"Ellery," he said. "Finch."

"Well, Ellery, the truth is I don't want to die here. And I think you and I might be able to help each other, if" — she pointed at the metal figure — "you've got more tale-made treasures like that."

"Nobody wants to die here," he said. "Everyone's trying to escape. What does the fox have to do with it?"

"Think. What do you need to escape?"

"A door."

"*Money* and a door. I know a place where we can make some coin off that fox and anything else you might've picked up. How's this: I get forty percent for taking you there and making the introduction. And for giving you the idea in the first place."

"Is your buyer in the Hinterland?"

She smiled, relaxed but with a hint of the shark beneath it. "My buyer is not."

"Meaning you can get us out of here? You know a safe way out, a guaranteed way?"

"I do."

"You get thirty percent." Finch took the red bottle and drank. The liquid inside tasted like rum made out of electrocuted sugarcane. "And I get to bring two people out with me."

Iolanthe pulled out a pocket watch on a long chain and consulted its face. From

194

where Finch sat, it looked completely blank. "Forty percent, and I can personally guarantee the safe passage out of your two people. But they can't come with us."

Her hand, when Finch shook it, felt rough and solid, the hand of a woman who'd navigated alien waters in search of tales to tell.

She held his fast. "Meet me here tomorrow at sunrise. Bring your two friends and anything you've got to sell. And say your goodbyes. It'll be the last you'll see of this place."

~17~

A twenty-four-hour diner held down a corner two blocks from the apartment, serving bottomless drip coffee and cheap breakfast combos to construction workers and old people in jogging suits. I knew Sophia would be late, so I skimmed a few chapters of *The Changeling* while I waited. When she finally showed, she looked small, the larger-than-life outline of her rubbed down. She still wore the dress she'd had on at the party, the fabric so dark I couldn't tell if it had bloodstains.

"Trip," she said, falling into the seat

across from me. It was her nickname for me — Alice-Three-Times, Triple, Trip — and I always felt a blend of affection and irritation when she used it. When the waitress came, Sophia revived a little, ordering chocolate-chip waffles and mushroom omelets and Canadian bacon for the both of us. I could already see her calculating how to get away without paying the bill.

"We are paying for this breakfast."

She winked, but it was half-hearted. "Is it breakfast if the sun's not up?"

The food came, and it looked to me like pieces of a plastic playset. I watched the chipped glitter of her nails around fork and knife, too up in my head to swallow more than milky coffee.

What was Finch doing right now? Where was he doing it? Outsized possibilities played across my eyelids. *Sometimes the image of you hits me so hard and sudden I believe the only explanation is you're thinking of me at that exact moment, too.*

"Hey."

My focus snapped, breath drawn in like I'd been caught at something.

There were half-moons in her lip where she'd bitten it. The skin around her eyes was blue paper. "You got me here. Why aren't you talking?"

"Jesus, Sophia." The words slipped out sideways as I focused, really focused, on her face. "You look like shit."

"Back at you."

"Sorry. I just . . . I wish you could sleep."

"Don't. I don't even remember how it feels."

I was raw, eroded down to skin and nerve. My eyes filled before I could check myself. "Oh, Soph. What do you *do* all night?"

"You know, I've known you a while now, and this is the first time you've ever asked me that." She said it without judgment, but it still felt like a cut.

"I'm sorry."

"Does that help me?" She sighed, put down her fork. "It's harder now. With the Hinterland gone, it feels harder. This world is so dim, I can hardly see. Sometimes when I look at people their death is *all* I can see."

198

"You've never told me how I'm gonna die." Saying the words felt like passing my fingers through flame, daring it to burn me. "Do you know? Can you see it?"

"Ask me instead if I can see your life."

"Can you —"

"Yes." Her golden eyes held mine. "It's the color of oil. Black until you look close, then every color. Sometimes it looks so dark. Sometimes it looks like a pearl."

"Can you see everyone's life and death, all the Hinterlanders?"

She tensed. "Are you asking about the murders? If I knew?"

"Not because I'm blaming you. Not because I think it was your fault."

"Of course it wasn't my fault. Was it yours?"

She asked the question so lightly. *It'll be okay if it is,* her voice said. *I'll like you anyway.*

I squared up and looked at her, hands resting on the table. "I've got nothing to do with this."

After a moment she nodded, and returned to her waffle.

"I've got proof if you want it," I went on. "Someone tried to kill me, too. A couple nights ago, on the subway."

"It's weird more people don't die on the subway," she said equably. Then, "Wait. Are you serious?"

I pointed at my chin, scabbing over. Then I told her everything, right up through my conversation with Daphne in her hotel room.

"So it *is* one of us," she said. "I figured. Shit, what if it's Robin? He loves rhymes, all that high fairy-tale formality. And he's mad as a hatter, besides."

"Right, but can Robin freeze people alive?"

"Oh, yeah. Damn. It would've made him so much more interesting." She shuddered, her expression bright. I felt perversely pleased that I'd thrilled her with the story of my own near-death.

"So I'm right? They did all die that way — like Genevieve?"

"That's what I heard."

"And you didn't think to tell me?"

"I didn't hear about any of it till after

Hansa died. Then you showed up at a meeting out of nowhere, and . . . I wondered. I guess I was waiting, maybe, to see if you had something to tell *me*."

"You really thought . . ." I sighed, laying my head back against the seat. "If you thought I did it, they must all be thinking it."

"Some of them. Maybe."

I remembered Robin, all the shuttered faces at the wake. That whisper in the bloody bathroom. *Alice-Three-Times.* "Some of them, definitely."

"Let me take care of it," she said. "I'll tell them it wasn't you. They'll believe it, coming from me."

I swallowed it down, that little stab of nonbelonging. I'd *chosen* to walk away. "Who else could it be? Can anyone else do what I can do? Does anyone else have a reason to want, you know, *body parts?*"

She gestured dismissively with her fork. "Fairy tale something something. You know how it goes."

"Right — exactly. It's like something in a fairy tale. This isn't just violent, it's specific. There's got to be, like, some ice

201

king who used to collect his wives' ankles running around the city."

"Their *ankles*?" She ran a finger through a comet scatter of spilled sugar crystals. "What the fuck would you do with a bunch of ankles?"

"I don't know," I said, impatient. "But I can't go home till I figure it out."

"Till you figure out —"

"Not the fucking ankles." I wiped a hand over my mouth, frustration rising. "Did you not see what I saw tonight? Are you not scared?"

"Scared." She said it thoughtfully, like it was a word she was looking up in a dictionary. "To die, you mean? No, I'm not scared."

"Well, it's different for you. You can't, you know. Die."

"Yes, I do know," she said dryly.

I thought about Finch, somewhere far away, remembering a better version of me. Ella on the couch, dreaming of a land of red rocks, where we could see the whole curve of the galaxy from our backyard.

"You told me," I said carefully, "that I should be sure."

"Don't," she said swiftly.

"Soph. I can't even go home. Someone tried to kill me, they might try it again. And I always *hurt* her. My mother. Again and again. I never mean it, but what does that matter? After this, after I figure this out, I think I've gotta go. For real this time. Leave the Hinterland behind."

She nodded, and for a moment I thought she understood. Then her lip curled back like a cat's. "Do you really think that's how it works? The Hinterland was never a place, it was always *us*. Wherever you go, *that's* the Hinterland."

Hearing my fears spoken aloud made my anger rise. "I grew up *here*. I spent my whole life here, I was *raised* here."

"How many lives did you spend in the Hinterland? How many dozens? You think you're special just because somebody from this world loves you? That's not how it works."

"That's exactly how it works," I spat. "That's the point of the whole goddamn world."

"It's not our world."

"It's not *yours*."

A waitress came by with a coffee carafe, looked at us pitching toward each other over the tabletop, and kept walking.

"You said I had a choice," I hissed. "You said I was the only one who did."

"That's right. And you made it."

"I almost killed a man. Here, where it counts. I saw a dead girl in a bathtub, her body frozen. *Mutilated.* I almost got killed myself. Don't you care that I could've died? I thought you were my friend!"

Her hand shot out and gripped my wrist. "I *am* your friend. Your fucking friend, your *only* friend. You ungrateful ass."

I tried to pull away, but she squeezed tighter, the bones of my wrist bowing like saplings. "You asked me what I do all night. Ask yourself what *all* of us do. Daphne and Robin and Jenny and the rest of us, do you think we sit around wondering who we are, how to live? Go to funny little part-time jobs, like you? Do you really think we don't use what we've got to live the best we can live, and have fun however we want to have fun, because we *can?* We don't have mothers waiting at home for us, making us tea. We don't have years and years of life in this place behind us and a *future* ahead."

She leaned close to me, as close as she could get across the table. Her empty eyes were fathomless, nothing and nothing and nothing all the way down.

"I'm not getting any older. Death will never come for me. Instead I'll just rot. I can *feel* the rot coming. It'll start here." She pointed at her forehead, at her heart. "I'll go black and green. I've got nothing in my life but time, and I still don't have time for this: one foot in, one foot out, *poor me.* How come, with more than any of the rest of us have got, you always make out like you've got so much less?"

When I said nothing, she fell back in disgust. She plucked the untouched waffle off my plate and slid out of the booth. "Thanks for breakfast."

I watched her go. I couldn't move, couldn't think of what to say. I sat there in the grainy diner light, breathing in the smell of hash browns and coffee and hot batter, thinking of the day I learned her tale. The day I learned she was deathless.

We were lying in Prospect Park in the shifting shade of a blackgum tree. It was one of those endless late fall afternoons, breezes mixing cool and cold, everything you could see stuck on the bright edge of dying. And I was happy. Really, uncomplicatedly happy. Watching the hours drift by with my friend, my first real *friend,* who wasn't Finch or some kid briefly foisted on me by coincidence — same apartment complex, same lunch period, same need for protective social cover. I felt settled in my skin.

"Dogs in strollers," she was saying. "Dating people you met on a phone. Coupons."

She was naming Earthly shit that didn't make sense to make me laugh. After about the twentieth thing ("Vending machine hamburgers. *Why?*") she fell quiet a while, long enough that I thought she was asleep. Then she spoke.

"I want to tell you something."

Her voice was so serious I started to sit up.

"No. Just let me say it like this."

I lay back down. I listened to her fingers stripping fallen leaves, the wind imitating the ocean.

"I want to tell you my tale. Of the time when I was called Ilsa, and the night I fell in love with Death."

I looked straight up into the tree's skittish leaves, and the pieces of hard sky between them, and listened.

~18~

I was a girl born for bad luck. That's what they told me, in the village where I grew up. Full of hard old men and harder women, and winters so lean you could see your bones through your skin by the end of them.

I don't know how it is for you, but I have memories of my tale from above and below. Do you know what I mean? I remember all the parts of it that the Spinner spun — my brothers dying one by one, my father long gone, my mother growing old in front of my eyes, old before she was thirty. I remember — everything that came after.

But I remember other things, too. Little ones. Things the tale couldn't have had any use for. Like shooting a rabbit right through the eye on my very first go — I wasn't even aiming for it, I'd never have gotten within a mile if I'd tried. I cried and cried. One of my brothers painted pretty things for me, made a little doll I liked to carry around by its seedpod head. That can't have been in your grandmother's storybook, could it?

That's not important, though. What I meant to tell you about is Death. He's a wily fucker, slippery as oil, and he's been taunting me since I was old enough to know it. I caught him when I was small. I shouldn't have seen him, only the dying ever do. And he was there for my father, not me. But I saw him, all right, and he knew it, and slipped away like a back-door man. Six times after that he came for my family — for all my six brothers, one by one — but he never had the nerve to let me see his face again.

There were tricks you could use to catch him. To delay him, confuse him, turn him away — water and earth, copper and heartwood. I tried them all, but nothing worked.

I grew up trying to catch Death, but Death never turned around and caught me. He let me get grown enough to marry, old enough to try to have my own family — to make more of the living I could fight Death to keep. But then the boy I meant to marry got sick, and I knew Death was on his way. *That wicked old wolf,* that's what my mother called him. But I'd seen him, and she hadn't, and she got it wrong. He had skin the color of chestnuts dug out of the coals and eyes like . . . like the shine of sun on rain, when they both come at once. Or like a cat's eyes when you look at them from the side, that clear kind of silver. Eyes that see everything, and skin you so fine you don't feel it till you're already bleeding.

By then I'd decided he would not take another thing from me. I grew up with nothing six brothers hadn't gotten to first, I had to scrap with starving boys just to get my share. I wasn't about to let that pale-eyed bastard take my husband before I could even marry him.

I came to my betrothed's sickbed with offerings: the soul of a songbird, songs to scatter ashes by. Then I crushed the offerings under my foot, because fuck Death. He can be killed, just like any man, and I'd be the one to do it if it came to that.

And he showed. He came for the boy I loved, and I was there waiting for him. I was ready to die just to show him I meant it, just to prove you can't take absolutely everything from a girl who's got nothing.

But what he took was my hand. In his. When he did it I forgot every little thing: the boy on the bed. The smell of sickness. My dead father and stolen brothers and my skin all sticky with sparrow's blood. Death walked me right through the wall of the sickroom, and into another part of the world, a palace where a king lay dying. I watched him take the king's life: it took the form of a little colored light. You could just look at it and know what kind of man he'd been, what kind of king.

We traveled all over the Hinterland that night, taking lives away. I saw how heavily they weighed on Death, how he wasn't a master but a servant. And I guess I fell a little in love with him. With his *life:* the freedom, the duty.

I was different by morning. When Death dropped me back home, back into my tight fist of a life, he told me the boy I loved would live. That his life was a gift to me, for serving a night as Death's companion. Like showing someone the entire sea, then giving them a thimble of salt to remember it by.

After that night, I forgot the boy I loved. Thom, his name was, but I made myself forget that name. I waited for Death to return to me. I followed sickness like a plague wagon, and waited for accidents. You never had to wait long, in our village. But Death stayed away. He passed over our village for an entire season.

I figured out then that he was as stubborn as I am, and I'd have to go find him myself. By then I knew I didn't really love him, but I needed him to know he couldn't do what he did. You can't tease a girl with the whole of a world, then think she isn't gonna come after you for another taste.

I thought I'd set a trap for him. I'd bait the trap with one of the things he carried, in that canteen around his neck: all the little lives he peeled away, all those colored lights.

It was an accident the first time. I killed someone who was trying to kill me. Not that I'm making excuses for it. I won't make excuses for any of it. When that man's shitty little flicker of a life didn't draw Death in, I thought I'd try again. And again. I'd make myself Death's rival, if he wouldn't take me as his companion. I killed the worst kinds of folk at first. Then I stopped worrying so much. I'd kill anyone who struck me wrong, whose face I didn't like. Without meaning to, Death had taught me the trick of it: a person's life hides in their face, right there in plain sight. You can reach in and grab it if you've been taught how. I'd watched him all that night, I was a quick study. Before him I couldn't even see their life-lights; after I couldn't look away. They told you everything: who they'd been and would be. If they deserved what I was doing to them. If they didn't.

Death got wind of what I was doing eventually. I bet it made him mad. I still like to think about that, even though, I'm warning you now, this story doesn't end so well for me.

It wasn't all bad. I saw all the corners of the world. I saw its shores and its mountains and its valleys and every town. But I knew it through the creatures that lived in it, most of them as miserable as I was, and I never managed to just settle. Live another kind of life. I guess I couldn't have, not while the Spinner was watching, but like I said, I'm not making any excuses.

Then there was the night I met a little old man who made me an offer so good I should've known the only thing to do was bury him and his offer at the bottom of the Hinterland Sea. But I was desperate. By then I had a canteen full of stolen lives, and the weight of them was killing me. Sometimes I wish they'd finished the job.

The old man showed me a way to enter the land of Death: he gave me something to drink, something that turned the world's colors to gray, till all I could see against all that foggy nothing was a length of golden thread. Right there, at my fingertips. I pulled myself along it, hand over hand. I followed it through water, right down into the land of Death. I walked through his cold mineral forests, past lakes of frozen fire. The lives around my neck were whispering to me, as if they knew Death was close and thought he'd give them peace at last.

I walked into his ugly palace, unafraid. Well, a little afraid. It was a trap, of course. Everyone I'd ever killed was waiting for me in Death's hall. I thought they were there to kill me, too. When I saw the way Death looked at me — like I was nothing, like the life I'd turned over to finding him meant *nothing* — I think I wanted them to.

But Death wanted to set the price I'd pay. He wouldn't let them kill me.

Instead he took something from me. Something so small you never think you'd miss it. The thing that hides behind your life-light: he took my death. Perfect punishment, right? Who knew Death was a poet?

Life is all that's left to me now, much good it does me.

~19~

I sat alone in an all-night diner, no idea where to go next.

I read the rest of my book. I ordered toast and ate it, after Sophia's picked-over feast had been cleared away. I drank my coffee; it'd have to do me for sleep. When I couldn't put off leaving any longer, I stood, dropping a tip big enough to cover the hours I'd spent squatting.

Outside the air was a soft blue-gray and the birds were testing their voices. I let my fingers close around my pocketknife as I watched a few cars go by. A man on a bike with a radio lashed to its handle-bars, scattering timpani. A woman in a cleaner's uniform, shouldering a heavy purse. In a bus shelter across the street, a little girl in a hooded sweatshirt leaned against the dirty plastic, looking down at her feet. I watched her a while, but she never looked up.

And all the time I was worrying at a riddle: Where do you go when you have nowhere to go?

If you're Hinterland, you go to the Hell Hotel.

Maybe it was a bad idea to get any closer to Daphne and our bloody-fingered brethren right then, but I had the thought that it would be better to embed my-self among them than to always wonder where they were. Or maybe I was just out of ideas, and incredibly tired.

This time, the lobby was empty. Nobody sat behind the desk, or came when I rang the bell. I waited, impatient, the duffel bag I'd stuffed the night before slung over my shoulder. There was a board of keys hang-ing behind the bellhop's desk, more keys than empty spaces. When nobody showed after a few minutes, I chose the first three digits of Ella's phone number — room 549 — and headed to the fifth floor.

If I'd stayed in this room when I was eight, just after reading *A Little Princess,* I might've loved it. It felt much higher than it was, like a garret tucked away into the eaves. Or a pigeon's nest. Decades of smoke had baked the walls as yellow as teeth, and a single painting hung on them like a poppy seed: a tiny, intense portrait of a mermaid sunning herself, her hair layered on with a paint knife.

There was a tuft chair and a dresser and a desk with a Bible in it, half-hidden under an age-stiffened issue of *TV Guide.* The bed was lumpy, the bathroom not to be spoken of. I made a mental note to pick up Clorox wipes. I set my toothpaste and face wash next to the sink and drank a mugful of water. There was no reason for it to taste different here than at home, but it did.

When I couldn't think of anything else to do, I lay down and looked out the window. From my bed I could see the gray face of the apartment building across the street, and a sliver of sky. Somewhere, someone was listening to music. You couldn't tell from which direction the bass was sneaking in. I had to work later, I remembered dimly, though it was hard to believe any part of my life might remain the same. I felt much farther than a few miles from home.

I drifted off around eight a.m. and woke up gasping. I'd been dreaming something. It had the deep-water texture of a hotel dream, anonymous and heavy. Inside it, someone had been speaking to me. I could feel their words inside my ears, but I couldn't recall them.

Before I left Brooklyn, I'd sent Ella a text to confirm I was alive, then turned off my phone. When I turned it on to check the time, it jittered with notifications I didn't want to read. I looked up the nearest reputable hotel on Google Maps and texted her a link.

Here's where I'm staying. Just for a little while. I'm safe and I'm sorry and I love you.

Seconds after I sent it, the phone began to ring. I held it to my chest, letting it vibrate through my sternum. After it stopped, a text came through.

Come home.

I turned it off again.

It was already past three, and I had to be at work in an hour. I headed down to the lobby, figuring I'd find somewhere to eat before heading to the bookstore. Felix was back behind the desk; when he saw me he beckoned me over.

"Hey," I said. "I should tell you, I took a —"

"Room 549?" His eyes were flat. They gave nothing away.

"Oh. Yeah. You weren't here, so I just . . ."

"It's not a problem. Daphne told me you were coming."

I frowned. I'd decided that morning to come here. I hadn't told anyone, not even Sophia. "Daphne said I was coming? Are you sure?"

He was writing my name and room number in a red leather–covered book, pretending he was too busy to hear me. "Check your mailbox, by the way. It looks like you've got something."

My hand was on his arm before I knew

what I was doing, grabbing up a fistful of sleeve.

"I've got a letter?"

Whip quick, he peeled my hand away. "Watch yourself, ice queen," he growled. The thing that sparked in his eyes might've been anger, or it might've been fear. He jerked his chin toward the elevator. "Mail's that way."

An archway to the left of the elevator opened onto a corridor lit by a single orange-shaded bulb, honeycombed on either side with wooden mailboxes. I traced my way to box 549. Inside it was a heavy ivory envelope, unaddressed. I teased out the trifolded page and read it standing up.

Dear Alice,

It's hard not to think of these letters like I'm writing in a diary when I don't know if you're reading them, or if they're really just for me. I had a therapist once who made me keep a diary, except she wanted me to bring it in each week and read it to her. So mainly I just used it to write Dragon Age *fanfic. I won't do that to you.*

Instead I'll tell you a thing I can't stop

thinking about. When I was little my mom used to make me pray, and I'd always pray for magic to be real. And when I wished on stars or at 11:11 or blew on a dandelion I'd say it in my head: let magic be real. *But ever since I found out it's very very real, I don't wish anymore. I don't pray. I want things, but I don't wish them. I don't know what to think about that. I don't know that I really have a point. I'm just thinking about it because the world keeps getting bigger, so much bigger than I thought it could be even when I was wishing. I'm using* world *as a euphemism, of course. I just realized I've seen almost as many worlds now as I've seen states in the U.S. My dad would hate that. He always acted like life ended outside of New York. I've thought about writing to him, too, but I wouldn't know where to begin. It's better writing to you. I like pretending I'm talking to you. I like imagining you making your don't-waste-my-time face when I do it. That was a good face. Generally speaking, you've got a good face. Now I'm just rambling.*

Maybe I should tell you more. About where I am. Why I am. What I'm doing.

I left the Hinterland. Did I tell you that?

It's hard to remember what I've written and what I've just thought about. I'm talking to you all the time in my head now. When I go to sleep and when I wake up.

Days run together, but I guess it's been a couple of months since you left. In my head you're in New York now, and it's May. You're sitting in Washington Square Park eating a paleta from a cart and you're wearing what you were wearing that time I saw you in Central Park, those jeans with the holes in the knees and that striped shirt. You're using my letters as bookmarks.

I want you to know that, all promises aside, I'm going to write to you again.

It took me a while to see anything but the letter, hear anything but my own breath.

A couple of months. As the days counted down on my side of the divide, just *two months* had passed in the Hinterland. Finch was seeing me through the haze of sixty days, while out here, nearly two years had gone.

I hid a while in the cool of the corridor, hearing the words in his voice. Unsure if I was even remembering it right. How did the magic work? Could I write back to him somehow? I turned the letter over and dug a pen out of my bag, pressing the page against a bare patch of wall.

What would I say if I was sure he would read it?

I forgive you.

Do you forgive me?

I talk to you all the time in my head, too.

Maybe I'd pick up somewhere in the middle, wherever we'd left off. He'd always done more of the talking. It was a minefield for me, making conversation. I'd spent too much time with people who forgave me my conversational sins: Ella, who loved me anyway; Sophia, living by the arcane rules of another world; Edgar, so deeply eccentric he wouldn't know inappropriate if it jumped out of a first edition and bit him.

Finch was different. We'd wanted things from each other, we'd been using each other. He seemed stable enough to steel me when Ella's disappearance left me entirely alone, and I thought I was trespassing on his kindness, his curiosity, and, yeah, his crush, but the terrain between us was more complicated than that. When I learned he'd been using me for my magic — for my *proximity* to magic, my ability to pull him into the whirlpool of Althea's worlds, which looked a whole lot prettier from the outside — I might've shut the door on him.

But he put himself in the way of the wrong kind of enchantment, and got himself killed.

Or so I thought. Instead he recovered, somewhere, somehow, and dragged me kicking and screaming — and scratching, if I remembered it right — from my tale. I'd barely had time to thank him. I'd barely had time to let the new shape of him impose itself over the old one in my head. The Finch I carried around with me was somewhere between the narrow, restless prep school kid I'd known, and the scarred, strong, steady-eyed man I only got a glimpse of.

That version of him had looked so grown. So complete. But I bet he was just wearing another kind of armor.

Here's what I would write to him. If I knew how to deliver the letter.

I always knew magic was real. It might be cheating to say that now, but I really think I did. I just didn't call it that. I didn't think it could be benevolent, except in books. Magic was a bully that made my mom cry and followed us at night. In the daytime, too. It was the thing in me that made it hard to get calm again, once I got angry.

One time I counted it up, and I'm pretty sure I've seen thirty-one states. Some places I've only seen their gas stations. Some places that's all there is to see.

I wrote fanfiction, too. If you find me ~~I'll let you read it~~ I'll tell you what I wrote it about. If you find me I'll tell you whatever you want to know.

~20~

Janet wanted to meet Iolanthe first. In-grid didn't want to go at all. She wasn't like Janet — a transplant, a born wan-derer. Her roots here went all the way down to the world's bedrock, even if that bedrock was turning to smoke.

"We don't know where the door in the tavern goes," Finch said tightly. "But the fact that it smells like everything you want to get home to is a pretty big tip-off it's dangerous, right?"

"Yes, thank you, I've read my share of fairy tales," Janet snapped. "And while we're on the subject of devil's deals, who exactly is this person that popped in out of nowhere, ready to save our lives?"

"A traveler," Finch said, though he knew that was oversimplifying things. "She wants money, and she thinks I can help her with that."

"A traveler, listen to him. Do you know what you're talking about? Do you think we're playing a game?" Janet's chill had frayed along with the Hinterland. For the first time Finch feared he wouldn't be able to convince her, that she wouldn't come at all.

"The door in the tavern feels *wrong*," he half shouted. He hadn't fully admitted it before, but it did. It had a furtive feeling, an oiliness. Even the round hobbity cuteness of it felt like a vicious joke.

"So our options are these," he said, speaking low again, calmly. "We stay. Hope the Spinner fixes things. Or we take our chances tomorrow morning and go. Because none of us is walking through that door."

Finch didn't sleep much that night. None of them did. He heard the burr of Janet and Ingrid's voices through the wall hours past dark. They would decide without him whether to stay or go, all he could do was wait and see. His tiny store of belongings was packed, and all the inscrutable treasures of the Hinterland. There wasn't anything more he could do. Finally, restlessness sent him outside.

Night was tipping softly into day when the front door creaked open behind him. Janet was always after Ingrid to fix that creak. She settled beside him, already dressed in her jeans and open-necked shirt, her trim-cut coat, relics of the Earthly life she'd abandoned decades ago.

Traveling clothes. The fearful grip on his heart eased away. They sat together while the light went blue, then violet, then the powdered silver of pine needles. The Hinterland and its relentless beauty stopped for no one.

Just before sunrise the three of them walked together across the women's land. Ingrid unlatched the gate on the goat pen and bent over to pick a teacup-shaped flower. She tucked it into Janet's hair. Their path to the tavern was circuitous now, winding around great starry gaps in the land. Iolanthe was standing out front of it in her black on black, including a cloak with copper stitching at the neck, running a thumb over the empty face of her pocket watch.

First she made Finch show her all the things he'd taken from the broken tales.

"Good Christ," Janet murmured as he did it. "That's quite the arsenal."

Iolanthe's eyes were alight as she ran her hands over all the little treasures he'd plucked from the Hinterland's wounds. It filled him with pride to see her lift one, then another, holding a walnut to her ear and shaking it, weighing the balance of a speckled yellow egg. Then she picked up the dagger.

"Hello," she said. "You're going to make this a whole lot easier."

It was an age-stained thing of yellowing bone Finch had taken from a pretty three-story manor house in the town where Hansa had lived. Words ran over its hilt, carved in a language he couldn't read. Iolanthe shrugged an arm free of her cloak, then paused.

"Almost forgot: I made you a promise."

From an inside pocket she brought out two small booklets. They were bound in the same shade of green leather as *Tales from the Hinterland,* the print across them embossed in the same gold. PASSPORT, their covers read, above the unmistakable shape of a Hinterland flower.

Alice, Finch thought. She'd had that flower tattooed on her arm. The memory was sharp as an embroidery needle.

Janet practically snatched the passports. Finch could see her hungry mind clicking away. "How do they work?"

"The door." Iolanthe pointed toward the tavern. "Keep them against your skin as you walk through it, and you'll get to where you're going. I'd hold hands if I were you. Tightly."

"And if you walk through the door without a passport?" Ingrid asked grimly. "What happens to you then?"

"Hard to say," Iolanthe said. "But I wouldn't trust it, would you?"

"What about Ellery?" Janet put an arm around him. "Can you guarantee he'll be safe?"

"No." Iolanthe smiled to soften it. "But

I can guarantee he'll be interested. Good enough?"

Janet looked at her coolly, then turned to him. She touched a new cut under his eye and a healing one below his lip. Gently, she cupped his chin, looking at the scarred-over line on his throat.

"This is what you want." She said it without inflection, not a question.

Finch had gotten used to not looking at what he wanted head-on. He'd learned the dreadful lesson of being careful what you wish for, and had taken pains since then not to wish for too much. Nothing more ambitious than to save one girl.

And to dismantle, as it turned out, one entire world.

"I want to see what's next." They felt like the safest words he could say. He felt Iolanthe's eyes on him, and refused to be embarrassed. He brought his arm around Janet, then held the other one out to bring Ingrid in.

It was okay to leave the Hinterland if they weren't in it. If another world waited for him and Alice was free and he'd drunk so deeply already of this place's orderly and chaotic magic, he could go. He could let go.

And if he left, part of him whispered, the Spinner couldn't follow. He'd be free at last of the fear that held him by the neck, the sense that her revenge, when it came, would take him out at the knees.

"Walk through the right doors," Janet told him. "And perhaps a few wrong ones."

She tilted her head and ran her thumb tips under his eyes. "When we see each other again, heaven knows where, you can tell me everything. And if this young woman is to be trusted, we can thank you both for our lives."

Iolanthe's forearm was already bared. She held the bone knife in her left hand, loose and easy. Tossed it a bit, to get a better grip. With a motion like she was mincing garlic, she made three cuts just above her elbow.

Janet breathed hard through her teeth and Ingrid stepped back, muttering. The cuts welled and spilled, running red over Iolanthe's sun-browned skin. She stepped closer to the tavern wall and, using her finger as a brush, painted a line of blood in the space between two timbers.

"Stop staring," she said after a minute. "It doesn't help."

The lines she drew were faint, the blood stretched as thin as it could go without breaking. It wasn't till the line climbed over her head that Finch understood what she was doing.

She was drawing a door. The bone dagger, the blood. The door. Finch knew this story. He'd read it in *Tales from the Hinterland*.

If Iolanthe was weakened, the only sign of it was the way she caught herself, briefly, against the wall, before pulling a square of fabric from her bag.

"Tie this around my arm?"

Finch did, wincing as he drew the ends together tight.

"Now." Iolanthe looked close at the dagger, at the words running over its handle, then read them aloud. Their syllables were bright and distant; they swooped and dove like seabirds, lingering on the air before drifting away.

The blood on the wall shifted like a

shadow, becoming the seams of a real door. Through those seams, a gray light glowed.

Iolanthe drew her head up and shook out her cloak and looked, for a moment, very solemn. "Ready?"

~21~

After my first night's sleep in Hell, I woke up too early with a stranger's voice in my ear.

A girl's. Stucco-rough but somehow sweet. I could still hear what she'd said, I could almost remember it . . .

Then I woke the rest of the way, and it was gone. I thought about swimming up yesterday from my blackout nap, the feeling I'd had that someone was talking to me then. And I wondered.

But not too hard, because I had bigger things to wonder about. First, I reread

Finch's last letter. I read it twice. Then I pushed it aside because I could lose a whole day to that mystery, and there just wasn't time. I had to figure out who among the Hinterland had ice in their hands and a taste for dismemberment.

I could hear Sophia's voice in my head. *Look at you, Nancy Drew.* She'd never say that; she'd never even heard of Nancy Drew. I guessed the voice I heard was really my own. I guessed I should call Sophia to talk about last night, and Ella to beg her forgiveness. I did neither.

I decided what I did have to do was learn what had happened with Hansa. She was the only one of the four I felt like I knew, at least a little, and if I was looking for a pattern here her death seemed the most likely to break it.

But the idea of sniffing around her grieving parents, once I tracked them down, made me feel sick. Even worse was the idea that they might think I'd been the one to kill her. Though Sophia had promised to unsmear my name, I didn't know how long that would take. Who would and wouldn't believe her. And whether she was still up for helping me after last night.

When all my thoughts started going into soft focus I put on a clean shirt and headed out for coffee and food. I walked till I found an open pizza place, then ate a big foldable slice of rubbery margherita while searching out caffeine. It was half past seven by then, commuters bleeding from every subway entrance. A thousand different faces to get caught on, but the one that hooked me was a little girl's. She wore sunglasses and a hoodie and was sitting on the edge of a gutter punk's blanket, just out of reach of his dog. I couldn't tell whether they were together, but she was paying him no mind.

Something about her was so familiar. I stared a minute, trying to place whether and where I'd seen her. Then I had it: she'd been waiting at the bus stop across from the diner last night. And the night before that, she'd been in Central Park. Watching me from beside the path.

"Hey," I said, almost to myself. I started toward her, but didn't make it too far. As soon as I got moving, she vaulted herself off the blanket and flew down the street.

"Hey! Wait!" I took a few running steps, then stopped. She was already a block away, moving fast as a whippet through the crowd.

My heart pounded and my thoughts went sharp. She could run, but I knew who she must be. And I knew where to find her.

Not many kids came through from the Hinterland. Hansa had been one of them. Creepy Jenny was another, with her baby-doll face and those keen little in-turned eyeteeth. And then there was the Trio.

In the Hinterland they'd had other names: the Acolytes of the Silver Dagger. The Red, the White, and the Black. But here, everyone just called them the Trio. They weren't little girls, exactly, that was just the form they took. It was odd to see one of them alone, but these were odd times.

I only knew about them what Sophia had told me: that in the Hinterland they'd answered to their own kind of deity. Here, they'd found their way to the Christian God, though I doubted it was a mutual thing. They hung out at a church in Midtown, and tended to show up when they had a message for you — the garbled, prophetic kind. The kind you'd damn well better heed. I waited a little longer, but the girl didn't come back. When nothing worse showed, either, I headed to where I knew I could find her.

Times Square in the morning looked oddly clean. Massive video billboards cycled silently overhead, and tourists clustered on the corner of Forty-Fourth and Broadway. The place I was looking for was weathered stone with a big rose window, its imposing face half lost behind construction scaffolding. A church, lovely and unlikely, tucked among the anonymous hotels and overpriced diners above the square. The schedule by the entrance said I'd missed matins, but when I tried the doors they opened.

Ella never took me to church, and there'd been a time when I was fascinated by them. I couldn't believe they were free, that anyone was allowed to walk inside a place that looked so much like a museum or a castle.

This one's entrance was cool and hazy

241

with incense. Beyond it was the great glittering mouth of the church itself, yawning wide to reveal its treasures: rows of polished pews and the Virgin in her nook, mosaicked arches and filigreed screens and wooden carvings of figures who must've been holy men, but could just as easily have been depictions of the Green Man, the Erlking, the King of May. Saints glared out through solemn eyes, and stained-glass windows cast dim jewels over the ground, and I was starting to see how an ex-Story could find solace here, in a building so replete with ancient tales.

There were a few tourists here and there, lighting candles or taking sneaky photos, dwarfed by the gold-and-marble altarpiece. Nobody who could be the Trio, I thought. Slowly I walked to the front of the room, a faint *tock tock tock* taking up slow residence in my head.

It was the sound, I realized, of heels on wood. Looking over the pews I saw that they weren't quite empty: three heads just peeked over the top of a bench on the left side. The heads were hooded, from left to right, in red, white, and black. One of them must've been kicking her feet against the pew like . . . well, like a bored kid in church. I was a few rows away when the kicking stopped and the heads clicked on their necks like something out of Camazotz, turning in unison to look at me.

"Hello," said the child in red.

"Alice-Three-Times," said the child in black.

The child in white said nothing, but you could tell she was thinking plenty. She showed her milk teeth in a smile that made me colder than consecrated stone.

I scanned them, trying to figure out which had been following me. The one in red, I thought. She'd changed her hoodie.

"Hi," I said, a little breathless. "I think you have a message for me."

Red and Black leaned forward to look at each other. White kept staring.

"Well? What is it?"

"You can ask us anything you'd like." Red.

"Perhaps we'll answer. Perhaps not." Black.

White said nothing, but the other two tilted their heads into her silence, and laughed.

"Is that the message?" I slid into the pew in front of theirs and turned around, facing them over its back. They had eerie little oatmeal box faces, like an illustrator's idea of how a wholesome child might look. If the illustrator were terrified of wholesome children.

Red studied my face. "You're afraid of something."

"Isn't everyone?"

She smiled, a little meanly. "You have more to be afraid of than they do."

"Okay. Does it have something to do with the murders?"

"With the deaths, you mean," said Red.

Black bowed her head. "We honor their sacrifice."

"What sacrifice?" I said. "I'm talking about murder. The four Hinterlanders who were killed."

"Great change requires great sacrifice."

"And tales change their shape, depending on who's doing the telling."

I tasted metal. "Don't talk about this in riddles, all right?"

All three held up their left palm, oath-giving style, as Red and Black talked between them.

"No riddles. *You* say it's murder."

"But we say they chose to die, and knew what they were dying for."

"They go on to a great reward, in a better world."

I seized on Red's words. "A better world? What world is that?"

"The world of the kingdom of Heaven," she said primly.

Black spoke next. "*If* they can make it. We do pray for all of you, not just ourself."

"Thanks," I said dryly. "So you've thrown the Spinner over for God?"

"The Spinner never spoke to us. God does."

"Oh, yeah? What does God tell you?"

Black shrugged. "He moves beneath the green and the gold. The blue and the brown. The red, the white, and the black."

245

"He sacrificed a piece of his very self, just like Genevieve. Just like Hansa."

I didn't like to hear the dead's names in their mouths. "Murder isn't sacrifice — they didn't want to die. Saying it was a sacrifice implies there's something they died *for*."

Red turned to Black. "Assumes she knows everything, this girl."

"And knows less than most."

Red looked back at me. "Don't you know the story of Saint Alixia? He cut off pieces of himself to feed the gateway between Heaven and Earth, to keep it always open for his kin. He cut off pieces till he fell down dead, and his blood became a river. His wife paddled down it to her divine reward."

"That's not a real story," I said, though I supposed it could be. You never knew with saints.

"We've nothing more to say to you, child."

"Child?"

"We've nothing more to say," Red repeated. "You asked your questions and we answered them. If you won't listen, bother us no more."

"Let's take her out of our prayers," Black whispered.

There was more I wanted to say to that, but a harassed-looking man was hurrying over, hem trailing behind. He clapped his hands gently, looking past me.

"You three cannot be in here. I've already told you, no unattended children in the church."

The thing in white piped up then. Her voice was bell-sweet and lightly turned. She looked not at the man but up, like she was practicing her Joan of Arc. "'Truly I tell you, unless you change and become like little children, you will never enter the kingdom of heaven.'" Her voice flattened, and her eyes met his. "Never, not ever. *Never ever.*"

Whether it was the scripture or her spooky little face, the man fell back, uncertain. "Well, that's . . ." Without finishing his thought, he swept off toward the altar.

"Our advice to you," said Red, turning back toward me.

"Is to *listen* when your betters speak," said Black.

White looked at me, and I held my breath.

"And to remember every story is a ghost story," she said. She reached out and pressed one cold little hand to my chest. Its nails were painted ballerina pink. "If you're looking for answers, seek out your ghosts."

The painted eyes of the saints watched me walk away. The lit candles guttered as I passed; I wondered what would happen if I trailed my fingers through the pool of holy water.

I looked back, just before opening the door, at the three dark beads of their heads over the pew back.

Four. For a moment, I thought I saw a *fourth* head. Then the door behind me opened and the sun sliced in, and I blinked the vision away.

~22~

What did Finch think they'd find through the door?

A goblin market. The wood between the worlds. An underworld of smoke and fire.

Not this: a few rippingly painful seconds spent falling through an icy fog. Then his body tipped onto dusty stone, hard through the patched-over knees of his jeans. He was certain he was upside down, clinging like a spider, till the world righted itself. Iolanthe was already standing, swatting the dust away, as Finch rose slowly to his feet.

They stood in a cracked courtyard circled with crumbling pillars, under a blank gray sky. But *courtyard* didn't feel like an old enough word. It was an agora, then, vast and ancient and empty. Finch couldn't tell if it was night or day, or whether those words had any meaning here. The pillars were neatly spaced, flanking wide stone roads, each angling steeply upward toward the broken teeth of the city encircling them.

This world was dead. Finch thought he understood what that could mean, having watched the disintegration of the Hinterland. But that was a *bleeding* world, running with life and rage and sentient stars, bucking against the insult of its own collapse.

He hadn't understood what death could look like when the corpse was made of stone and wind and dust and all the million, million elements that sifted and slept the big sleep under a voided-out sky. The weight of it was unimaginable.

Iolanthe's hand was friendly on his shoulder. Her calm was a lifeline, and the casual lilt of her voice. "Scary, isn't it? We can't stay too long without shelter —

it gets under your skin out here. In your head. But look around while you can, hardly anyone gets to see a fossil world."

Finch found his words at last. "What happened here?"

She was turning in place, looking at each road. Something about the one directly to Finch's right must've appealed to her, and she started toward it. Far, far above them — though it was hard to say how far, because of the place's surreal flatness — stood a palace of high gray towers, edgeless against the sky.

"A parasite happened," she said. "Now follow me, and save your breath. It's a long walk."

The city seemed distant till suddenly they were in it, among the falling-down slabs of walls and shops and houses. They walked in silence, but inside Finch's head was a rising fire. A building whose windows were great black eyes had on its roof a stone symbol like a thumbless hand, clearly some kind of long-fallen temple. There was a moment when he thought he saw a sign of life — an undulation in his vision, like the flicker of distant light —

but Iolanthe didn't seem to notice it, and then he wasn't sure.

The towered palace, when they reached it, was surrounded by an expanse of open pavement cracked into gray mosaic. They picked their way across it, toward the structure's arched, iron-girded doors. There, Iolanthe looked again at the blank face of her pocket watch. She replaced it and pulled a key from her bag — bronze, ridiculously oversized, straight out of *Alice in Wonderland*.

"Skeleton key," she said.

"Who the fuck *are* you?" Finch replied.

She looked at him to see if he was kidding. He was not. "Now you ask me?" Her face was half in shadow and half in gray light. Tramping in her cloak through this hollow land, she looked more like the progeny of Prospero than the grungy wanderer he'd pegged her for.

"I'm a traveler," she told him. "A survivor. Most of all, I'm the person who got you into this gray fart of a world, and I'm the person who's going to get you out. Good enough?"

"For now."

"Oh, good. Now stay close, it's gonna be dark for a while." She cranked the door open with her outlandish key, and they slipped through. Finch hadn't noticed the enervating breeze soughing in his ears till they stepped inside and it was gone. Immediately his head felt clearer.

Iolanthe slid through the dark. Her cloak had metallic stitching on the back, too; Finch followed its faint radiance. Through a series of connected rooms like the sections of a centipede, down a long corridor, and into the sudden gray light of a window-paneled atrium, where, at last, the air was filled with the scent of something familiar.

Books. The drowsy odor of paper and leather and dust and age, and none of the scents you'd expect: of mildew and water damage, pages gone to rot. They stood in a library.

Finch darted ahead. The books climbed up and up, shelves alternating with windows through which he could see scraps of the building's towers. He hadn't seen this many books in one place since before the Hinterland. Janet had a yellowing collection she cherished, and the refugees a teeny lending library that boasted the pooled resources of Earth's displaced travelers — *Wuthering Heights, Go Tell It on the Mountain,* a Turkish translation of *A Wrinkle in Time* — but that was fifty titles at most. These brimming shelves tugged him in like a moon. He almost didn't hear Iolanthe's mild "Careful" as he pulled down a book.

It was gray as the rest of the room before he touched it, but once it was in his hands he could see that it was bound in pale blue, embossed, front and back, with an intricate spiderweb. Tiny women were caught in its net in various attitudes of peril: arms up, heads thrown back, hands to mouths. They looked like a pack of Fay Wrays. It was creepy enough that he paused, before opening it anyway.

The print was made up of intensely black, closely clustered characters. Though he couldn't read them, he could feel their inherent narrative thrust: they *wanted* to be read. They wanted to tell him a story. Staring at the text was like staring at churned-up water, slowly clearing, till he could see what lay on the seabed below.

What came into slow focus was a cautionary tale. A tale of silver scissors and red fruit, of green leaves and dark earth, of dangerous and endangered girls. It was, if he had to guess, a fairy tale.

He peered into the deep water of the book till he could hear the wheedling bite of the scissors and feel the sweet give of poisoned fruit and the leaves circling his brow were cool and wet like they'd been plucked just after a rain and —

"Hey, now." Iolanthe stood over him. The book was in her hands, firmly shut. Finch blinked, trying to remember when he'd gotten to his knees. "This isn't the book we're looking for."

Finch breathed to steady himself. "What was that? What the hell was that?"

"I had to let you do it once," she said, unapologetic. "So you won't do it again."

A card catalog stood between the double helix staircases. She chose a drawer near the bottom, flicking through it for a minute before emerging with a card. The book she wanted was two stories up, and she made Finch fetch it. He scurried up a wet dream of a library ladder, all sturdy wood and metal fittings. His perspective shifted as he climbed, books altering their size and height and sparking with roving flares of color, like optical illusions.

"Stop!" Iolanthe called when Finch had reached the second landing. The book she directed him toward gained heft and density in his hands, like one of those little Bibles made up of a zillion onion-skin pages. He tucked it under an arm and took the staircase down.

"What now?" he said, a little breath-less. Iolanthe had pushed her sleeves back again; Finch was worried she'd slice up the other arm.

"Now I show you a less bloody way of walking through a door."

"Jesus," Finch breathed. "Are all these books *doors?*"

"A book is always a door."

"Sure, yeah, but not a — usually not a *literal* door. Have you done this before? Have you gone into these books?"

An odd look flashed over Iolanthe's face, sharp as a sunbeam caught in a hand mirror. "I came out of one of these books."

The air in Finch's lungs went fizzy.

He'd suspected she wasn't from Earth, but it was different to hear it confirmed. This girl with the ice-colored braids and the wanderlust might have more secrets than he did. "Which one?"

She climbed up a few steps, leaned far over, and stuck a finger in the empty space between two books. "This one."

"What happened to it?"

Her face was still turned away. "It's been checked out."

"I'm sorry," Finch said softly. When she didn't respond, he went on. "Whose library was this? What *was* this place?"

"It belonged to a magician. A powerful one."

"All these books — all these worlds — were his?"

"Hers. Only one world is hers."

"Is? She's still alive? Who is she?"

"Shh. Come here." She walked back down and extended a hand. Finch took it. With her free hand Iolanthe fumbled open the book, and began to read.

The words weren't the fleet, wild-winged things that opened the blood door out of the Hinterland. They were slower, sweeter. They beguiled. Finch wanted to see when it happened, when the door appeared, but he couldn't keep his lids from closing.

"Keep them closed," Iolanthe said, her voice wobbling toward Finch's ear like sun through water. Her fingers tightened around his, and the pair of them stepped forward into something that felt like Finch once imagined a cloud would feel, back when he was a little kid looking out the window of an airplane. It was soft and giving and it smelled like the sweet wood of a cigar box. Then the air cleared, went thin and smoky and cool.

When he opened his eyes they were standing uneven on a cobblestone street, the cutout square of a doorway hanging in the air behind them.

~23~

Outside the church, the sun was higher, the heat heavy as a hand. Tourists and commuters in sweat-stained business clothes moved like sleepwalkers. My eyes caught on exposed arms and bellies and feet, the sweat-shining canals flowing between women's clavicles. The glare of it boiled together with incense smoke, the sad-eyed Virgin, the candles lit like so many life-lights. And the message the Trio had for me: that the deaths weren't murders, but martyrdom.

Martyrdom to *what?*

I backed into a square of shade and called a car, unable to bear the prospect of twenty blocks of hard sun, or wading through the morning rush in Times Square. A few minutes later a black sedan pulled up and the driver ducked her head down, looking at me.

Sun-dazzled and suddenly starving, I collapsed into its back seat.

Maybe martyrdom wasn't the crux of it: I'd almost been killed, and there was nothing I'd been ready to die for. The child in white told me to seek out my ghosts. Maybe that was the real message. But what did it mean? I sighed, craving the solitude of my room, ice water, and a shower. I lay my head against the seat.

And heard the click of the child locks. I looked up.

"What are you —"

"Shut up," the driver snarled. "Don't say another word till I say you can. And put your hands up — cross 'em, up on your shoulders, where I can see them."

Her face, what I could catch of it in the rearview mirror, had a wicked Morgan le Fay look to it, fleshy and lush. Her head grazed the top of the car, all of her built on a grand scale. She was Hinterland, of course, but I wasn't panicking yet; no chance was she the quicksilver thing who'd attacked me on the subway. Mainly I was kicking myself for getting in the wrong damned car.

"Look, what do you want?"

"I told you to be — *hey!*" She leaned on her horn and shrieked a string of expletives as a tank-topped school of pedestrians bearing Disney Store bags darted in front of the car.

"It's Midtown," I snapped. "What did you expect?"

"Shut up."

There was such focused rage in the words that I did go quiet. When I tried to sneak a hand to my phone she braked hard, glaring at me, and I pulled my hand back. Traffic was stop and go, past chain stores and Netflix ads and people dressed in unlicensed Anna and Elsa costumes and it all felt so surreal I didn't really get scared till she veered hard into a parking garage. Past the booth, attendantless, and barreling upward, around and around in dizzy circles through the dim, taking every corner too tight and making me dig my nails into my skin. Then we burst out into sunlight glinting off chrome fenders and pearlized finish, so assaultive after the dark I didn't see the man right away.

Sitting on the hood of a parked car, holding a dark metal wrench.

And it struck me that I should be arming myself, if I could.

Cold, I was thinking dizzily, squeezing my eyes shut and pressing my fingers into my collarbone. *Cold, cold —*

The woman flung open the door and dragged me out by my arm and a fistful of shirt, throwing me onto the ground. Glittery bits of it dug into the heels of my hands and my bare knees as I pushed up, tried to push to standing. Then she had me again, her hand palming my neck like I was a kitten. She forced me to kneel and I felt the beginnings of it: that burn in my throat, that ice-pick ache in my eyes. The man stood in front of me with his wrench over his shoulder, black boots planted. Him I recognized. Brown skin, dressed all in green. I'd seen him in meetings before, even heard him talking about his daughter, but it wasn't till now that I put it together. The cresting cold in me guttered and fled. I pressed my palms, placating, to the ground.

"You're Hansa's parents, aren't you?"

The hand on my neck tightened and jerked, shaking me till my vision snapped with stars.

"Listen to me," I gasped. "I didn't do anything, I —"

Then she was lifting me, easy as a puppet, hauled up under my armpits. When I was back on my feet she moved next to the man, looming over him by a head. He flexed his hands around the wrench, and she held her own hands up like they were weapons, like they were as deadly as mine. I believed it.

"Tell me to my face you didn't kill my daughter."

I looked straight into her wild blue eyes, ready to deny it. As they met mine, caught mine, I felt an aqueous click in my brain. A hypnotic tug that reeled me in and sent me tumbling headlong down a cool blue hallway the exact color of her eyes. When she spoke the words again, they came from inside my head.

Tell me you didn't kill my daughter.

I couldn't look away, couldn't blink, couldn't move anything but my mouth.

"I didn't kill Hansa. I didn't touch her."

Her pause was long, and I was falling. Or maybe I was suspended, in an endless tunnel of light. My body felt warm and weightless, sheathed in calm, panic scrabbling at its underside. Then a jerk behind my belly button heaved me up and out of that serene blue place, dropping me back onto the rooftop of a Manhattan parking garage, sweat-sticky and spitting curses on my hands and knees.

"What was that?" I half screamed.

The man looked down at me, impassive, the wrench now at his side. But the woman was even angrier, crouched beside me.

"If you didn't kill her, *who did?*" Her breath was hot on my face.

"That's what I'm trying to find out!"

"I'll know if you're lying. Do you want me to find out if you're lying?"

"No, no." I put up a hand, scrambled backward. "I'm not lying. Whoever did it, they're trying to make it look like it was me. Whoever did it, they tried to —"

Kill me, too, I was going to say. But suddenly I wondered. If whoever was doing this was trying to frame me, why would they want to kill me? Which half was I wrong about?

"Tried to *what?*" she said, pushing her face into mine.

"They're trying to do *something,*" I said, changing course. "Why else would they do what they did, taking pieces away?"

Her big vivid mouth went bloodless. Behind her, the silent man shifted.

"You're going to find out who did it," she said. It wasn't a question, it was marching orders. "And when you find out, you're not going to do anything else about it until you come to me."

I made myself look right at her when I spoke. "If you do one thing for me first."

"You think you're in a position to bargain?"

"I just have a question. If you'll answer it. I just want to know . . ." I swallowed, trying to put my suspicion into words that wouldn't enrage her. "What was Hansa like at the end?"

"At the *end*?" She glared at me. "She was curious. Funny. Odd. Happy. She was a child."

I nodded, but I couldn't think how to ask the question I really wanted the answer to: Would she have martyred herself? If so, for what?

"Not at the end, though." The man spoke for the first time. His voice was soft. The woman turned on him, and a little steel went into it. "You know it's true.

"At the end she was angry." He looked at me. "She didn't want to lie about who she was anymore. What she was. She didn't understand why we had to."

I braced myself. "Is there any chance she might've . . . chosen this? That it might've been part of something bigger, even if she didn't really understand it?"

The woman's body was taut as a tiger's. I didn't dare look at her. But the man seemed to be thinking, turning over my words. "Our daughter did not want

266

to end," he said carefully. "Never, never would she choose that. But. It's possible whoever took her life tricked her. That final day, next to her body, we found a packed bag. All silly things, cookies and books and coins. I think she thought she'd be traveling. Perhaps she believed dying was the first step of the journey. Death isn't the end, in the Hinterland. I wish we'd taught her better than that here."

He reached into his pocket, and I flinched. But what he brought out was a compass. He pressed it into my palm, then pulled his hand back fast like he wanted to be clear of it.

"Take it," he said. "If you're really trying to find out who did this, use it. It steered Hansa right, till it didn't. Perhaps it will help you."

~24~

The door they'd come through clung for a moment to the air. Through it Finch could see the weary illumination of the last world, turned grayer by the contrast. Then it winked out like a firefly.

He turned, and for a delirious moment thought they were back in the Hinterland. But this place had a shabbier, used kind of feel — less cozy medieval, more Dickensian. They stood at another crossroads, a six-cornered intersection of rubbly little streets lined with lit windows. The sky was an early evening color, and it was a relief after the dead world to breathe in cooking smells and breezes and even the murky contents of the standing puddles between cobblestones.

Iolanthe, too, breathed like she'd set down a heavy load. "Glad to be out of there. You good?"

Finch nodded wordlessly. He wasn't sure he was. He wasn't sure he was made for travel like this, barely leaving a footprint in one place before you were off to the next.

Scooting them out of the way of traffic — a man on an oddly balanced three-wheeled cycle, who ignored them from beneath the brim of his hat — Iolanthe swept off her cloak. She folded it into a bundle so impossibly tight it made Finch remember she'd been a sailor, and tucked it into her bag. Over her black jeans, bleach-stained black T-shirt, the exposed black straps of her bra, she pulled on a high-necked black dress. It fell around her heavy hips with a swish.

"Camouflage," she said.

Finch looked down at his patched-up Frankenjeans, the blue Hanes T-shirt he'd won from Lev in a particularly intense game of Egyptian Rat Screw. His shoes were more duct tape than canvas. And his skin was brown, which hadn't signified much among the refugees of the Hinterland, but might mean something in a place that looked and smelled like a scene from *Great Expectations.*

"You're fine," she told him. "This place is used to travelers — think of it like a port city. It's just, they do have certain ideas about ladies here."

On *ladies* she dropped like a bob into a curtsy that would've been ironic, were it not so deep and perfectly done.

Who the fuck are you? This time Finch said it in his head. He was biding his time.

Now properly attired for who knew what, Iolanthe led them down the widest of the roads, still so narrow he doubted this was a world built for cars. There was more foot traffic the farther they went, and more shop windows open to the evening, selling food and clothes and tools and toys. Finch searched the faces of the people they passed, but they were a diverse, disinterested crowd, and after a while he paid more attention to the windows.

"Don't look too closely," Iolanthe said sharply. "They'll make you buy something."

"I have exactly zero dollars," Finch said, though it wasn't true. He still had forty-seven U.S. dollars and thirty-eight cents in his wallet, which he was too superstitious to toss.

She threw him a look. "They don't want your money."

Iolanthe barreled down the street, looking to neither side. Afraid of losing her, or of invoking some binding buyers' rule of the market, he followed, but things still caught his eye: a window full of small, densely focused paintings of mermaids, and another hung with gossamer-weight butterfly nets, handfuls of jeweled insects stuck into their webbing. The blue eyes of a man selling tins of tea; the man was leaning forward, smiling, when Finch ripped himself away. In an alcove between shops, a puppet show played out beneath a dusty curtain. Two jointed wooden puppets clacked over a painted backdrop of a familiar city skyline. The girl puppet had a cap of pale hair, the boy a cloud of dark. Between them they held a green book, its title written in tiny gold print.

"Wait," Finch said, slowing down, but Iolanthe grabbed his hand and tugged him into the thickening crowd.

"If you stop, they'll want you to buy something," she called back.

They walked deeper in, past increasingly urgent sellers and their wares — twitching piles of ballet slippers, bumpy fruits, a window full of telephones (candlestick, rotary, princess, tablet) that made Finch do a double take — before stopping in front of a shop he'd have missed on his own. Its window was frosted glass, firmly closed. Iolanthe rapped on the door beside it, winking conspiratorially at Finch. As if he were in on the joke. As if he had any idea where they were, and who they were about to see. He gripped his bag in front of him, packed in the Hinterland less than twenty-four hours and exactly two worlds ago.

The woman who opened the door was

Baba Yaga to the life, with eyes like milky jade, straight-up George Washington teeth, and the leathered skin of an aging French film star. She was built like a sparrow but moved like a battleship: slow and deliberate, with a hand to her back.

"You," she said crankily, eyes on Iolanthe. "Back from nobody knows where, dragging I don't know who, selling gods know what. Nervy little bitch."

"Hello, Grandma June," Iolanthe said comfortably. "I know I've been away too long and you thought I was dead and I'm a dreadful child for never bothering to write, but here I am anyway. Can you forgive me?"

The woman flapped a dismissive hand. "Depends what you've got for me. Come in, before you stand still too long and the market thinks it's caught two buyers."

"Is that really your grandma?" Finch muttered.

"Hell, no. Watch your back around her, she'll steal the gold from your teeth if she thinks she can get away with it."

The door shut behind them with a sinister snick, and Finch blinked in the abrupt gloom. Though it wasn't really gloomy; it was the stained red of a forge, or the inside of a dragon's belly. The place was a curiosity shop, or else a really, really esoteric thrift store. It was full of delicately balanced metal instruments, and pieces bristling with exposed circuitry, and the kinds of carved wooden objects that look like they've got a trick to them: a secret compartment, a hidden blade.

"Well." Grandma June bustled behind a countertop and turned on a lamp, casting a circle of clean white light over the three of them. "What have you got for me?"

Iolanthe presented Finch with a flourish, like she was whipping a drop cloth off a statue. "A scavenger, fresh from the Hinterland."

"Hinterland? Scavenger? You're telling me that place is in a state to be *scavenged*?" The old woman rubbed her bristly chin. "Serves her right, doesn't it? Well, don't stand there blushing. Show us what you've got, this isn't my first time."

Finch stuck a hand into his bag, pulling out the first thing he touched — the spyglass from Hansa's cottage — and placing it on an open square of countertop.

Grandma June's brusque air dropped away. Her hand shot out to grab it, then stalled midway. Carefully she plucked and lifted it, like her palm was a grocery scale.

"Well? Did I do good or what?" Iolanthe's eyes crinkled.

June ignored her. "I've seen the seed before the bloom. I've seen the babe before the bones. But I've never seen one of these."

"What is it?" Finch asked, itching now to snatch it back. He wasn't sure, suddenly, that he wanted to sell.

The woman handed it over. "Look through it."

Finch already had, in the Hinterland, but now he tried again. "Nothing." He executed a slow turn. "It's not even magnified."

She took it back and touched an invisible catch, and the thing snapped open, revealing a second section. "Now look."

Finch peered through it dutifully, and gasped. He felt like he had the first time he'd ducked his head underwater while snorkeling with his parents in the Seychelles: from the mundane surface to a riotous world of colored fins and scattered light. Just like that.

"How am I seeing this?" he said. "*What* am I seeing?"

"That's the past," she said, her voice disembodied, floating. "You might be looking at yesterday, or a year ago, or ten."

"Longer," Finch said. He was watching a girl with milk-glass eyes, tracking her path through a transformed shop — brighter, tidier, full of different unnameable things. She was fourteenish, light as a dragonfly, her skin the color of buckwheat honey. She perched on a cluttered tabletop, then turned. Impossibly, she fixed Finch with her pale green gaze. It sparked like an ice cube down his back, and he dropped the spyglass to his side.

"Well?" June said hungrily. "What'd you see?"

"A girl. Really, really pretty, with eyes like yours. I think she might've seen me."

"That was me!" she crowed. "I thought

you looked familiar. I *was* pretty, wasn't I? Too pretty for anyone's good, least of all my own.

"One more thing," she said, taking the spyglass back and opening it to reveal a third section.

"The future." She narrowed her eyes. "Look if you'd like, but keep your findings to yourself. I'm old enough to have a fair guess as to what's next for me."

Finch made to take it, then shook his head. "I believe you."

"Clever boy. The spyglass alone is worth plenty on its own, but let's see what else you've got."

The next few hours were full of wonders. Iolanthe sat cross-legged on the floor, grinning, as the old shopkeeper showed Finch what his treasures could do.

She showed him how to prick his finger on the frail golden needle he'd taken from a crumbling tower, then laughed at his panic as the thing spun around him, weaving a shirt right onto his back. The child's boot was a charm, for the health of the child who wore it. If you polished the mirror it would show you what your true love was looking at right that second; Finch's heart flip-flopped, and he pushed it back without peeking. When Iolanthe put out a hand to look into it herself, Grandma June snatched it away.

"Not you. Not here."

Iolanthe's lips thinned before she made herself laugh. Finch noted the odd exchange, filed it away.

The walnut the old woman shook her head at.

"Unpredictable. There could be a dress of stars inside it, or a cloak of ashes. Or a white cat. Or just a walnut."

She picked up the silver pen carefully, tapping its point with the ball of her thumb. When she wrote with it, the words disappeared into the paper, each swallowed up as she wrote the next. She clapped her hands.

"Oh, this is good. It's a general's pen."

"A what?"

She knew he didn't know anything, she just liked making him ask. "Generals use them to write reports back to their king or queen without fear of interception.

You can write a letter to anyone, on anything, and one way or another, the letter will find them — and never fall into the wrong hands. It doesn't leave a mark on your end, either. Of course they're used more commonly for trysts, or separated lovers." She smirked at the look on his face. "Well, well! If I didn't know better, I'd say I just convinced the boy to keep it for himself."

He shrugged, like, *what can you do?* and put it into his pocket. "You never know when you might get a chance at a tryst."

"Wise words," she said. "Now look: these scales are used by sailors in storms. Often lead to drownings among the lovestruck, but summoning a mermaid is the most reliable way to change an unfriendly tide . . ."

Finch was paid for his treasures in bound stacks of leaf-green paper, tissue-thin.

"What is this?"

"We call them fairy gold," said Grandma June. "It's a joke that stuck. Whatever world they're in, they become that world's currency. And they keep their form till

279

they've passed through seven times seven pairs of hands."

"You're telling me that after . . . forty-nine people have touched them, they turn back into little pieces of green paper?"

"Right. Long after they could possibly be traced to you."

"Yeah, but what about the forty-ninth guy?"

"Save your tears for the fiftieth. Would you rather I pay you in stock?"

Iolanthe elbowed him hard. He took the fairy gold.

Before they left, Grandma June caught up Iolanthe's blank-faced watch in her knobby fingers. "How about this? Looking to sell?"

Iolanthe snatched it back and shoved it down the front of her dress. "Not today, grandmother," she said in a voice like iron.

After that, Finch decided he'd keep an eye on that pocket watch, too.

When they walked out, his treasure bag was empty, the unsold walnut in his jacket and the general's pen in the front pocket of the new shirt the needle had sewn for him. It was nice. A little piratey, but soft. A first day of school feeling was coming over him, that imminent sense of being left behind. This, he figured, was where he and Iolanthe parted ways, once they'd split up the money. He wondered whether one of those books in the gray library told a tale that would drop him back on Earth, and whether he was ready, finally, to read it.

But Iolanthe said nothing as they made their way up the street. It was nighttime now, the sky scattered with strange stars, and half the shops were closed. The windows still lit held darker promises than they had before the stars came out.

Finch didn't stop to stare. He was too distracted. He felt the metal of the general's pen, warm through the weave of his shirt. He felt the weight of it, heavy as words unspoken.

In his mind, he was already writing a letter.

~25~

Come home.

Ella's last text to me before I'd turned off my phone. And I wanted to, so badly. I wanted to kick the bottom of our front door to unstick it when I came in, and fit my fingers into the grooves of the fugly hand-thrown pottery mugs we ate our yogurt from. I wanted to see the crown of Ella's hair under the living room lamp, the sides of the couch too high to know what she was reading till I came in close. I wanted her to flip back to the pages with folded corners, to read aloud the lines she'd liked and had saved for me. I wanted to slip back into our domestic routine like it was warm wax.

Instead I walked on shaky legs to the parking garage's elevator, my body feeling like it had been run through a laundry wringer. I texted Sophia as I went.

If you're working on clearing my name work faster. Hansa's parents just threatened to kill me with a wrench.

Then, because it looked a little more dire typed out than I thought it would: I'm sorry btw. Does it suck that your best friend's such an asshole?

Seriously though I'm sorry

She still hadn't gotten back to me when I walked into the hotel lobby. Felix was gone from behind the desk, replaced by a pink-haired woman I'd never met. Even her brows and lashes were the color of bubblegum. She looked like something in a bakery window, a cake that bit you back. When she spotted me her face went from bored to pin-sharp. She had a phone in her hand, and I was pretty sure she used it to take my photo. I threw her a dirty look as the elevator doors closed.

The air inside it pushed against my ears. As the elevator rose the pressure climbed, climbed, then cracked like an egg when the doors opened. I was left rubbing away the memory of pain, and the sense that I'd been about to hear something when the pressure let up. That if I'd just listened closer, words would've broken through.

The hallway was empty as ever, and I wondered who slept behind these doors. Who read or stared or waited for some unfathomable thing. Were they fearful? Were they angry? Were they trying to figure this out, too?

In my room I checked under the bed and inside the closet before stepping into the shower, because I'd been on the receiving end of vigilante justice once today already, and that was enough. The shower I took was so cold it made me gasp, but when I stepped out, the mirror was fogged all the way over. I stopped, one foot out and one foot in, because words were written in the fog in slashed uppercase letters, like a scattering of toothpicks.

YOU'RE NOT LISTENING.

I stared a few seconds, my skin prickling over in goose bumps so sudden they hurt. Then I banged my elbow yanking my towel down and around me, and slipped out of the bathroom sideways. I pulled clothes on over damp skin, the grossest feeling in the world, and hightailed it to the lobby.

The pink-haired photo-taker was still at the desk. She looked a little scared as I stalked over, a little thrilled.

"Hey. Is this hotel haunted?"

Her face relaxed. "Oh. Yeah. Of course it is."

"By who?"

Now she looked downright skeptical. "Really? By *us*. By Hinterland. You think only the living came through?"

The ex-Stories carried ghosts with us. The figurative kind, mainly — all those who hadn't made it here, or hadn't chosen to come. The echoes of our stories, all the things we'd done or hadn't when the Spinner still held us in her grip.

Some of our ghosts, though, were literal.

Fairy tales were thick with them. Slain brothers, punished parents, a skin-crawling volume of dead brides, all those white-wrapped girls perched on the spindle point between maidenhood and the wedding night. I couldn't believe I'd never considered that some might have slipped from the Hinterland after the rest of us.

The pink-haired girl's name was Vega, and it didn't take much prompting to get her to tell me how I could summon a ghost.

"You could lay out a dish of cat's milk," she said, ticking it off. "Just don't let your reflection show in it, whatever you do. Reciting poetry can do it, if the ghost likes your voice. Burn a bridal bouquet, that one's easy. Pull out your eyeteeth and hold one in each hand. Let's see, what else?"

"I think that's enough," I said hurriedly. "Really helpful, though, thanks."

I started to walk away, then stopped.

"Did you take my picture earlier?"

"Um." She fiddled with the ends of her hair. "Yes?"

"Why?"

"Because you're her, right? Alice-Three-Times? The one who . . ." She made a series of furtive hand motions. "*You* know."

"I'm nobody," I said firmly. "I didn't do anything. If anyone asks, if anyone talks about it, you tell them that. And watch out for yourself, okay?"

"Okay," she said, looking disgruntled. Then, in a louder voice as I neared the door, "Another thing you could try is having sex. Ghosts are drawn by desire. Or they might just be nosy."

Faced with the decision of coming back with a bunch of flowers or downloading a dating app, I headed to the good bodega a few blocks away, where flowers were sold but cat's milk was in short supply. I grabbed a bouquet and a dollar lighter and a carton of whole milk just in case, and threw in two Kit Kats because I hadn't eaten in ages.

Back at the hotel, Vega had left her post. I dropped a thank-you Kit Kat next to her bell and headed upstairs.

YOU'RE NOT LISTENING, said the message in the mirror. I hadn't been. To the voice following me in and out of dreams, to the Trio, the words of the little one in white: *Every story is a ghost story. If you're looking for answers, seek out your ghosts.* But I was ready to listen now.

I could attempt the summoning in the lobby, but Vega struck me as nosier than a pervy ghost. And I didn't like the idea of inviting the dead into my room. The hallway, I decided. I'd head up to my floor and pick a patch of carpet.

I waited till dark, then crept out of my room, a clutch of cheap carnations hanging from one hand and the milk in the other. In a bag around my wrist was the lighter and a paper coffee cup. The hallway had the aggressive, destabilizing sameness of hotels everywhere, even the haunted kind. I walked down and around, till I found a little alcove holding a dusty rubber plant and a sconce with one burned-out bulb. I pushed the plant into the corner. Then I knelt, filled the coffee cup with milk, and lifted the lighter.

And realized I hadn't thought this through. What would I do with the flowers when they really started to burn? How quickly could I stamp out the carpet if it caught?

Fuck it. I held the lighter up to a carnation's frilly cup. The flame lapped at the petals, but they didn't catch. Then it popped and blinked out, the lighter's hot metal burning my thumb. I dropped it, cursing, and tried again. And again. Finally I pulled the receipt from my pocket and lit that, sticking it in among the flowers.

The flame took. The flowers released the barest breath of green before starting to stink. When they were just fiery enough to make panic bite at my neck, I started to recite.

"I went out to the hazel wood, because a fire —"

I shook my head and started again.

"Out of the ash," I whispered. "I rise with my red hair. And I eat men like air."

Daphne flashed in front of my eyes. I blinked her away.

And I thought of the ghosts who might be gathering over my head, even now. Thumbprints on their throats and bellies bright with blood. Yellowed lace, embroidered slippers. Eyes full of retribution. Or jealousy, because I lived.

Good thing I'd had a goth period. Or maybe I *was* a goth period. At any rate, I could still dredge up some Poe.

"The ring is on my hand, and the wreath is on my brow." I raised my voice, and the hand holding the bouquet. "Satin and jewels grand, and many a rood of land, are all at my command, and I am happy now."

The words were already spooky in the quiet room. But the last handful of them *bent,* refracted as they hit my ear, making my voice sound strange to me. The flowers smoldered, orange rills and blackening petals. I waited.

"Do you think it worked?"

The voice, right by my ear, made me shriek. I looked at the girl sitting cross-legged beside me and almost did it again.

She was, in fact, a bride. Her hair had been red, I think, her face lushly freckled. A wedding dress gripped her by the neck. She was a glass chess piece in a thousand shades of blue, hands resting on her knees.

She nudged at the milk with an incorporeal toe. "What am I, a fairy?"

"I . . . um . . ."

"Why don't you try pouring it on the flowers."

It took a few startled seconds for me to understand. Then I dropped the flaming carnations and tipped the entire gallon over them. Milk doused the flames, drenched the carpet, splashed and seeped onto my jeans. The bride rose a few inches off the ground, as if the milk might damage her dress.

"Sorry," I gasped. "I didn't mean to . . ."

"No harm. I hate this dress. I didn't even die in it." She looked down its long white body. "I died in a nightgown."

What do you say to that? "It's a pretty . . . it was a pretty dress."

"It was a monstrosity. I was the *first* bride, you see. Before they learned to stop wasting the lace. Just a harbinger, really. A lesson for the final bride."

"What happened to her?"

"Nothing good."

I crouched in milk, beside the wreckage of burnt flowers, but I didn't dare move. "Thank you for coming," I said, too solemn, sounding like the host of the world's saddest dinner party.

"Took you long enough to invite me." Her fingers dipped into the mess of the milk. "Next time try whiskey. It made my husband's breath sour but it looked like a jewel in the cup. I've always wanted to taste it."

"Why did you want to talk to me?"

"I knew your grandmother. In the Hinterland. We were friends."

Althea. "She wasn't really my grandmother."

"All the same. She asked me to tell her my story. I hadn't known I had one."

"Well, she wasn't doing it to be nice. She was stealing it, to make money."

Her voice cut its teeth against the air. "Two things can be true at once." She wavered out, then in again, like her attention was elsewhere. It probably was. Maybe she could split herself into two pieces, or three, or ten, make the lights blink on Broadway and a phantom wind whistle down Second Avenue, all while sitting here with me.

"That's really it? You wanted to talk to me because of Althea?"

"No. I'm *willing* to talk to you because of Althea. She helped me once, and a debt weighs heavier than a wedding ring. What I have to say has nothing to do with her."

She closed the lit lamps of her eyes, appearing to breathe in deep. Then she flickered out completely. Every light in the place pulsed, one by one, like her spirit was a kite whipping through them. Then she was back in front of me, gaze keener than the rest of her.

"I forget," she said, "what we were speaking of."

"You have something to tell me." My fingers made impatient indents in my thighs. "You've been trying to speak to me."

"Oh." She considered, tilting her head to the side. And tilting, till it hung unnatural, and I could see the mottled bruising around her throat. "Yes. I've been wanting to tell you that you're haunted. Did you know it?"

My heart squeezed, quick as a fist. "Haunted by who?"

She reached out one thin blue hand and gently, gently placed it on my chest. The feeling was awful, an ice cream headache right down to my spine. "Ghost within, ghost without. How do you carry it?"

"What are you talking about?" I kept my voice level, just barely. "Who's haunting me? What do you mean, ghost *within*? What does this have to do with the murders?"

"I mean just what I say, and that's all you'll get out of me." She smiled, brightening as she did. I could count her freckles now, and see the gap between her front teeth. "I get to speak in puzzles if I like, it's the purview of the dead."

I was suddenly curious. "Are you happy, then? You don't want to . . . to rest?"

"Rest where? In the Hinterland the dead could walk Death's halls. We could eat at his table. If we pass on here, we only —"

"Stop," I said quickly. "Please." There were still some things I didn't want to know.

"You'll learn for yourself in time," she

said coolly. "And when it is your time, consider making a haunting if you can. This world is a far better place to be dead. I *love* it here. I curdle their milk. Beat the eggs in their shells. Turn their clothes inside out and rattle their windows with stones." When she smiled, her teeth glistened like bits of sea glass. "Here, they call me nightmare, hallucination, curse. They don't believe in ghosts."

"So you really know nothing about the murders? No hints, even? You can tell it in riddles if you want."

"It's not such a disastrous thing, dying," she said tartly. "It's very nice once you're used to it." A tremor ran through her, like she was a flicked water glass, and she started to fade. She was dim as an Edison bulb when her eyes snapped back to me. I could see the long hollow of the hallway, visible behind her lips.

"One more thing. You have a friend who waits for Death. Yes?" She didn't wait for me to answer. "Tell her I talk to him sometimes. Tell her she won't have to wait too long."

~26~

Finch wrote a love letter. At least he thought he did.

Back in the towered castle in the fossil world, in a spare gray bedroom on the second floor, he circled a few times before sitting down, gingerly, on the edge of the bed. He pulled out the silver pen, and for a long time he just thought.

About New York. About the first time he saw Alice, the spark that grew into curiosity, then fascination. That tumbled into and out of nightmare. Her skeptical eyes and cropped hair and husky, hard-won laugh that sounded twenty years older than her voice. He touched the pen to the blank inside cover of *I Capture the Castle,* the book that was nearest at hand when he'd packed, and the only one he'd taken from the Hinterland. Ink bled steadily into the page from its point, wicking away.

I am lost, he wrote.

I am lost and stupid and doing this all wrong. He watched the words disappear.

Then he was off, writing in a fever, the words vanishing into the page, barely remembering what he'd said from one line to the next. His head was full of giddy images of Alice. Her face tilted over the letter, the elfin bend of her ear peeking through yellow hair. Her fierce gaze eating up his words.

When he finished his eyes were so wide he could feel them drying out. Every time he closed them, a firework burst in his chest: of anticipation and anxiety and a kind of sweet panic. He recognized the feeling from the time he dropped a carefully copied-out Neruda poem into his ninth-grade crush's locker.

"Jesus Christ," he whispered, laughing at himself, then rolled over and shoved his face into the pillow. It smelled like dead people's dandruff. He said her name into it, and felt shy.

Earlier that day — though Finch wasn't sure how to account for days stretched across multiple worlds — Iolanthe had walked him to the six corners, then left him there as she darted back down the street. She returned carrying two bottles of a carbonated lemony drink, not sweet, and a stuffed, greasy-bottomed bag that smelled like heaven. They sat on a curb and ate right there.

"You don't want to eat in the gray world," she said, around a mouthful of something midway between a bao and a knish. "Death gets into everything, makes it taste like black licorice. It's the same way in the Hinterland, in the land of the Dead."

Finch was going *hah, hah* to cool his mouth after biting into a boiling-hot pastry; now he stopped short. "Wait. You went to the land of the Dead?"

"Of course. I went everywhere."

"That's . . ." *Amazing,* he could've said. *Incredibly foolish. Terrifying, to be frank.* "Extremely metal," he finished finally. "How'd you get in?"

"I followed the Woodwife." She looked at her hands, neatly sectioning her knish to let the steam out. "How about you? How did you get in?"

Finch stilled. He hadn't told anyone he'd gone into the Hinterland's underworld. He thought he never would. Those were dark days, best looked at sideways: his nihilistic expat period, when life was one long string of double-dog dares that could've killed him.

"I followed Ilsa's golden thread," he said quietly. "In, and out again."

"I knew it. I could tell right away — that you're like me, that you've come too close to it." She smiled faintly and touched her neck where his was striped with a scar. "I think you've come too close to Death more than once."

She had no scars he could see, but right then Finch had the oddest vision: of Iolanthe as a creature many times mended.

He could almost see the cracks in her carapace, and the light that came through.

"I think you have, too," he said, then looked away, unsettled.

They didn't speak again till they were done eating. Iolanthe stood, pulling out the book that had brought them there.

"Brace yourself," she said. "The doors can be rough on a full stomach."

Back in the dead world, Iolanthe assigned them each a room on the castle's second floor. He figured they'd be massive and opulent, like the library, but his had the constrictive, smoke-stained feeling of a chamber built in an age when everyone had ten kids and died before they were thirty. He'd had the sense, closing the door, of sealing himself away in a tomb.

He wrote his letter to Alice. Lay down, got up, lay down again. When he peered out the window, a glassless circle the size of his two hands cupped, he saw the kingdom laid out like fallen dominoes. Again came the tricksy flicker of distant movement. Finally he climbed under the bed's moldering blanket, certain he'd never sleep.

The light hadn't changed when he woke chilled with sweat, his body turned like the arm of a clock and his covers kicked to the floor.

In sleep he'd flown over the Hinterland, the land wrinkled beneath him like the surface of a globe. He'd watched as mermaids beached themselves, singing torch songs, and the last of the castles came down. It could've been just a dream. But maybe he'd seen a true vision of the world's last gasp. Still caught in the drifting headspace between sleep and dreaming, he wrote Alice another letter. It felt like he was talking to himself; it felt like she was right beside him. He wasn't sure which instinct to believe.

The dream and the letter left him with a heartburn hurt and the need to move. He laced up his shoes, slipping out of his room and past Iolanthe's. He figured he'd poke around the library. But halfway down the stairs he heard a woman's voice.

Iolanthe's, coming from below. His stomach seized, but when he found her,

she was alone. Sitting at a long table singing a wordless song, breaking between
verses to drink from her red glass bottle.

Finch stood in the shadow of the stairs.
Against all odds, he knew the song. Ingrid sang it sometimes, on late nights
with Janet in her lap and a glass or two
of cider gone to her head. Ingrid had put
words to it: of hope and longing, and the
distant shores of home. Iolanthe's voice
turned it into something else. Something
raw-edged and utterly alone. He could
taste the salt on it, imagine her singing it
as she sliced through the Hinterland Sea.
A flyspeck on its waters, the stars peering
down. When he couldn't take any more,
he crept back up the stairs.

Her room was next to his, a similarly
medieval bolt-hole of rough walls, pictur-
esquely lumpy bed, and washstand and
basin. Her bed was undisturbed, her bag
propped carefully against its foot. Before
he could lose his nerve, Finch crouched
down and opened it.

Inside, impressively rolled, was an all-
black rainbow of clothes. An offbrand
Walkman and a handful of unmarked
tapes. Toiletries, an array of currencies

302

in a leather pouch, four packs of Silver Siren brand cigarettes. Canteen, hair-brush, needle and thread. And below all that, wrapped in a pair of long johns, the things he figured he was looking for. The things she thought worth hiding: a book, a photo, and a little metal rabbit.

The rabbit looked like a game piece. It was heavy, its fur filigreed and its eyes inset with minuscule pink stones. He put it gently aside and inspected the photo. It was different from photos on Earth. More intense. It looked less like paper than a dark and bright window onto a breezy day when a younger Iolanthe had grinned, squinting, into the camera, snugged up against a slender, dark-haired man who looked like Rimbaud. His face held the kind of temporal beauty gener-ally reserved for those who die young.

He stared at the photo awhile before placing it carefully back into her bag. Then he turned to the book. It was a children's picture book. *The Night Coun-try,* it was called, with illustrations the saturated colors of candied fruit.

This is not a fairy tale, it began. *This is a true story.*

Finch paged through the book. It was a tale sparely told, of a mischievous little girl, the daughter of a court magician. When her kingdom is descended upon by a plague of golden locusts, the little girl and her best friend, the king's youngest son, steal her father's books to try to discover a way to save it. First, they accidentally enchant every mirror in the castle to say true and embarrassing things to anyone who looks into them. Then they summon a lazy demoness who tries to lead them astray. Finally, they find a spell that could save them: a spell that conjures a door into another world. That world is called the Night Country, and in its fertile air the children rebuild their kingdom as they please, simply by dreaming it up.

They create a world without vegetables or tutors or bedtime. Full of rainbow-flanked ponies and candy fountains and an underclass of hardworking gnomes who build them stained-glass cakes and clockwork wonders, like a beautiful pantomime princess to read to them and an old wizard who sends them flying around the room. In the end, they don't let anyone else into their Night Country. They shut the door, leaving their parents and siblings and everyone else to the plague of the golden locusts.

Finch closed the book, feeling uneasy.

Then he reopened it. Just to see the illustrations one more time. There wasn't much to the story, but it gave him a feeling he couldn't place. He'd just reached the bit where the king finds the first golden locust inside his royal egg cup when the door swung open.

Iolanthe hung in the doorway, her posture dangerous. He crouched in place, her open bag beside him. For a long time they just looked at each other.

"Did you read it?" she asked brusquely.

Finch nodded.

"Good." She stayed, lightly swaying, in the doorway. "It's a true story, you know."

Finch wasn't sure whether he should stand or remain seated. He settled for rising up on one knee. The pieces of what he knew about Iolanthe were stirring together like alphabet soup: The missing book in the library that she came out of. The picture book in his hands, and the pocket watch in hers. Her sail across the

Hinterland's storied sea, and her journey through its underworld. The photo of the beautiful young man tucked away like a secret.

"Who are you?" he asked her. Not for the first time. He should've demanded a better answer before walking through a door traced in her blood.

"I'm like you," she said. "One of the lost. A wanderer, worldless."

"How do you know I'm worldless?"

"Same way I knew you'd seen a door into Death, and walked through it." She knelt beside him and put a fingertip to the line over his throat, pressing closer to keep it there when he recoiled. "Same way I knew this would work, you and me."

He spoke around the permanent gravel in his throat. "What do you mean, work?"

"You're a searcher. We both are. Trying to get back something we lost — a home that no longer exists."

She said it like she was a seer. But Finch was used to people telling him stories about who and what he was. It had been happening all his life.

"Actually I'm thinking about getting back to a girl," he said. "So I guess you don't know me too well."

That broke the spell. Iolanthe fell back, her laughter short and surprised. "So let me get to know you." She held his gaze, still so near he could smell the liquor on her breath. For an awkward moment he worried she was hitting on him. Then she grabbed the book.

"True story," she said again, pointing to its cover.

"What part of it is true?"

"Maybe all of it. But the part that matters, the Night Country, *that* is true. I meant for you to read it. It's what we're waiting for. It's what we're seeking."

"We? *We're* not seeking anything. I don't even understand what that means."

"A world made to order, full of everything you'd like. That's what a night country is. Doesn't that sound pretty? Doesn't that sound nice?"

It did, for a minute. Finch's mind sparked like a flint against all the things he wanted. Then the sparks went out.

"It sounds like a nightmare," he said.

Because it did, when you thought about it. A world where you glutted yourself on your own desires till you were as awful as the little girl in the picture book. There were enough worlds that could make you into monsters out there. Why make another one?

"It's the very last secret," Iolanthe whispered. She poked him again, this time in the chest. "How many can say they've walked through a world made from pieces of their own heart? I saw your face when I talked about sailing the Hinterland Sea. You wanted to do that, too. And now you never will, oh, well. You want to read every book in the library, visit every world. How can you say no to the Night Country? You can't," she answered herself. "It'll be one more thing to haunt you."

"Don't touch me," he said, rubbing his sternum. "Back *up,* I can't think."

She sat on her ass, feet on the floor and eyes amused. "Sorry. I'm drunk. But I'm also certain. I'm inviting you to be my companion. Not *that* kind of companion, we'll get you back to this girl. But first: let's have an adventure."

"Why would I go with you? I know nothing about you. What's with the pocket watch? Why didn't Grandma June let you look through the spyglass? Where do you even come from?"

"You need to hear my sad story to trust me?" She shrugged. "All right. I come from a world you've never heard of, so it's no good my telling you its name. I lost someone I loved and it was at least a little bit my fault, and I ran away from that. I ran so far I couldn't find my way back. I've been gone so long I don't know what I'd be finding my way back *to*." Her voice went a little mean. "How about you? Think that girl will still remember your name? Your face? Time gets slippery when you start walking through doors. She could be married by now. She could be dead."

Her words were infecting him with a buzzing, low-grade panic. Alice married, Alice dead. Alice thirty years old, say, smiling at him politely. *Letters? What letters?*

"So why would I let any more time pass?" he asked. "If too much has gone already?"

"Because if you do this for me, with me

— if you do this for yourself — I'll make sure you get exactly where you need to go, and *when*."

"That's something you can do?"

She held up her pocket watch. "I've got a few tricks."

"But why do you . . ."

"Because I'm scared." She laughed a little. "I'm finally going to get what I want. And I'm scared now. Don't make me do this alone."

The last scavenger hunt Finch had gone on took him to a heavily fortified castle at the foot of the ice mountains. Its moat swam with annihilating mist, but its drawbridge was down.

He'd run across it. He'd moved through a torch-hung hall that felt like something out of a video game. Down a winding staircase into echoing dungeons, and below them into a crypt, each walled-in corpse marked by a bigger-than-life-size statue that peered at him with glimmering enamel eyes. He'd taken a rusted metal crown from the head of a surly-mouthed queen, and a misty orb from the hand of a mage.

Crouching next to this slippery, avid-eyed woman in her faded blacks, Finch felt the same way he had walking through that castle's courtyard. It was addictive, that cocktail of trepidation and desire, walking on when you knew you should turn back. Saying yes when the right answer was so likely no.

"First promise me," he said. "After the adventure — promise you'll get me back to her."

~27~

"Pick up your goddamn phone, pick up pick up *pick up.*"

Sophia did not pick up her goddamn phone. And the ghost hadn't come back. Not when I'd yelled for her, not when I'd recited "The Raven." I thought about running out for whiskey, but I didn't want to waste the time.

Instead, I walked the winding hallway and let myself back into room 549. I'd shower again first, then head to Sophia's place. I stank, like curdling milk and burnt carnations and the solemn breath of the dead, and my ears rang with the ghost bride's prophecies. *Ghost within, ghost without. Tell her she won't have to wait too long.* I threw the chain and security locks before stripping down and stepping into the shower.

The water took ages to get hot. I looked at it running around my feet and saw

Genevieve in the bathtub, blue and white

I closed my eyes. Counted to ten, twenty, thirty. Imagined Ella's hands in my hair. Soaped away the outward traces of the night. But when I left the bathroom, I could still smell something awful, like the scent had crawled into my nose and roosted there. Or like it had been in the room all along, covered up by everything I'd just showered away.

I took a step forward, and stopped.

There was someone in the room. In the bed.

"Soph?"

No reply. I watched the long lump under the bedclothes, waiting for them to sit up and reveal themselves. The covers were over their head, but there was something showing on the pillow, the unlikely color of cotton candy.

Hair. Pink hair. I sagged against the wall, relief and confusion striping through me. It was the woman from the front desk.

"Hey. Vega. Wake up."

No response.

Gingerly I walked toward the bed, wondering if she was messing with me. "Vega. Hi, good morning. Night. Whatever." I poked where I thought her shoulder might be. "Excuse me. I've had a very shit night, and I need my bed back."

Nothing. My body was trying to tell me something, pumping a queasy poison into my stomach and my limbs, telling me no good would come of staying in this room, but I didn't listen. Instead I pulled the blanket back, and back, peeling it away from the figure on the bed.

First I saw the full fall of her flossy hair, then her startled, mottled face. Ice crystals gathered under her skin, bruises raised like the ghosts of old traumas. Her mouth hung open and there was so much

Blood. A broad black road of it. Maybe

there'd be even more if she hadn't been frozen like a butchered animal before she was cut. Before she was *plundered.* The blood came from her mouth, from the root of her stolen tongue.

If I screamed, I couldn't hear it over the sound in my head.

Bare feet and a towel, running down the carpeted hall. The elevator or the stairwell, each felt equally perilous; I chose the elevator. Four floors up and down the hall to Daphne's room.

Her caps were off, and her lipstick. The fine needles of her teeth flashed behind her pale mouth.

"Another?"

I nodded, wordless.

In my room she turned on every light, pulled the blanket over the dead, opened the window. Took a bottle from her robe pocket and put it into my hand while she made a phone call. I drank it down. Much later, when my head was clear enough to think, I figured it must've been something more than alcohol, something she got from Robin, I'd bet, because from that point on I felt okay. I felt *detached,* like I was watching a movie. The liquor turned up all the lights in my head and took the fearsomeness from the shadows. The room filled with people whose faces I couldn't keep straight, till I realized they were three people with the same face: the creepy milk-pale brothers who lived with Sophia.

They'll take care of it, Daphne told me, her words pressing funny on my ears.

It was the body. *It* was a woman who was alive a few hours ago, till she made the mistake of talking to me.

More activity, lights turned higher — no, it was the sun coming up. Then the room was empty and my bed was stripped, and when I looked at my face in the mirror the imprint of Daphne's lips lay over my temple, like she'd tried to kiss the worst of my thoughts away.

Her words before she kissed me came trickling through, hours after she'd spoken them. *They'll think it was you.* Then the kiss, cold and glittering, as the room turned gray. *Watch yourself carefully now, they all think it's you.*

■■■■

I let myself into Sophia's building, twitching with nerves and sleeplessness. Banged on the apartment door till Jenny opened it, then immediately slammed it with a shriek.

"Go away, murderer!"

"Jenny, goddammit, I didn't do anything! Get Sophia!"

"What, so you can murder her? No way!"

I rested my head against the door and changed tactics. "You really think I can't kill you through a door? I'm fucking *dying* to. *Get her.*"

A few seconds of silence before she spoke. "She's not here. And that's not my fault, so you just leave me alone!"

I believed her. Jenny would sell her own mother up the river for a peppermint stick.

Now I was walking down Seventh Avenue, tracing my night, looking for pockets of lost time. I reviewed my path at the wake, ran my nails over the sealed black box that held my memories of the night

317

I broke into the apartment in Red Hook. I hadn't seen my attacker on the subway, but I'd heard them. I couldn't have been fighting myself in the dark.

Unless I was losing more than just time. Unless some crucial part of me had come undone.

I was heading back to the bookstore, planning to sleep behind the desk till Edgar got in. The hotel was two kinds of haunted for me now, and whoever killed Vega had no trouble getting into my room.

I saw her right away when I turned onto Sullivan Street. Half a block down, back against the bookstore's front window. When she spotted me she stood up straight and rushed forward, her arms half open like she didn't know if she wanted to hug me or hit me.

"So you are alive. You unbelievable, irresponsible, thoughtless *asshole*."

I was already crying. Just the sight of her face had done it.

"Mom," I said, and ran into her arms.

I didn't know till that morning that some bars stayed open twenty-four hours.

I don't think either of us could've handled the grind and chatter of a coffee shop, and I didn't want to talk on the street. So we found a no-name place with a lit Amstel sign in the window and an unlocked door. Inside, we breathed the sour overlay of decades of spilled beer and watched a bartender cutting limes down at the far end of the gouged-to-shit bar. The only other patron was slumped next to the sleeping jukebox, one hand around a bottle.

"Tell me," she said.

And I did. I was exhausted, clinging to reason. I wanted someone to hold all the unwieldy, sharp-edged pieces of my slipshod investigation, to tell me what they meant or just to take the weight for a while. I wanted someone to tell me I was *good,* way down at the very bottom where it counts, and not capable of the things some of them thought I'd done.

I told her about the meeting in the psychic's shop on graduation day, what I'd drunk at Robin's. Red Hook, the necklace of blood. I told her about the murders. The shortest version, no details. It was harder to save her when I got to the stalled subway car. She gripped the table's edge and glared at me, gesturing fiercely for me to continue when I faltered.

The knife, the rhyme; the Hinterland, the ice.

The hardest thing was telling her I'd gone to Daphne when I was hurt, instead of coming home. Then I had to tell her about the wake, Genevieve's body and the blood on my knees, and that was even harder. I told her just about everything but that Finch was sending me letters. For now, those were just for me.

I thought she'd look wrung out when I was done. Broken. Instead she looked hard, her eyes flinty and her mouth pressed thin.

"It's not me. I would never — I don't understand how it's happening, but it's not me."

"Of course it's not," she said, her voice so scornful and certain I breathed deeply for the first time in days.

"There's one more thing." My stomach turned; it was, quite possibly, the ugliest thing. "The person — the murderer — whoever's doing this. They're taking something from each body. They're taking a *part*."

Ella was holding her lime and tonic loosely, rolling it from hand to hand. Now her hands went still.

"What parts?"

Her voice was taut.

"Um. Feet. Hands. And Vega . . . Vega's tongue."

"Oh," she said in an altered tone.

"What? Does that mean something to you? What does it mean?"

She lifted a hand, signaled to the bartender. Reluctantly he sloped over, tossing a dirty towel over his shoulder.

"Can I get a glass of whiskey, neat?"

"We don't serve till eight." He looked pointedly at the clock hanging over the bar, a giveaway from some prescription drug company. "It's seven forty-five."

Ella pulled out her wallet and laid two twenties on the bar. "How about you give me the whiskey now, and you take my money at eight?"

He shrugged, poured a long few fingers of Wild Turkey into a Solo cup because it was that kind of place, and took the money.

She picked up the cup and drank half of it down, not even a wince. Then she placed it gently back on the bar.

"Do you want to hear a story?"

In my family, that was a loaded question. I wasn't so sure I did.

"There's a tale I almost forgot I knew. Althea told it to me once, a long time ago. Did I ever tell you —" She stopped, shaking her head. "Of course I didn't. I never told you shit about my mother. I *still* don't, even now."

"It's okay. It's hard for you, I get it."

"No, you don't. You never will. It's nineteen years' worth of complicated, and we're not getting into it now. I grew up in the Hazel Wood, remember. I grew up in that cracked-up, *fucked*-up, broken place. Between two worlds. Not of one, not of the other.

"You can't imagine what it was like, living there with her getting sicker and sicker. And those creatures crawling in from the woods, and me sneaking out, half convinced I was one of them. But that's —" She took another swallow. "That's a story for another day."

It wasn't. We both knew she'd never tell me the entirety of that tale.

"It wasn't easy being Althea's kid, even before we moved to the Hazel Wood. But one thing I'll say for her, she could spin a hell of a bedtime story. Stick with you for months. Give you nightmares for years.

"Althea and the Spinner, they were . . . not friends. Old adversaries, at best. They used to meet for tea sometimes, at the edge of the Halfway Wood." She smiled at the look on my face. "Didn't expect that? Well, boredom makes strange bedfellows. This was after my stepdad died, long after people stopped coming to stay. Althea would get all dressed up for it, like she was Norma Desmond or something. Even when I was little it was hard to watch. And she'd come home and tell me all the things they'd talked about, like it was this normal social call. I guess for her it was. I guess it was the only kind of social she got. The Hinterland treated me like a mascot, like a little changeling kid — untouchable. Althea, though, they messed with. Or worse than that, ignored.

My god, you cannot fathom the depth of her loneliness.

"Okay," she said, putting down her cup. "Okay. So there was one day when Althea came home from one of her tea parties and told me a story. She told me lots of stories, enough to make you sick on, but this one I remember. Because she told me — and she said this like it was an *honor* that she knew it, because even if she resented the Spinner she drank her Kool-Aid, too — she said it was the very first tale the Spinner had ever told.

"This story is called 'The Night Country.' And it is not a fairy tale."

~28~

There's no shortage of spilled blood in fairy tales. But this is not a fairy tale.

It's a love story.

In a real world where blood was red as apples, as bitten lips, and spilled just once, there was a girl.

Always. Of course. A girl.

This girl was not a victim or victor. Not a maiden or a princess or a mother or a witch. She was a girl with chapped knuckles and curious eyes that saw everything. She was not a good person, by which I mean she was not good at being a person, which was okay because she lived in a world where girls were not expected to be good at anything. She was uninterested in the limitations of her sex, so she ignored them. Her obsession was with uncovering the workings of her world: what lay beneath.

Though not a princess, she was the daughter of a powerful man, a magician, and a dead mother, so perhaps this is a fairy tale, just a bit.

With no mother to raise her, the magician supposed she could raise herself. He gave her freedom, and trust, and a library to roam in. Though not a whimsical child, she was drawn to his books of fairy tales. Such tales exist in all worlds. She loved them not for their enchantments but for their shapes, their ruthless black-and-white symmetry. She was often left alone, but she always had her books, and she was never lonely.

Her father was a very bad person, but very good at hiding it, and had become powerful by his importance to the rulers of their world. One after another, these rulers died, and always he was there, invaluable and discreet, to guide their successors, until at last none was left to rule but him, with his strange and lovely daughter.

Because she was very lovely. And wise enough to know it was dangerous to be so, in a world where she prized knowledge and the freedom to seek it above all. As her father, who was proud in his way of his brilliant daughter, and allowed her access to the tools of his arts, turned his mind to affairs of state, she was left to her own devices.

There was no wolf to mislead her in the woods, no stepmother or enchantress. There were only her books, her curiosity, and the iron of her will.

The first magic she learned was the art of wearing different faces. This was a world where small magic was common, and those who could used it to smooth their way. But transformation was not a small magic: once done, a magician could not return to the face of their birth. The girl peeled herself away from the face she'd been born with, trading it for a plain one that would allow her to do as she pleased without notice. Her eyes, only, she couldn't change — silver-blue eyes, their color as unlikely as summer ice — and her father knew her by them when he saw her again. He said no words of damnation or praise, but pressed a hand to her unfamiliar cheek. He was not a tender man, and it was not a tender gesture, but acknowledgment of what she'd done: one magician honoring another.

From that day he left her to her work. He never spoke of marrying her off, but waited greedily for what knowledge her studies might uncover that he could profit by.

And he did. Her abilities became greater, deeper, more insidious. She was born the beautiful daughter of a commoner, and had become the plain daughter of a self-made king, and it seemed that nothing could stop their rise.

Until something derailed it. This girl was uncommon: intelligent, without sentiment, cold. But she was not entirely heartless. And love, unexpected and unlooked for, came her way.

It happened like this: on occasion her father would prevail upon her to give some demonstration of her magic, an impressive public display to shore up support and quiet the discontented. He took credit for this magic, which was as she wished it. She liked being nearly invisible, working in her library and her laboratory, learning to separate matter from reason, and to convince the physical world that it needn't continue to do the things it had always done, just because it was habit.

On the third anniversary of her father's rise to power, he requested that she put on a display in his hall. She made hypnotized spectators dance ten feet above the ground, twirling in elegant pairs. She coaxed static sparks from their clothing and rolled them into a lightning bolt that crackled across the ceiling and back, before unraveling and returning to the places from whence it came.

For her final act, she lifted all the jewels from the gathered attendees' ears and wrists and throats and fingers, gathering them into a spangled cloud that clustered and hummed. She meant for the jewels to whirl up into the shape of her father's sigil.

But something was working against her magic. It bent the will of the jeweled cloud. Instead of forming her father's sigil, it picked itself out into the shape of an abelia: a bell-like flower. Then it shivered out like blown pollen, each piece returning to its master.

The audience thundered their approval, not understanding the error. The girl's cheeks reddened as her father looked at her, ferocious and brief, before turning a benevolent face to the crowd.

But her heart was a shivering cloud, too: only another magician could've disordered her display, one even greater than she. And by doing so, they'd both shamed and honored her: the flower was her namesake. Like her dead mother's, her name was Abelia.

The second time it happened she was alone.

She could not, to her frustration, change the paths of celestial bodies.

That was a magic even her father's grimmest grimoires could not condone. But she was learning to alter the *appearance* of the skies. On a moonless night she stood by the edge of the lake behind her father's palace, her sleeves rolled up and her hair tied back. Borrowing the light of the stars, she made a counterfeit moon and ran it through its phases.

But as it waxed it deepened in color, from champagne to wine. Her arms ached and her eyes streamed, and still she could not make it pale. In its fullest form, it sprung five arms, and a star spun out of orbit to serve as its pistil.

"Abelia," said a voice from behind her, as deep in color as the altered moon.

She turned, and her life was changed.

What drew the girl to the mage was his magic. What drew the mage to the girl was her ambition. To him, ambition smelled like a drug, like opium and amber, and hers was bottomless. He, too, wore an altered face, but while hers was built to go unnoticed, his was made to please, because it costs less for a man to be pleasing.

From that day, they worked together. Her ambition ran into his like a tributary into a river. He reminded her of her earliest wish: to peel up the corners of the world and see the workings that lay below.

Anyone who seeks to bend the world to their wishes, with words or science or magic or sheer will, must operate by a code. The girl was not good, but she had a code: she did not undo what she could not put back together. But rules can be rewritten, letter by letter, by a man with a velvet voice, who touched her mouth with his thumb tips and said her name like it was dipped in honey.

When he asked her the first time, he said it lightly.

Hands, he told her. There's so much magic in hands. If we needed them — if you needed them — could you get a pair of hands?

Yes, she said. Of course. The city has no shortage of corpses.

Not like that, he said, choosing his words as delicately as grains of rice. There's a power in ending a life. In the dead giving of their body to make something new. An ending births a beginning, becoming that much more powerful.

The girl understood, then, what he was asking for.

She took one hand from her seamstress. Clever hands, neat and quick. She took another from her cook, blurred with scars but strong. And her lover was right: the women were alive, then dead, choking on poison on Abelia's sitting room floor. That was their end. But when Abelia took their hands, it became a beginning, too. She could feel in the hands' heaviness all the knowledge that pooled there, all the ability. She wrapped them in yards of heavy satin and had a rider carry them to her love. The rest of the bodies she disposed of.

All of it was easy after that.

One foot came from a housemaid who'd always moved lightly through

the castle, with the darting joy of a bird. The other from a messenger boy who spent his days running between the castle and the city.

When her lover asked for a tongue she solved two problems at once, cutting it from the mouth of her father's silver-tongued right hand. He'd grown too powerful of late, too sure of his place. She didn't tell her father it was she who'd solved his problem.

For the pair of eyes the mage requested, she ventured into the city, her anonymous face her disguise. A man in a tavern there was bragging of all he'd seen in his travels, how far he'd come from and where he'd been along the way.

She gave herself a lovely face and form just long enough to lure him into an upper room, where she took his life and his eyes that had seen so many wonders.

Now, her lover said when she'd given him all these things. He could not hide the thrill in his voice. Now we need only a heart.

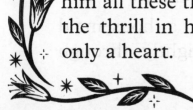

This was harder for the girl to obtain. She did not lack nerve, or even appetite. But she could not decide on the heart. A good one — but who could tell what secrets might lie inside it? A hard one, then — but what rotten softness might hide within?

She considered the riddle so long her lover grew impatient. If you don't have the stomach to do this, he warned her, I'll find one that will.

The girl did not like to be threatened. She didn't answer his threat, because she hungered to know what great magic he was building, whose purpose he still hid from her. She only bit her tongue and noted, with a scholar's fascination, how a slice of the love she bore for him shriveled and fell away.

The arrogant magician hadn't noticed it when her magic exceeded his own. He did not understand that by teaching her ruthlessness, he'd made her more powerful. And he didn't recognize that her ambition had grown greater than her love.

Finally, impatient with her, he chose

a heart himself. The finest heart he could think of: the heart of a king.

When she learned he'd killed her father, the mage imagined she would cry, as women do. Be angry with him. He imagined she would rage, strike out with attacks he could easily defend against, and require many kisses to return her to herself.

But his imagination was limited.

When he showed the girl her father's heart, she did not need his words to recognize it. It was shaped like her own, just barely scarred with love. The scars belonged to her, and those on her own heart, faint as they were, belonged to him, her father, not to this man she'd briefly thought worthy.

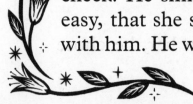

She knew, too, that her heart would not be scarred again. Her father was dead, her heart impermeable, and the man before her already gone to dust in her mind.

She lifted a hand as if to touch his cheek. He smiled, that it should be so easy, that she should already be tender with him. He was not ready for the knife in her other hand. With strength born of fury and a hand driven by magic, she divided him from himself. Her face was set and steady. She did not seem to hear his screams.

She knew enough of magic to guess at what must be done with the pieces she'd gathered: the eyes, the tongue, the hands, the feet. She laid them out in the semblance of a body, and in the center of them she placed her father's heart. Her hands were still red with her lover's blood, and it touched the pieces like a covenant.

It was not long before the pieces shivered and shook, and the air among them thickened with gristle, with tendon and blood and bone. When they stood up together, they formed a figure, that did the thing it was made for: it pierced the wall of the world. It made in that wall a door to what lay beyond, a great nothingness waiting to take form. The figure breathed in the life of the world behind it, and blew it into the gap.

Then it moved aside for the girl to step through.

Before her, stretched out like a sleeping beast, lay the thing her lover had used her to kill for. A new world, waiting to be given form: a night country, fresh-made, created through magic and blood. As she stepped onto its giving ground, she felt it opening its arms to her. She became its master, and its servant. It laid its cuts on her unreachable heart.

She looked around at the soft black canvas of her world, and submitted to its pull. She knew only order, and magic, and the books of enchantments she'd raised herself on. Love had burned out of her at the root.

Grieving and angry but never uncertain, she made an ordered world. A world that ticked and turned like a clock. She filled it with fairy tales.

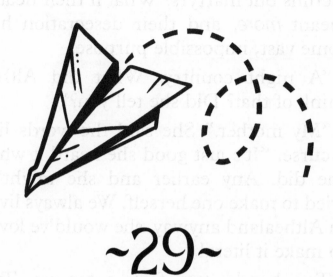

~29~

The bartender sliced his finger halfway through my mother's telling, shouted once, and disappeared into the back. The drunk in the corner groaned as the jukebox clicked to life, playing an old Flamingos song. The Spinner was gone, but her stories weren't; they could still leak poison into the air.

"So you think that the Spinner — and now you think someone's trying to . . ."

"I don't know what I think."

The bleak landscapes of the tale pulsed in my mind in shades of red and gray. The

Trio said it first: what if the dead weren't victims but martyrs? What if their deaths meant *more,* and their desecration had some vast, impossible purpose?

"A night country. What did Althea think of that? Did she tell you?"

"My mother." She said the words like a curse. "It's just good she heard it when she did. Any earlier and she might've tried to make one herself. We always lived in Althealand anyway, she would've loved to make it literal."

Two hands, two feet, a tongue. Two eyes, a heart, and blood to cover them. This was *it.* The piece I'd been looking for. But I had to get my mother clear of it.

"Or maybe," I said, my voice rusty, "it's just a story."

Ella fixed me with a stare that could wither an acorn. "So says the literal *Story.*"

She never referenced my origin like that. It stopped me short.

"I'm not saying someone didn't hear it and believe it," I said. "That they're not trying, even, to do what she did. But the Spinner told a lot of tales."

"And all of them true."

And all of them true.

We looked at each other, but I wasn't seeing her. I was trying to picture it, to imagine its outlines: a night country. A world built on carnage and sacrifice, made to order — but by who?

Ella swallowed the last of her whiskey. "I know you're not at the Best Western."

My eyes refocused on her tired face.

"I called the front desk, asking for you. Didn't want to tell me one way or the other, but I figured it out."

I caught a drop of condensation as it ran down the side of my cup. "Why didn't you believe me?"

"I just had this feeling you were lying to me."

"Why didn't you say anything till now?"

"I wanted to see your face, I think." She studied it. "I wanted to see if you'd try to keep lying."

"Why —"

"*Enough* with the questions. It's time for you to come home."

"When this is done. When this is done, I'll come home."

She cursed softly, looking at the ceiling for strength. I wondered who she was looking for up there. Certainly not Althea.

"What does *done* look like to you?" she began quietly. "Is done when you're dead? What will you do if you figure out who's doing this — turn them in? Stop them? You think they'd put up with that, any of them? It's time to stop playing at whatever it is you're playing at. It's time for us to *go.* You don't owe anyone here shit. Anyone but me."

"You just said they might be trying to make a whole new *world,*" I said incredulously, my act cracking. "You think I can just walk away?"

"You might *be* a Story," she said, ignoring me, "but I *know* Stories. Sophia and the rest of them are not like you. They're as different from you as an eagle from a canary. They're not built to survive here, and honestly? Good riddance."

"Mom, just stop!" I grabbed her wrist hard. And though it was her bones in my fist, it was my wrist that ached, where Sophia had grabbed me at the diner. As fast as I reached for her, I let go. I could taste acid in the back of my throat.

Blank-eyed, she rubbed her wrist. Rolled it.

"You know what," she said. "*No.*

"I've always excused your temper. It was easy to blame it on what you were. But now this is you. Just you. The Hinterland is gone, and neither of us can blame the Spinner anymore for how she made you. We are done with that." Her eyes were darker than I'd ever seen them. "If you touch me in anger again, I will fucking touch you back."

"I messed up," I said, low. "I did. I wasn't thinking, I —"

My breath gave out before my words did, juddering away as the panic rose, nibbling at the edges of my vision. "I'm sorry," I said. "Just, just *wait.*"

I bolted for the bathroom — tiny, rank, walls papered in ancient stickers. I thought I'd vomit, but I couldn't. Bent over the sink, I palmed cold water onto my face, breathing out, breathing in. I looked like shit in the mirror, my pupils sharpened to black beads and my skin yellowed by the light.

I stared at my face, hating it in pieces, all the parts of me that would never look the way I felt. Mouth that would've been sweet set in anyone else's face, the heart curve of my hairline. Eyes like a creature of the woods, set to startle. At least the hair was right, the kind of untamed mess that happens when you leave short hair to its own devices. It was choppy and rangy and in between, and it looked like *me*.

"What are you?" I asked my reflection in a choked whisper. "What fucking are you? What do you want to *be*?"

I had a vision then, a memory so saturated in color and sensation you could almost call it a flashback, of my mother cutting my hair in the bathroom mirror. A photo of Jean Seberg propped on the sink and the burn of her exhales wafting past my eyes, when she used to smoke while she trimmed.

I breathed in, breathed the memory away. Then I tucked my overgrown ends behind my ears and left the bathroom. But my mother was already gone.

■ ■ ■ ■

I was walking back toward the bookshop, along the rustling edge of Washington Square Park, when I felt something in the air. A funny cold little poke, as if someone had pushed aside the atmosphere like a curtain and stuck a finger through. A moment later, a paper airplane pirouetted over my shoulder like a Blue Angel, landing nose first in a laurel bush.

I looked back, just in case a little kid was about to come running after it, but the sidewalk was empty. I swore I smelled a sinuous note in the air, the scent of *not New York*. Not laurel leaves or pollution or street food or perfume, but something compounded of the molecules and stardust of far, far away. Maybe I could catch it next time, I thought. Catch that little rift in the air with my fingernails, and peel it back to find him.

For now, I could unfold the airplane and read his letter.

~30~

Dear Alice,

Soon I'll need a break from magical things. I'll want to walk through a door that's just a door. I'll want to talk to a stranger who's in no way mysterious. If you could see the view from where I'm writing this, you'd understand why.

Fuck it, I think I want all that now. Right now, I want to read books that stay on the page and ride the subway and eat dim sum and I want to hold your hand. I wonder if I'd be brave enough to say this to your face. I think I would. I asked you out once, remem-

ber? I kind of want to take that sentence back, but that's not the way the magic works.

I'm almost ready to come home. I've got a way to get there, too, or at least the promise of one. There's just one more wonder I'm out to see. It's something out of a book again. It's called the Night Country, and I don't want to explain it till I've seen it. Someone called it the "very last secret," whatever that means. I guess it means I won't know what it is till I get there. It'll either be heaven or it'll be hell, but either way an adventure.

I want to write to you again, but what I want even more is to watch your face when you look up from a book one day and see mine. One day soon. I'm gonna be so shy when I see you again. It's just, by now I've said as much to you in letters as I did in life.

Be patient with me, okay? When I see you and my tongue tangles up. Be patient.

I'll see you after the Night Country.

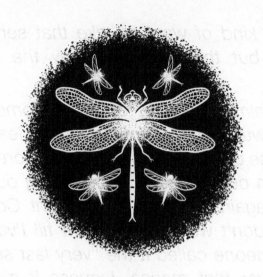

~31~

How did stories seep through the walls between worlds?

They came in through the cracks. Althea's stolen fairy tales, those bloody little coils of princesses and kings, they *made* the cracks.

But the tale of the Night Country. Ella telling me here, Finch hearing it there, wherever *there* might be — it made me nervous. More than nervous. The coincidence of it was sand beneath my skin.

When we'd first met, Finch and I, our meetings sang with a strange resonance.

Something grew up between us, something gossamer fine. We'd torn it down, with my stupidity and his betrayal, and then the different things we wanted divided us. Now here we were, years and worlds between us, and still he could find me by letter.

And one tale could find us both. Already fairy tales had brought us together, imprisoned us, spilled our blood, and carried us ruthlessly apart. What might this one do?

I left Ella a rambling voicemail. I called Sophia, again, then sent a text.

I know you're not talking to me but this is important. Please please please just tell me where are you??

She didn't respond. For hours, as I dozed fitfully in the back room of the bookshop and sleepwalked under the sun and read Finch's latest letter again and again, my eyes blurring and my hands gripping the page.

When she finally responded the relief hit me like a sugar rush.

I'm not not talking to you.

I stared at my phone and understood,

suddenly, how Ella must've felt, trying to chase me down by text and getting nothing but a cursory message after hours of silence.

Okay but we need to talk NOW something's happening. Where are you?

Her response was unexpected.

Going to a party

There was a delay, long enough that I knew she was debating it, then:

Want to come?

Send the info, I texted. I'll see you there.

Party could mean a lot of things, and I barely knew how to dress in the best of times. I changed into jeans and my cleanest shirt and put lipstick on, a burgundy that made me look like a little kid sneaking wine at a dinner party. Then I rubbed it off and put on eyeliner instead. With my mouth still bruised with leftover color and my hair a tangled cloud, dark below and pale at the roots, I looked older. Sophia would never make it past seventeen, but I was already on the other side. From here on out, I'd be leaving her behind.

Unless she left me behind first.

She hadn't said whose party it was, or how she knew them. It was in a condo building in Tribeca, so new you could smell it. The entrance was all wasted space, granite walls and complicated light fixtures and the trickle of water running over stone. A bored guy sat behind the front desk, staring at his iPad.

Ten stories up, the elevator opened onto a hallway spilling over with strangers and sound, the door across the way held open by a woman's back. She leaned against it in spike heels and a short red dress, eyes tilted up, laughing at something a man was yelling over the music. As I edged past her, into the apartment, she looked at me and stuck out a pointed tongue. Quick as a wink, then her attention was back on the man. My feet stuttered but I couldn't place her before she let the door swing shut.

Stepping into the party felt like stepping into a mouth. There was art on the walls that looked real and a bar set up in the corner, which already made it way fancier than any party I'd ever creeped around the edges of, and either everyone was having fun or they were determined to look it. The music filled my head, loud and bright and beating like a heart, and I'd been there two minutes but already I couldn't breathe. Across the room, doors opened onto a patio. I tunneled toward it.

It was cooler outside, the air braided with cigarette smoke and performative laughter. I put my elbows on the railing, looking out. The sky was black with a red echo, like Ella's hair after she rinsed it with henna. A pair of women to my left were laughing too hard to talk, and on my other side a man sat on the railing smoking a joint, his feet hooked around the bars. I hadn't seen Sophia yet, and was starting to wonder if she was here. This wasn't her scene. She didn't know people like this.

I'm here, I texted. Where are you?

I waited for her answer, watching a guy with pornographic chest hair struggle to get a lighter out of his painted-on jeans. My phone twiched twice.

We're everywhere

We're all around

Dread dusted my skin like moths' wings. I looked up and combed the crowd.

352

Nobody I knew. Good-looking strangers in expensive clothes, with haircuts so ugly you just knew they cost two hundred bucks. I took a last breath of the balcony's weird red air, and plunged back into the party.

It took a while for me to notice them.

There was no dance floor, but people danced in pockets, here and there. And wherever the dancing was too wild, too off-key, wherever it struck a note of odd discord, I saw them. A dark clock of them, counting down in a circle around me. *Hinterland.*

The man with the blue-black beard and trim suit running his tongue up a woman's neck: Hinterland. The girl who looked about fifteen, in a dress that might've been a nightshirt, jumping in place and screaming like she was at a punk show: Hinterland. And the narrow-cut boy in black, and the crone with the razor-blade smile, and the woman in the tiny green dress, her hair the color of fresh blood. Daphne. Blazing a rippling path through the party, tugging people's heads to turning.

Behind me, someone trailed their fingers over my bare arm and I swung around, expecting to see Sophia. It wasn't Sophia, but I knew her. I'd last seen her in the hotel lobby. Dark skin and silvery hair, her eyes lined in the same starry color. She was one of the seven sisters who moved together in a pack, always gloved, always whispering. Her gloves were off tonight, her nails filed to rose-thorn points. She smirked at me, mouth malevolent, then slipped on through the crowd, her hands seeking exposed skin. The way she moved made it look like she was dancing, but it was deliberate. She executed a dizzy turn, running an index finger over a woman's clavicle.

She wasn't alone. Her six sisters moved like pewter-headed matchsticks through the crowd, one of them climbing the stairs to the loft, all of them touching, touching, people turning around in confusion or anticipation, smiling at them or pulling away.

I looked at my arm where her touch had been, expecting to see something left behind: a bruise, a trail of iridescence. There was nothing.

"I can't believe she touched you." Sophia spoke into my ear.

Relief threw me off balance. I grabbed her arm. "You're here."

"I told you I would be." Her face was tense. "Alice, you should go."

"Not till we talk. I've been *looking* for you, where've you been?"

"I'm sorry about that. I really am. But right now, you need to go, or things are gonna get bad for you."

"Things aren't bad enough?"

She nodded toward the sister who'd touched me. "In the Hinterland their touch could make you hallucinate. They could make you see anything. They're not as strong here, but still. You should go."

My heart went hummingbird. "But they're touching . . . they're touching *everybody*. What are they trying to do?"

She spoke the words slowly, like she wanted me to really hear them. "Whatever they want to do."

There were easily a hundred people here. More. What would the sisters make them see — make *us* see? And what

355

would it do to all these bodies, in this tight space?

"Why are *you* here, then?" My voice was small. "What are you trying to do?"

Her gaze flicked over my shoulder. "I'm looking for a friend."

I grabbed her hand. "You found me. Come on. There's stuff I have to tell you, and I have to tell you *now.*"

"I can't go, but you'd better. They can only mess with your head if you're close."

I had more to say, but just then every light in the room — every bulb and candle flame, the glowing end of every cigarette, the lit screen of every phone — shuddered and *lifted.* Blue and silver and orange and gold, rising to a soundtrack of gasps and screams. They shook out damp-looking wings made of light.

Dragonflies. The size of postage stamps and playing cards, rising over our heads. The crowd looked up, mouths open in awe or shock or fear. When people lifted their phones to take photos, the fresh illumination gathered itself into winged form and flew away.

"Are you seeing this?" I asked Sophia.

She shook her head.

I should leave. I knew I should leave. But it was just so beautiful. The dragonflies moved like the Hinterland stars, they wheeled and sparked. People lifted their hands and the insects lit on them softly, catching their faces in cupped circles of light. When I lifted mine, Sophia slapped them down.

"Whatever you're seeing isn't real," she snapped. "Pull yourself together."

I watched a man in a flat cap catch a dragonfly between his palms, tilting it from hand to hand like a Slinky. Then he yelped.

"It bit me!"

He shook his hand hard, but the thing held on. It got bigger. It curled its wings around his hand. The music was loud, his scream louder, but I swear I could hear his skin sizzle.

More screaming. From across the room, then just behind me, then over by the door, like car alarms going off in rounds after a thunder clap. The dragonflies scuttled up sleeves and down shirtfronts, wrapped themselves around faces and necks and — I turned my head away, horrified — slipped into screaming mouths.

On the wall behind Sophia hung a massive canvas painted the mellow green of verdigris, its bottom half covered with little black slash marks the shape of swollen penne pastas. From the corner of my eye, I saw them tremble. I saw them move. My skin creeped and a scream pooled in my throat as they swarmed into a ball, then marched in a teeming black line off the canvas and over the wall.

Ella and I had roaches in Texas. Big fuckers, the kind that scattered when you turned on the kitchen light. The kind that *flew*, skimming over your hair and making you lose your mind. I wanted to lose my mind right then. I pointed wordlessly at the wall, pressing my lips together tight.

Sophia looked. "There's nothing there," she said grimly, grabbing my arm. "Time to go."

But we couldn't. The crowd had become a mob. There was more happening here than I could see; the sisters must've planted a different nightmare in each head. A woman in a beaded dress clawed at her front, ripping at the stitching, beads flying off her like water drops. A man bent over his knees, vomiting up a stream of light, like he'd swallowed a dozen vindictive dragonflies. Someone writhed on the ground, another person stamped and screamed. Panic spread like tear gas, till you couldn't tell who the sisters had touched and who was just infected by the screaming.

And above it all, around it, their faces blissed out or wicked or utterly unconcerned, the Hinterlanders. Felix was there, I might've seen Robin. The seven sisters moved like priestesses, possessed, and Daphne was up on the bar, dancing madly, wrapped in her falling red hair.

Godless. Nora's words at the wake came back to me, an icy jet turning my stomach cold. With the Spinner long gone and the Hinterland dead, she'd feared its creatures and their acts would grow wilder, godless.

It's happened, I thought. *We're here.* Then the chain of little paint bugs was skittering toward me, over fallen bodies and around dancers, and I couldn't help it: I screamed.

Sophia pressed her hands over my eyes. "You're fine," she said. "You're *fine*. Nothing real is happening here. I've got you, got it? You're fine."

I couldn't see her, but her hands were warm as a compress, her winey breath sour on my face. The rational line of her voice drew me back from terror, and other thoughts got in. I remembered why I was there, what I needed to tell her. I steadied myself.

"When we get out of here — I need to talk to you."

"Talk now. Distract yourself."

Screams of anguish, sugary laughter.

"Death, Soph. If he . . . if he found you. If he wanted you to — would you go with him?"

"Alice." She said it with such tenderness.

My knees bent a little, but I stayed up. "You could wait," I said. "Till I'm old. If I get old. We could go down together."

"Is that what you wanted to say to me?"

"That, and . . . I don't think they're

360

being murdered. Or, I don't think that's all it is."

She kept her hands over my eyes. Around us the partygoers shifted and shrieked, we rocked like a boat on a tide.

"I talked to my mom. She told me a story." I wasn't sure how to tell it, didn't want to try to in the middle of this haunted room. "Have you ever heard a tale called 'The Night Country'?"

Her hands fell from my eyes. Her face was too vulnerable, soft as a mollusk. "What did you say?"

Then a scream came from above, and we both looked up.

A woman teetered at the edge of the loft, in a blue dress and bare feet. She was half screaming, half laughing, hysterical and high, her hands grappling at some invisible thing around her throat.

"Oh, shit." I held up a hand. "Oh, *wait* —"

She went down. Sideways, almost slipping over the railing but instead she hit the stairs, tumbling in an awful slapstick pinwheel.

I didn't see how it ended. Sophia

wrapped an arm around my neck and the other around my waist and pulled me in tight.

I spoke into her shoulder. "Tell me. Tell me that wasn't real."

"Shh," she said. *"Shh."* She tucked my hair behind my ears, the gesture so motherly I went still. Then she kissed me on the cheek, soft and open-eyed, and if I blinked I might've missed it: swimming in the lacquered amber canyon of her left eye, a round black absence. Like a freckle on her iris. If it had always been there, I'd never noticed.

The insects crawling around my feet were gone, the wicked dragonflies winked out. Maybe even the sisters had had their fill of fun. Someone turned the music off and the lights on as people blinked at each other, stunned, or started to cry. They clotted around the bottom of the stairs, they pulled out their phones. I looked around for Daphne, but couldn't find her. Voices rose, and someone flung open the apartment door. Half of them were turning toward it, the other half rubbernecking the woman at the bottom of the stairs.

I was a coward, I didn't want to see. Didn't want to know how bad it was, what the Hinterland was responsible for.

"Come on." When I turned to grab Sophia, she was gone. I looked for her, but the pack of bodies was carrying me toward the door. If I didn't follow, they might've lifted me off my feet.

The scream of sirens came up from below, spiraling and distant and moving in. The crowd moved like a many-headed animal, bypassing the elevator, going straight for the cattle press of the stairs. I lost myself in the pack of strangers, shouting and crying and shoving in their rush, but human to their cores.

~32~

There was more than one trick to the pocket watch. Iolanthe told him the next morning, when they'd ventured into a pastoral world for breakfast and for the kind of air that felt good to breathe. The book she'd read from to get them there had been in a language of trilling runs and hard stops, which tickled the ear to hear it. When he opened his eyes, they were stepping into a meadow so idyllic it looked like a Thomas Kinkade print.

He lay down beside an honest-to-god haystack while Io went off to drum up some food — jerky, milk in a skin, bread with cheese and honey. All of it, even the bread, even the honey, tasted of goat.

In the lazy golden shade of the haystack, she pulled out her watch. It wasn't completely blank, he realized: it was pearlescent, colors chasing themselves over its face.

"Wait for it," she said.

A minute passed, and something showed: a string of numbers like a digital display, pinkish but unmistakably there. They darkened to red as he watched, then faded slowly to nothing.

"Call numbers," she said. "Corresponding to books in the library, corresponding to worlds. Everywhere, in every world, a version of the Night Country tale exists. When the numbers show like that, someone in that world is reading the story, or hearing it. When the numbers turn solid, you know: that's a world where someone is *building* it."

"It has to be built?"

She'd taken a big bite of goat-flavored something; her "Yes" sprayed him with crumbs.

"And we . . . what? Jump in there and steal it?"

"Think of the picture book. The girl and the boy work together to make their world. It's better that way, with more minds."

"So you're saying we'd be doing these random strangers a favor by appearing out of nowhere and trying to take over their world?"

She thought about it, dusting off her hands. "Yes."

"But you say you can *build* a night country. How? Why don't we just build one our —"

"Look," she said testily. "I've got the magic watch, I'm telling you how this is gonna go." Then, seeing his face: "No, no, we're partners. Sorry, what did you want to know? How do you build a night country? That's the thing, I don't know how to do it. But somebody, somewhere does. We'll find one in time."

He should walk away. He knew he should. But the key was in the lock. Strange treasures awaited him beyond the door. And he'd already told Alice he was doing it, so. He didn't want to go to her empty-handed. He had his green stacks of fairy gold, his magic pen, the mysterious walnut. He had a few new tricks — he could make goat cheese, drive fence posts, speak passable German. He'd gotten pretty into whittling for a while. But he didn't think Alice wanted his carved rabbits that looked a hell of a lot like bears. Instead he would bring her what she loved best: stories. He was collecting all the tales he'd tell her when he got home. He was becoming his own kind of library.

Those were strange days. He and Io dipped into and out of worlds, spending a day or an hour or an evening in misty mountain villages, ruins sliced into gold and gray pieces by the falling sun, cities crisscrossed by elevated trains, or wreathed in strange overgrowth, or veined like Venice with waterways. She chose the books carefully, picking worlds where they'd be safe, where they'd blend in. Finch didn't know how she knew, and she didn't tell him.

They talked a lot, but she didn't tell him much. Only tales of her travels through the Hinterland, and a little bit about her life when she was young — reckless, mischievous, underdisciplined. She loved to hear stories about New York if he could make them funny, but he took her lead, never sharing too much about himself.

A week passed. Two. One navy-blue night, drunk on clear liquor served in tiny glasses in a shanty bar on the edge of a vast red sea, Finch cracked open the walnut he'd taken from the Hinterland, which Grandma June gave back. He wanted to see the dress of stars, the meticulous white cat. What came out instead was a man's voice, bellows deep and touched with stardust.

The moonless child will die
And the starless child will fall
And the sunless child rise higher
than them all

The startled bartender made a gesture at the two of them — that world's way of warding off the evil eye, Finch guessed — and turned their cups over to show them they were no longer welcome.

"A dead world's prophecy," Io said, standing. "Were more useless words ever spoken?"

She took out her watch to consult it, as she always did, and her face changed. She held it up.

Numbers blazed off its face in solid black.

The silence between them swelled, then was shattered by the bartender, inviting them in her own language to kindly get their asses out of her bar. Finch laughed a little, looking into Io's anxious eyes.

"Here we go."

Back in the library her face was grayer than the walls. She didn't let him fetch the book, even though she looked two steps from keeling over. On shaking legs she found it, with shaking hands she took it down. They'd been shocked sober by the pocket watch, but she was four-thirds of the way back to drunk by now, taking continual nips off her bottomless red bottle.

Before she opened the book, she gave him a look. A hard, bright-burning look too packed full of feeling for him to master. It made him put a hand on her arm.

"We're good," he said, peering into her eyes and trying to make her believe it. Oddly, her fear made him less afraid. He felt like a man lifting a sail, shouldering a pack. Walking on down the road. "This is *good*. It's the very last secret, right?" He squeezed her arm. "We're ready."

One more inscrutable look, and she opened her mouth. Her eyes searched his. He thought she was going to say something, something important.

But her head dropped, and she opened the book. Holding it so he couldn't see its pages, she read the first words. "Once upon a time."

He startled. "Really?" None of the books had been in English before, or in any language he could identify.

She ignored him. "Once upon a time, there was a man and a woman and a vast green land, with cracked places where the land rose and became rippling stone, and broken places where blue water came in. And the man made stories of the earth and the woman told stories with the stars, and with the children she bore the stories multiplied."

"Wait," Finch said. His voice was distant from him, it seemed to come from a place outside his body. "Where are we going?" But the magic was already lifting them, taking them.

"Shh," said Iolanthe, and began again. "Once upon a time . . ."

~33~

Cities go wrong in the summertime. That's what the cops would tell themselves, the EMTs, all the bodies gathered together to tend to the girl at the bottom of the stairs, as good as pushed by the Hinterland.

The wrongness is in the atmosphere: strange skies, the wheedling nature of the breeze. Heat putting the screws on till the city feels like something set to blow, a place where everyone waits like frogs in a pot with the fire on low. The police would chalk this up as one more of the city's human horrors. There were enough of them that the Hinterland could blend in. That the mass hallucination would be written off as a drug in the drinks, an airborne attack. But I knew the truth. I knew we were poison.

Once I got free of the stairwell I kept my head down and slipped away to the river. The lucid fairy waters of the Hinterland felt very far from this mess of dead leaves and trash, freckled by the lights of passing boats.

I looked around — at the grimy water, the garbage on the ground, the man asleep on a bench behind me, aging and filthy in a world without pity. The city's beauty receded, until all I could see was the grime on top. The way everything and everyone here existed in their own lonely sphere, untouchable.

I called Ella, but she didn't answer. I texted her one more time.

I'm coming home soon. I promise. I'm almost done.

I didn't know why, but it felt true. Whatever I was waiting for, it was coming soon. For better or worse.

Back at the hotel, I opened my windows as high as they'd go, let my room fill up like a dish with night air. It felt like a dare coming back here. It was too dangerous to stay; I had nowhere to go. I should've been packing my stuff, but instead I looked out the window, over an insomniac stretch of city.

Here's what I'd say, if I could write Finch a letter.

Stay. Stay where you are. Let me find you.

My mother wants to run away. She wants to rewrite our life in a place with more empty spaces than people, where the air smells like hyssop and dust.

But not me. I want to find you. I want to walk between worlds with you. I wouldn't mess it up this time, I wouldn't hide inside my own head. I wouldn't let you hide inside yours.

How is it that I don't even know you anymore? How is it that you're so far away?

A sound startled me, making my head snap up. Something slid under the door, skidding a foot over the carpet.

A letter. I half ran across the room, my heart flooding with heat. The letter was

scribbled in blue ink on old hotel statio-
nery, folded into fours. But it wasn't from
him.

*Alice I lied to you when I said you're not
special just because someone loves
you. I lied to you a lot I guess but can
you blame me when you always believed every damn word I couldn't resist
it. I'm sorry I didn't stay with you tonight
but I'll see you again soon. It won't be
me exactly but you'll know I'm there.
I'll be the wind maybe or the trees or
the water or the sky even. I don't really
know how it works. Alice I'm tired and
I haven't been good in a very long time
and that's another thing I lied about that
I didn't ever want to be good. I think this
is the right choice for me. I think this
world is the wrong one.*

*There's going to be a time soon when
someone's going to ask you to walk
through a door. Say yes. Behind it
will be a bright new world bigger and
more beautiful than this one and with
no cages not one. Just freedom and a
place to be happy where you can live or*

*die or just be quiet. This world will be
gone and good riddance.*

*I'm sorry I couldn't wait for you but look
for me and I bet you'll find me. But even
if you don't don't worry. I wanted this. I
want this.*

Love,
Sophia

I read it fast, too fast, the words running
up on each other's heels. By the time I
threw open the door, Sophia was long
gone.

*This world will be gone and good rid-
dance.*

My mind rattled the words. Picked over
the story my mother had told me. I closed
my eyes and her face showed itself in the
dark. She was telling me the tale of the
Night Country, a cup of whiskey in her
hand and dusty sun falling on her shoulders.

*The pieces shivered and shook. They
formed a figure. It pierced the wall of the
world.*

The figure breathed in the life of the world behind it, and blew it into the gap.

Into the Night Country. It wasn't built only on flesh and bone and blood and the tawny muscle of the heart. It was a parasite, feeding itself on the life of the world it was built in. *This* world.

I started toward the elevator, then ran back for my phone. Sophia didn't answer my call, didn't answer, didn't answer, each ring shrilling in my ear like a scream. I was stepping into my shoes, shoving my wallet into my jeans. Everything I owned smelled like sweat and smoke. I was on my way to the hall when something buzzed in my pocket.

The compass Hansa's father had given me was rattling like a phone on vibrate. When I pulled it out, the rattling stopped. I studied its face. The needle strained in one direction — behind me, due southeast — like a dog on a leash. I folded my fingers around it and made for the elevator.

Outside, I paced the streets on foot, eyes glued to the compass, praying she hadn't taken a cab. Breezes tangled around me, just me, leaving the trash and the dirt untouched. I swear I saw the ghost bride watching from the crook of a streetlamp.

The sidewalks emptied as I walked. The darkness deepened, then tipped over the dividing line, inching up toward morning. The sleepless city slept, the stars losing themselves in the whitening sky. My footsteps were muffled but I could hear my breath as clearly as if my hands were cupping my ears. I felt like I was walking through a dream, but my dreams felt realer than this.

I was on an industrial block when the needle jackknifed, swinging toward the building to my right. It was the size of a small warehouse, its face fronted with tiles of reinforced glass. It stood out against the sky like a crisp-cut Halloween decoration. More than empty, it looked abandoned. But there was a side door, a brushed metal rectangle gone lacy with rust. Someone had propped it open with a brick.

Maybe Sophia. Or whoever was waiting for her.

This piece of city felt like an underdeveloped Polaroid. Only the building was sharp. I held my breath as I opened the door a little wider, easing myself through.

There was a trick Ella had taught me, for waking up scared in the dark: stay as still as you can, letting your eyes adjust, waiting for all the hidden things to show themselves. After a few long breaths I could make out a clumsy skyline of spinny chairs. A rolled carpet and an unplugged coffee machine on a countertop. I was in some kind of office, stinking of mothballs and roach spray.

And something else. A metallic, abattoir scent that told me I had to *hurry,* had to keep going, had to find the black heart of this place.

Beside the chairs was another door. Its knob turned in my hand, letting me into a hallway, windowed on one side. The smell was stronger here and there was someone just stepping clear of a slice of light.

There then gone, but I saw them. Their shape was imprinted on my sight. Small and furtive and somehow familiar. There was something to the sighting that made my mouth go dry, made my heart leap with more than fear.

I followed them. The floor was poured concrete, spattered with mysterious stains, and my shoes moved quietly into and out of the shadows. I heard nothing, then a breath, such a perfect in and out that I knew it was deliberate. A bread crumb dropped at my feet.

I followed it. Hard to the left, into a corridor lit by a red EXIT sign. The door at the other end was just closing. I ran to wrench it open before it caught, and found myself in another office, a wire-glass window on one side looking out over the street. There was a closed door on the other end, but I didn't think whoever I was following had had time to go through it. Headlights from a passing car strafed the room, lighting all its corners.

Empty. I swore and pulled out my phone to try Sophia. Distantly, beyond the next door, I heard the generic jingle of her ringtone. Before the first ring faded, I was hurtling through the door, into a room with a ceiling as high as a gym's, pale stripes of sky falling through skylights. The smell was stronger here.

I still had the phone to my ear, listening for the next ring. When the call picked up I nearly dropped it.

"Hello?" I squeezed the phone hard. "Sophia?"

Silence. Then an intake of breath and . . . a *giggle.* That giggle burrowed right into my brain, filling it up with an electric terror. It made neon shapes in the air.

"Who's there?" I whispered.

"Scratch scratch, little mouse," they whispered back. The call clicked off. When I tried Sophia again, it went straight to voicemail.

She was close. She was with someone I *knew,* I knew that laugh and could almost place it. I would find them both, I would dig through the dark. There was nothing in front of me but shadows and faint wedges of moonlight. I opened my mouth, took a step.

A door bobbed up from empty air.

~34~

Finch thought sometimes about the things he missed.

Showers. Real coffee. Soup dumplings. New books. Opening his eyes under the serene blue roof of a chlorinated pool, seeing the wobble of the distant lights. He missed dogs. The closest thing the Hinterland had was a roving tribe of mad cats, who slipped serenely into and out of the tales and looked so knowing he'd tried a few times, quietly, to start a conversation with one of them. No dice.

Despite all that, he didn't think he really

missed life on Earth. He told himself he was glad to let it go.

But when Iolanthe's words opened a new door, and the molecules of the next world came through, he knew. When he breathed in the chemicals and metal and dead skin dust of the place that had made him, he understood he'd been telling himself another lie.

~35~

The door wasn't there, then it was. A crooked rectangle like a child's rendering, its seams all lined with light. It hung there a moment, defiant.

Then — it opened. Behind it was a wedge of chilled gray air the color of stone. Another day stood through that door. Another world. Was it the Night Country?

A woman stood in the doorway.

First she was just a shape, singed at the edges with light. Then she was a stranger stepping through, all dressed in shabby black, her pale blond hair in braids. Her eyes had the amoral shine of a cat's. If she was surprised to see me, she gave no sign of it. She was a puzzle I might've kept staring at, but there was someone else coming in behind her.

Someone dazed and thin and taller than I remembered. His eyes were wide and his arms outstretched like he was walking into cold water.

I went still as snow.

There was so much I'd remembered wrong. He was leaner than he had been in my mind. Hungrier. He *moved* like someone hungry and restless. His jeans were worn to whiteness. He'd cut off his hair.

He hadn't seen me yet. I had a little time to get my head around this. I had a few more seconds to get it right.

~36~

They were back on Earth. He knew it the way you know the shape of your body in the dark. He knew it by the specific way its gravity worked on him; he'd forgotten exactly how the air felt here, but his body remembered.

He let that air run through his fingers and felt a nameless grief pass through him. For something lost, something found. He was no stranger to nostalgia, but the feel and flavor of his abandoned world made a new kind of music in him, an endless complicated pain in his heart.

Io had stopped a few yards in front of him. She was looking at someone standing just beyond the door, the light of the last world shining full on her face.

A girl. She was petite, dressed like him: old jeans, tight T-shirt. Her hair was messy and brownish and she stood at odd attention, like she'd just received an electric shock. All that he took in at a glance. What he really saw was the way she was looking at him.

Like she knew him. Like she wanted to rush him. Hide from him. Kill him, maybe. Her gaze was so ferocious he didn't notice at first how pretty she was, and when he did it was the beginning of the next revelation. The big one.

She was older. (His heart tugged; they'd lost time, more than he'd thought.) Sun-freckled and toughened. Her face held different things, and she'd only looked at him this way once, just once: right before she turned and left him, to walk off the edge of another world.

He tasted her name on his tongue.

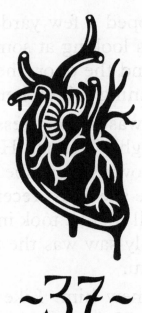

~37~

My old idea of him and the reality standing here in front of me warred for a moment then crashed, into this boy — this man — with scarred brown skin and radiant eyes and his face flickering confusion, slipping past fear, then lighting up like a thousand fireflies, soft against the dark.

"Alice," he said.

His names filled my mouth. I didn't know which one to say, and I thought if I spoke I'd cry instead. He stepped past the silent, flat-eyed stranger, coming so close I could see the dark line on his neck, where a knife had dipped in. I saw the swallow under it, the nervous pulse.

If I could talk with my fingers, I thought. If I could just touch him, *there,* where his life had almost slipped out, and *there,* the place I'd scratched when he dragged me free of my tale, and *there,* where a dream version of me had kissed him once, in a pulsing ballroom in the Hazel Wood. Each touch would be a letter. I wouldn't have to use any words. And maybe he did read my mind, just a little, because he swallowed again, and spoke.

"Did you get my letters?"

I opened my mouth, and my voice betrayed me: all my confusion and relief and fragile joy were in it. "Ellery," I said. "Finch. I got all your letters."

He smiled at me. Goofy, incandescent. He put his hands up and I knew what he wanted me to do was press my palms to his and let our fingers entwine. When I did, his folded so far over mine they nearly reached my wrists. He started laughing, and I did, too.

Laughing. It was hard to remember the last time I'd laughed over something good all the way through. But it scrubbed up against the rawest parts of me. I'd been something *else* the last time he saw me. Lost, yes. Messed up and confused. But full of hope. On my way home to Ella, love like a beam on water lighting my way. And he'd been a wanderer. Lost in his own way, but questing. He'd had a fairy tale land at his feet, and no reason to leave it.

What were we now?

"Hey," he said, catching the moment when my laugh turned south. He hesitated half a second, then pulled me in tight. It was such a *human* thing to do, it caught me by the throat. He smelled like a man who'd been on the road a good long while, with unsteady access to soap. He'd been back a minute, and already he was holding me like he knew me, like we weren't strangers at all.

He'd always had more armor than me, and less.

The woman behind him cleared her throat.

"You gonna introduce us?"

Remembering she was there made me

remember everything else. I shrugged out of Finch's arms, face hot, glad the light behind the door was fading.

"How did you find me?" I asked him.

"I didn't. We were looking for a place called — I told you about it in my letters — we're looking for something called the Night Country. I didn't know we were coming here. That you'd be right *here*." He looked at the woman behind him.

"How did this happen? Was it me? I wanted —" He turned back to me, smile so sweet and shy. "I wanted this. Did that mess up the magic?"

He didn't even look afraid. He still had the wrong idea about magic. He still thought it could be *nice*.

My stomach twisted. "This makes no sense. Finch, this can't be a coincidence. Why are we *both here*?"

Behind me, and very close, came that sugary giggle.

The joy on Finch's face lost its footing. "What was that?"

"Shh." I lifted my phone, letting the beam of its flashlight scatter the dark. I scanned the room once, twice. The third time it snagged on a face.

A pale oval, peering out of a drawn-up hood. It belonged to a child. She held one arm in front of her. Her chin was down, her eyes cast to the ground. And my insides went shivery, because I'd been wrong.

It wasn't the Trio who'd been following me. They'd never sought me out at all. The little girl I'd seen trailing me around the city was right here.

"Who are you?" I took a step toward her. "Where's Sophia?"

The child let her hood fall. Beneath it was a mass of blond hair.

She looked up.

And grinned as I finally got it, as I finally understood who I was looking at. The figure in the subway car, in Central Park, on the street. The giggle on the phone, so horribly familiar. The only creature with ice in her hands, enough to kill.

She was me. A younger me, me at age twelve. Feral and princess-haired. She wore flowered shorts and iridescent yellow jellies and a green hoodie. Her eyes were black from end to end.

"You."

"You," she echoed back, and snapped her teeth.

I took a step, heart pounding, head floating off my neck with the strangeness of it. Her mouth hung open a little and her gaze was as oily-flat as a selkie's. When we were close enough to touch, I reached out a hand. After a beat she reached back. Her fingers in mine were a curious numbness, smooth and small.

"Do you know me?"

She put one foot atop the other, balanced. "I am you."

"How do you exist?"

"How do you?"

I felt like a person pacing at a locked gate. I didn't know the words to get in. But I knew now that she was the ghost who haunted me. The one the Trio had told me to seek. The ghost of a past I once thought I could get clean of.

"Wait." Finch's voice was stricken. "That's *you*. I thought I *saved* you."

I remembered then that he'd watched me grow up. In the Hinterland, trying so hard to reach me.

"Why did you do it?" I asked her. "Are you building a night country?"

She narrowed her black eyes. "What's that?"

My head was filling up with hot sand. "You tried to kill me. On the subway. Why?"

"Nuh-uh." She was indignant. "I just wanted to meet you. Scare you. She said I couldn't let you see my face." My phone light made pinpricks in her beetle-shell eyes. "She said you'd be punished if I did."

"Who did?"

"Oh, don't play dumb."

A new voice came out of the dark. The speaker stepped into the flashlight's beam, beside little Alice. Arms folded, teeth sharp, red hair piled into a heavy topknot. There was a hunting knife in her belt. The light was in her eyes, but she seemed to see us.

"Alice," she said. "Ellery."

His name in Daphne's mouth filled my stomach with oil.

"How?" I spat.

Daphne smiled at me, jack-o'-lantern wide. "Don't you mean why?"

"I know why. I know about the Night Country. I should've known it was you. I should've known your giving-a-shit act was an act. I'm asking *how* — how are there two of me?"

Daphne put a hand on little Alice's shoulder. Alice looked at that hand like an animal debating whether it should bite.

"Silly girl," Daphne said. "There are *three* of you."

I felt Finch flinch beside me. He'd read my tale. I hadn't. "What are you talking about?"

"She was always inside you. All I had to do was ask her to come out. When you were sleeping, sweet in your bed. And your mother down the hall." Daphne bent over her knees like someone coaxing a dog to come closer. "I just talked into your ear till you tossed, till you walked into a dream you couldn't wake from, and I led her out of the deep. Alice-Three-Times, three little monsters like stair steps. The littlest one is still hiding." She gestured at my chest. "Can you feel her there? Does she burn?"

Ghost within, ghost without.

I'd thought one night that I'd seen Daphne in my room, as I was waking from a bad dream. My chest hurting like something broken. I'd been right.

"Who are you?" I took her in, the blood-and-cream beauty of her. "What *were* you?"

She flashed her awful teeth. "Wicked stepmother."

"Tell me the truth."

She let her chin rise. "I was a queen."

"No, you weren't."

She smiled. She grew a little smaller, I swore she did. "I was a maiden."

"No. You weren't."

When she shifted, the light played unkindly over her skin, sudden wrinkles by her lips.

"A crone, then."

"No," I whispered. "You weren't that, either."

"Clever, clever." Her eyes were blue. She'd always had the Spinner's eyes, and I'd looked right past them.

"You didn't have a tale, did you?"

"I had every tale," she said.

"Oh. Oh, my *god*," Finch said, half a step behind me but figuring it out now.

The Spinner smiled at him, shrugging Daphne off like a coat. Not much about her changed. Her hair was still red, her eyes as blue as they'd ever been. But the role she'd played for months was gone.

"Not a god," she said, winking at him. "And certainly not yours."

"You used her like a *weapon*. Used *me*." I looked at little Alice, and wondered if she'd minded. If killing for the Spinner made any impression on her at all.

"This is why you pulled me back in?" I asked. "Why you kept an eye on me?"

"Pulled you back in?" she said scornfully. "You never left. You were always where I could reach you. But I wanted you nearer, I wanted you scared, I wanted you to *see* the damage you could do. Back when you were just mine."

"What did you tell them to make them die for you? What did you tell Hansa?"

"I told them who I am. I told them about the Night Country, that they could help me build a new world. Was I lying?"

"They loved you. They thought you were protecting them!"

"I lit your candles," she said. "They're mine to blow out."

My voice was thick, the arm holding my phone up starting to quiver. "Where's Sophia?"

The Spinner looked past me, her Cheshire smile growing. The stranger Finch arrived with had been silent through everything, leaning against the door.

"Iolanthe," the Spinner said. "It's good to see you."

The woman inclined her head.

"Waiting on your payment, are you?"

"That's right." The stranger's voice was steady, her face honed as a blade. She wouldn't look at Finch.

"On delivery, as promised." The Spinner brought a hardback out from some-where and winged it over. "I wish you a happy homecoming."

The stranger caught the book against her chest, turned toward the door, then paused. "I am sorry," she said to Finch, still not looking. "I couldn't say no. But I kept my promise, didn't I? Here you are, back with your girl."

"You dirtbag," he said in a dead voice. "You absolute piece of shit."

The stranger shrugged. She walked back to the door they'd come from. Stepped through, closed it, and was gone.

"Where were we?" The Spinner smiled at us, pleasant and distracted. I couldn't believe I'd ever thought she was less than she was.

"A new Hinterland," I said. "That's what you're making, aren't you?"

Her laugh was scathing. She looked bleached in the light. "A new Hinterland? Just like that? You think it's so easy, to build a world? To wrestle with the dark and the light, to hang its stars and balance its moon and coax each blade of grass to grow? To fill it with pretty monsters who tell themselves stories, live their stories, *are* the stories, to make the time go and the sun rise and the heart of it hold?

"The heart of it." Her gaze clicked to Finch. "You ripped out my heart."

His face looking back at her was calm. He looked like someone who'd been waiting on bad news for a very long time, and was relieved it had finally come.

"You play a long game," he said.

"I've got nothing but time," she replied. "Nothing."

I looked between them and saw there was a chapter in their history I hadn't read.

"Tell him," she said to me. "Tell him the tale of the Night Country."

He shook his head, once. "I already know it."

"Not the neutered nursery story Iolanthe used on you like a hook," she snapped. "The tale of *my* Night Country. Of how I made the Hinterland. The very first tale I ever told."

"Where's Sophia? Tell me that."

The Spinner leaned over and said something into little Alice's ear. The girl nodded and ran out of the light. I felt sick watching her go, seeing the way she held her spindly arms out from her sides, chin tilted down, the stance familiar from every photo Ella took of me in those purgatory years between ten and thirteen.

Silence, then a heavy click. Banks of fluorescents switched on overhead, illuminating what had been hiding in the dark.

In the tale it sounded tidy as doll parts. Two hands, two feet, two eyes, a tongue. In reality it looked like a massacre. Like aftermath. The pieces were laid out in the vague outline of a body, it was true, but it looked so *sloppy,* so utterly profane. The ground bucked under my feet as I half walked, half swam toward the horror, scanning the pieces till I found what I was looking for.

The eyes. Dark gold, clipped from the optic nerves, their big-cat color unmistakable.

"Sophia." I said it like a prayer, passing a hand above them. Like I could close them, seal this last piece of her away from harm. The Spinner was the one who'd truly made Sophia deathless. Of course she was the only one who could give death back.

Finch kneeled beside me, throat clicking dryly as he tried to pull me up, pull me away. But I stayed. I saw Hansa's small foot and Genevieve's rough one, corded with scar tissue. Vega's chattering tongue, gone still. And I realized something was missing.

"My heart." I looked at the Spinner. "That's why I'm here, isn't it? So you can take my heart."

"Not exactly," she said. Then she leaped at little Alice. Roped her hair around her arm, dragged her head back, and drove the hunting knife into her chest.

~38~

My own chest exploded with pain. My head fell back, and my vision went white. Into the whiteness came something glittering. Ice: the distant ceiling of an ice cave. Then it changed, to the moving roof of a grove of trees. I blinked and it changed again: I saw the face of a crying child, in a misty wood. My tongue tasted like honey, like salt. I saw the four of us from far overhead: Finch crouching over me, and the Spinner over little Alice, hoodie peeled back, the front of her black with blood. When Finch screamed my name, I didn't know which one of us he was calling for.

Then I was back in my body, in my head, looking up at him.

"Jesus, are you okay?"

I tried to nod, but he was holding my face too tightly.

"She was a kid. She was a *kid.*" His eyes were shiny with shock. "How could she kill a kid?"

I tried to push up onto my elbows. My mouth tasted like blood and my chest felt like a crushed can but I talked as fast as I could. "She'll kill *everyone.* The Night Country is a vampire. Whatever you've been told, it kills the world it's made in. Do you understand me? If she takes Alice's heart, if she makes the Night Country, this world will fall apart. Like the Hinterland did."

"No," he said, his voice stunned and new. Like he'd just remembered something. "It won't be like that. It'll go gray. The sky, the earth, all of it. It'll be like Pompeii, like something out of a nightmare. This is your revenge, then?" He looked to where the Spinner must be. "A world for a world?"

I heard her voice from behind me. "Poetic, isn't it?"

Finch helped me sit up. I couldn't look at the boneless crumple of my younger self. The black-eyed shell of me, what I would've been if Ella hadn't stolen me away, hadn't loved me. Instead I looked at the Spinner, holding a freshly harvested heart in upraised palms, looking like a sorceress, like Circe, so packed full of malevolent magic the air around her seemed to ripple.

I leaned over and snatched up the closest piece: Hansa's foot, scraps of purple polish still clinging to its toes. I pulled my arm back, but before I could chuck it — to stall her, at least — the Spinner was running at me with the knife.

She ran it down the sunburnt line of my arm. The blade was a brute, dulled on the chamber of little Alice's chest. The Spinner dropped the heart in place with her other hand, then braceleted it around my arm and slid it over the slice, squeezing. I screamed at the rusty pain of it. Finch lunged at her, but she'd already let me go.

"And blood to bless it," she said, half shrieking it, and shook out her hands.

Drops of blood, my blood, flung themselves over the pieces. The foot I'd let fall when she cut me, the sci-fi meat of the heart. Sophia's golden eyes. Finch was talking in my ear, he was tending to my bleeding arm, but all I could hear was silence.

The silence of a turned corner. The wait between the drop and the crash. Maybe it won't work, I thought desperately. Maybe she forgot one thing, did one thing wrong.

Then the singing began. Pure tone, high and sweet and cold as a spring. It came from Vega's tongue.

I would never be able to explain it, how the air shuddered against the song. How it *unpeeled* itself, allowing something to crawl free of nothing. The tongue sang itself two rows of bright teeth. It sang itself a skull and the stacked ivory checkers of a spinal cord, the cage and cradle of ribs and pelvis. The long bones of the limbs swarmed toward severed hands and feet, one leg blooming odd and overextended to reach Hansa's foot where I'd dropped it. The busy bloody tumult of muscle and organ and tendon, so ripe I couldn't blink, couldn't breathe, then the relief of skin sliding over it like a paper window shade.

The singing stopped, but the notes still scraped against the air, arcs of hot sharp sound. I didn't think my ears would ever be empty of it. I was pressed against Finch, both of us so sweaty I couldn't tell what was him and what was me. When the body stood up we gasped in a breath together.

It was a girl. Bald-headed, its skin a calico patchwork, its eyes my dead friend's. Its heart drummed so loud we could hear it through its new-sprung skin.

It stood like a child. Back swayed, belly out, Sophia's eyes in its head a new kind of blank, washed clean of history. Finch was saying things under his breath as we stared, a stream of whispered disbelief, but I couldn't speak at all. This wasn't magic like I'd seen — the snarled labyrinth of the Hazel Wood, the unlatched cages of the Hinterland. It was older. Cruder. This magic was a blunt and wily animal, fed on horrors.

The creature began to move. First in a dizzy circle, like it was getting its bearings, bobbing on its one odd leg. Getting used to being alive, if that's what it was. Then — it began to dance.

None of us could look away: me, Finch, the Spinner. There were things so strange even she had to pay them witness. The creature's limbs swung on joints loose as baby teeth. Spectral red shoes swirled around its feet, kicking off sparks. It picked up speed, it began to whirl. Every other second it broke from its spin, making darts at the air like a hopped-up cat.

And then I got it: the creature was looking for a weakness. The air here was thinning. Lightening. *Lessening:* it was looking for the place where it might break through.

We felt the moment when it found it, when those searching fingers made a tear in the world's skin. The room's atmosphere swelled and popped with a tinny *huff.* The Spinner laughed, high and wild.

A black keyhole hung on the air. Floating, detached, I'd say *impossible* if that word hadn't been used up. The blackness spread, till it formed an archway high as a church door. The creature turned away from it, opening its mouth wide, like the boy in the fable getting ready to swallow the sea.

It took in a breath. I felt that breath beneath my ribs. All the colors I could see went flabby, watered like a cheap drink. Then it turned and exhaled all the life it had taken into that flat black doorway.

The dark woke up. A wind blew out. It smelled crackling and undone, and filled my hair with static. The patchwork girl moved more clumsily now, her purpose complete. She'd made the dark hungry; now it would feast on its own. She spun as she unraveled, gums receding, molars dropping like dice, jawbone falling after them. Ribs and intestines and tissue nibbled away by the air, till all that was left were the parts she'd been made of, falling to the floor in a harmless patter.

It was done. In the end, I hadn't stopped it. In the end, I'd barely known how to try. I could feel Finch beside me, his hand clamping a ripped-off strip of his T-shirt around the slice in my arm. I felt Ella distant from me, somewhere else in this city. I imagined her head lifting from her pillow, or from a book, if the eerie turning of the world had left her sleepless.

And I remembered another piece of the story she'd told me.

The Spinner had made the Night Country that became the Hinterland. But it hadn't become *hers* till she stepped inside it, imprinting herself on its land. I held that idea in my mind like a key. Like a blade. My mother had always worked so hard to arm me against the dark.

The Spinner moved toward the doorway, her face as soft as I'd ever seen it.

"Hello," she crooned to it. "Hello, again."

Her voice had changed. I think it was her true one. I think she might've forgotten about us entirely if we'd let her — she had her parasite, her cannibal, she'd fatten it up on New York and everything that lay beyond it, and we'd go out with a whimper. She'd gathered us here to watch her gloat, then to die with this world. That was her revenge.

Finch touched my uninjured arm.

"Don't," he said. Like there was anything left to wait for.

I spoke through gritted teeth. "We cannot let her go in there first."

The Spinner heard me and smiled. "Go ahead, then. Go on." My confusion made her smile thicken. "You're a Story, sweetheart. Potential, given form. Through that door is *pure* potential. You go in there first, it'll dissolve you like a sugar cube."

Before she was done speaking, Finch was on his feet. He was running toward the door. He trusted me that much, after everything.

She met him there, knife in hand. I saw him hold back for a crucial second, then duck away as she swiped. I followed, trying to put myself between them, pulling out my pocketknife.

Potential, given form. Fuck that. I held the knife like a killer in a slasher flick and, screaming, brought it down into her shoulder. It went in half an inch and stuck. She bared her teeth but made no sound. Finch had both hands around her wrist, holding back her hunting knife, as she drove a knee into his gut.

We grappled there on the edge of the infant world. But the dark had a mind of its own. It knew who it really wanted, among us three.

It reached for him. I know it did. With bare black arms the Night Country drew Finch into itself, and the Spinner screamed. I saw his feet touch down on the formless ground. I saw it when the place seized hold of him, the way he breathed in like a wave had just slapped him, his eyes going round as shooter marbles. Then the Night Country folded over his head.

The Spinner screamed again. She threw the hunting knife in after him, the knife in her shoulder, ripped out two fistfuls of her hair and threw that, too. She stamped her foot like Rumpelstiltskin. Then, breathing hard, she dove in after him.

Looking into the dark was like looking into black water. As unknowable. As frightening. I braced myself against the iron-laced air, and jumped.

~39~

Finch always thought he was the center of the story. Who didn't? And he was heart-broken every time he learned, again, that he wasn't. That he'd known nothing, or all the wrong things, all along.

He could've stayed on his knees listing his regrets as the Spinner swallowed the world, or he could respond to that note in Alice's voice, that said all hope wasn't gone, and made her words work on him like an incantation. *We cannot let her go in there first.*

So he'd run headlong toward an actual

black hole, the scariest thing he'd ever seen or imagined. It wasn't long, between deciding to do it and falling in, the Spinner screaming after him and Alice crying out and the jellied black air folding him up. But time slowed down for him. There was still so much he wanted to consider.

That Iolanthe had betrayed him. That Alice had gotten his letters. That his time on Earth was nothing but a layover. He couldn't actually think about the world ending. It should go in fire or flood or supervirus. Not like this: its life sucked out like soda pop.

Then he went into the Night Country and couldn't think about anything at all.

He was himself, falling through. Then he was — *bigger.* He landed on all fours in a soft black nothing, and his sense of himself expanded in all directions. He was water flowing into a basin. He filled the endless dark — he was it, it was him — until a stray thought floated by like a message in a bottle. He seized it.

I'm so thirsty. The thought came with words, and with the words came the water: his feet were wet, he was standing in a river. He could see it shining silver, then it was gone; his terror dried it up.

Terror and elation: he'd *done* that, spun something out of the Night Country's fertile air. He tried to hold reason around himself like a slicker, but the insidious air was the rain that got in, running into his nose and eyes and open mouth, as dim and drugged as the water of Lethe.

A teacup, he thought, and held it. Thin-sided, pink and gold, filled with an inch of milky tea. The last time he'd seen it was on the table of his mom's apartment, years ago, before she'd died but after the divorce.

"Coffee," he whispered, and the cup's contents changed.

Mom? he thought, inside his mind, but without conviction. She didn't appear in the dark.

He was glad. Then he shuddered, as the weight of this settled over him.

A new-struck world, his for the making. This was what Alice meant when she said they couldn't let the Spinner in first — they couldn't let her have a whole new canvas on which to paint her horrors.

What if she was wrong? The thought came crooked and cowardly. But what if it *should* have been the Spinner here, weaving reason out of the dark? He pictured all that she'd made out of nothing: the ice caves of the Hinterland, its deep woods and articulate stars. A secret part of him wished for them, and their ghosts rose up, spectral and shimmering, then drifted away.

The Spinner was a maker of worlds.

He was a boy in the dark with a teacup.

No. He fell to his knees. He dug his fingers into the ground, which was nothing before but became dirt under his nails as he wished for it. *Daffodil,* he thought. *Daisy, clematis, rose.* They grew from his dirty palms, petals raining from his hands and vines twining up his arms.

But he lost his words for the flowers, looking at them. They were red and yellow and blushing and white, and he couldn't put names to their faces. That terrified him enough that he clamped down on his mind, *don't think don't think,* and of course that made him think of

Blacktop. And a basketball drumming

416

A yellow dog with a red collar

A table with three plates on it, salmon and rice

His father looking at the newspaper, shaking his head

All of it but his father came and went in the dark. After, he felt rubbery, wrung out. Like he used to feel just before sundown on Yom Kippur, watching out the window as the sun slipped below the tree line of Central Park.

(Trees grew up in the air around him, then blew away into molecules.)

"No," he said. *"No, no, no."* Everything he dreamed up siphoned more life from the world he'd left behind. What had just died so his visions could take stunted shape? He pictured the steps of the Met emptied out, gone pale as ash. The sun bleached out like a stain, the streets of his city preserved below dead skies like insects under glass.

The city. His abandoned city, now lost to him forever. In dreams he'd walked through Manhattan with his mother again. Paged through bookstores with Alice. Memories and longings swelled up, and the Night Country wanted them. It was *hungry* for them.

He wasn't strong enough to deny it.

The city flowed from him. Streetlights, skyline, cherry blossoms and gutters and the sound of a street performer's violin. Benches and buses and stolen wine on a rooftop. Streets of pitted blacktop lined with trees and ice cream trucks and stars you could barely see. An afternoon in summer so still the clouds looked like paint on blue enamel, and cast shadows on sunbathers in the park.

The memories rushed out of him on the back of a sweeping wind. It was cold and had a thousand hands and they reached into every corner. It's a fearsome thing, to make a world. He was unmade in its making. The theft leached the black from his hair and the bend from his bones.

It might've stolen the bones, too, before it was through. But two figures came barreling out of the dark.

~40~

In her rage the Spinner ran like an animal, loping and low. Without her, I wouldn't know where to find Finch. Already the Night Country had carried him away from the door.

I chased her, forward and on. Time was elastic, it stretched and contracted. I would've killed for a streetlamp, a star. If I lost her, I'd be *lost,* completely. So I ran through the sandy pain of a stitch in my side, and the distinctive terror of running through the nothing space of an unmade world. Until finally something broke the

Night Country's long, formless plain: Finch. Still too far off. I couldn't go any faster and she'd almost reached him when something sprang up from the dark.

Trees. Birches elms sycamores, saplings delicate as wrists. The Spinner tried to stop herself but couldn't, reeling into the place their trunks had been — they were already gone. Stars blinked on like track lighting, then off again. We both stopped, waiting to see what the dark would spit out next.

A golden retriever burst from the air, ran a sloppy circle and vanished. A set table, a newspaper fluttering its pages. There was a pause, darkness bleeding back into the cracks the phantoms had made. I could hear her breathing. Then:

A city. Not all at once, but piece by piece. A yellow cab. A trashcan. A street cart and a cherry blossom tree and a building traced in mist and silver, rising into clouds the color of steamed milk. In a space the size of a single block, blistering the air, the city flashed and faded.

In the middle of it all, Finch kneeled with his head bent down, fingers dug into dirt, flower vines winding from his wrists to his shoulders. His hair was shot through with white, and when he lifted his chin, my heart folded over.

He looked like someone had stirred gray paint into his skin. Tendons stood out at his temples, his lips were scored. His eyes were losing their light.

"Finch," I said, my voice as cracked as the teacup he held in one hand, squeezed into shards. Blood ran through his fingers.

"It'll kill him." The Spinner's voice was bitter as walnut skin, relentless. "It'll be a hard death. He'll be skinned away from himself piece by piece. A new world is a void, it's a *hunger*. I withstood it — I shaped my world, poured into it all the things I could afford to lose. He doesn't know how. It'll hollow him out like an egg."

Finch heard her. His chin snapped up. All the swarming, erratic pieces of his city scattered and faded, till nothing was left but me and him and her and the velvety grip of the dark. When he spoke, his words laid themselves against the air.

"Once upon a time.

"Once upon a time there was a monster. She called herself a spinner, and she was. But she destroyed things, too. She made a world and called it hers, but didn't understand it when the people she filled it with wanted more. More than blood and death and a story they couldn't change." He looked at her. "She gave them all the worst parts of being human and none of the things that made it worth it."

The Spinner stood perfectly still, watching him through hooded eyes.

"So a hero came to the world she'd made."

She laughed. I did, too, but mine came soft and surprised.

"The hero unraveled a corner of her world, and the whole thing fell to pieces."

"It won't work," she said, her voice wound through with warning.

"So she made another," he continued, dogged, his eyes desperate points in his weary face. He still gripped the ground. "She did terrible things to make it, but in the end it wasn't hers. It pledged itself to

422

the hero instead. And the world turned on her."

Nothing happened. I could feel all three of us waiting, but the dark stayed dark.

"You'll die," said the Spinner. "You'll die killing the world that made you. Oh, this is *better* than I planned."

"The world found out her secrets," he whispered. "It showed her as she really was. It showed her to the light."

A light snapped on. Not a sun or a lamp but something in between, a molten ball of smokeless fire. By its illumination, the Spinner changed. Her hair shook out in yellow waves, her skin went the color of amber. She looked like *me*, once upon a time. Like a fairy-tale princess.

But her eyes. Still a frozen blue, they held the weight of centuries in them. Her shell was young, but the eyes peering out of it told the truth. She felt her face, fingers running over its contours. I could hear her thoughts clicking like beads.

Under her hands, her features solidified, strengthened. She looked older now, Ella's age. Then older still, grown and beautiful, lines at the eyes.

"Oh," she said. For the first and only time, I saw her look surprised.

Her skin loosened. It dropped at the chin and creased at the mouth. Those frightening eyes faded, wrinkled at the corners, and receded into seamed pockets, clouded over with a milky film.

"Stop it," she said. Her voice was an old woman's, but commanding. *"Stop it now."*

Her bones warped and contracted, settling into arthritic curves. Her voice creaked like a stair. "If I die, my children go with me. If you kill this body, you're killing them, too. You're killing *Alice.*"

A beat passed.

"Wait," he said. He didn't lift his head.

The world waited. The Spinner didn't die, she stood there in stasis. But I ran.

His hair was white all the way through, and I ran to him. Skidded to a stop in his patch of dirt. Before I could reach for him, a fence grew up between us, glittering with barbed wire.

"Don't touch me," he said, ragged. "I might kill you. I might *dissolve* you. You're a Story. I'm a Spinner."

I held on to my own arms. "Okay," I said. "It's okay." Words were meaningless. They were all I could give him.

"Alice," he said. He'd always liked saying my name. "What should I do?"

I looked at the slope of his shoulders and the soft of his mouth and the faded crackle of his beautiful eyes. "You should finish the story."

The Spinner waited, vision iced over with cataracts. She didn't beg.

"A cage," he said, in his roughed-up voice. "The hero captured the monster, and he caged her. She was so dangerous he used a whole world to hold it. The cage had golden bars, and in it the monster slept. She slept for an eternity. She didn't hurt anyone, and she dreamed of fairy tales."

The cage closed her in like a nightingale. The Spinner had no final words. She shuffled forward half a step, then lay down. She didn't move again.

Finch let out a breath. The fence between us dissolved, the light going out with an audible *click*. And he fell onto his side.

When I touched him I didn't die, or dissolve. His breath came shallow as varnish and his skin looked yellowed in the glow of the bars. I worked by their light, peeling his fingers back from the broken china, picking out the shards and wiping the blood away. My own arm had stopped bleeding, now it just hurt. His eyes were half closed and his breath came at odd intervals.

"Finch." He didn't answer.

He could die here. He could die here in the dark, and I would be all alone.

So I let myself fall, slowly. I let my head drift to his shoulder and closed my eyes.

"I loved your letters," I told him. "I'm bad at talking. I'm bad at just about everything. But I loved your letters. I wrote back to you, in my head. I've told you so much, I can't even remember what I've really said and what you don't know yet."

All my heart was in my words. My bruised, inhuman heart.

"Did you feel it?" I whispered. "Did you hear it, when I talked to you?"

A pause, then his cheek brushed over my hair as he shook his head.

"That's okay. I can tell you everything

again. But we need to . . . we need to stand up and find the door. Before . . ."

Before there was nothing left on the other side to find.

"Okay." I felt his breath as he said it.

Slowly I tilted my chin up. Too shy to look at him till the last moment.

His eyes weren't soft anymore. They were focused and steady and they held me in their light. In them I could see all the Finches I had known. The fanboy and the wanderer and the traitor and the hero. He said my name again, and raised his hands to cup my face.

A sudden breeze slid over my neck. I reached up and felt the bare length of it, and the shorn ends of my hair.

My body tingled like a bumped funny bone. My hair was shorter, cut right up to my skull, like it was when I'd met him. When I looked down I was wearing tight black jeans with holes over the knees. A blue striped shirt. Things I wore when I was seventeen.

Finch snatched his hands away. "*Shit.* I'm sorry. I don't know what I'm doing, I don't know how it works."

427

"It's okay," I said again, numbly. Lying through my teeth, through the horror of being remade by him. Of being reminded that here, I was nothing but Story stuff.

"No, it's not. I'm not — I don't want to change you, I just . . ."

"*Stop,*" I said, with more force. "Let's find the door."

"I'm the Spinner." He said it like he was sorry. "This is my world. I can *make* the door."

He didn't look strong enough to make anything, but he stood up slowly, holding his hands out like a conductor.

The door he made was plain, unpainted wood. It wasn't there, then it was. We stared at it, and we looked back to where the Spinner lay in her cage. She slept on.

Finch reached for my hand, before remembering. "Hold on to my shirt," he said.

I grabbed him by the T-shirt, and hooked a finger through the frayed loop of his jeans. That was how we walked out of that world.

~41~

We stepped through into cold and the smell of dust and a flare of white light I tried to blink away, before realizing it wasn't light, it was color. The warehouse wasn't the place we'd left, fluorescent-lit and enunciated. It was smudged out, a pale ruin. We stepped over a clatter of little bones: all that was left of the creature the Spinner had made, who'd scratched at the Night Country door and let us in.

"How far do you think it goes?" His voice was as wrung-out as the room.

My phone was dead in my pocket. I wrapped my hand around it anyway. "I don't know."

"I did this," Finch said. He spun in place slowly. *"I did this."*

"Don't you dare. Anything that's left, it's because of you. You did *that*."

His bones pressed too close to the surface of his skin. Both of us were filthy, we stank of blood. I reached up and peeled away a petal that had stuck to his cheek, and thought of the letter he'd sent in the heart of a flower.

"You need to end it. You need to close the door."

"End it?"

He looked so confused my heart spiked. "What's wrong? Don't you think you can? Do you not know how?"

"I know how to do it," he said, sharp and certain. "I can *feel* how to do it. But . . . you heard what the Spinner said."

The Spinner. Daphne. The monster and the woman who never existed. They blurred in my mind, a double image. "She said a lot of things."

"You know what I'm talking about. If I end it — if I kill the world, and the Spinner in it — what happens to you?"

Not just me, but all of us. If the Spinner died along with Finch's world, would her children really go with her? My throat ached thinking of Sophia, already gone.

"We know she's a liar," I said.

"I don't think she was lying about that. And what if it's too late anyway? What if I've already made too much? And I close the door and you die, too, and it's just me, all alone here, like some shitty episode of *The Twilight Zone*?"

His rising panic made me calmer. I thought of the silver tracings of his city, the soil and flowers and the sizzling golden cage. I weighed it against the entirety of this world.

I thought of Ella. I closed my eyes and reached for her, feeling for that thread that connected us. I couldn't feel it, but that didn't mean it was gone. I though it just meant we were untwining, growing into two distinct people, in the way that moms and daughters do. Maybe that was the most human thing that could happen to me.

"I don't think it's too late," I told him. "It's not too late."

"What if we just leave it? For now. Go out, see how far this spreads. Then we decide what to do."

"Finch," I said quietly.

"You can't make me," he said, just as quiet. "You can't ask me to do this. What'll it be like, if you die? How will you go? Do you melt? Disintegrate? *Fuck.* Why am I saying this to you?"

He straightened, like something had struck him. "I bet there's another world we could go to. Iolanthe" — his face flashed something complex — "Iolanthe showed me. There are whole shelves of worlds, too many to fit in a letter. Alice, you wouldn't believe the things I've seen."

"Okay," I said. "Let's go to another world."

His eyes widened, before he understood. I reached for him. I felt the scars over his knuckles and wondered about their stories. We looked at each other over our clasped hands, and the words we didn't say were *hello,* and *goodbye,* and a love song with no words to it.

Maybe in another world they spoke a language you could sing it in. Maybe I could find it. Alone, with Ella, with Finch. Maybe I'd stay right here, and live. Maybe I'd unwind altogether, dissipate into strands of story stuff, unpack myself like a Roman candle glittering with every last thing my mother had ever done for me, and the brown eyes of a boy who walked worlds, and the fast-working fingers of the creature who'd shaped me, so arrogant she'd nearly made herself a god.

Finch pressed his lips to my hands, one then the other. He looked at me and I remembered you could slice a moment into a million million stories, a million ways it could go. I figured this could be my very last page.

And it was the way his chest rose and fell. The shift of his Adam's apple beneath the scar on his throat. I had the weirdest feeling like I was swimming, held weightless by a bubble of enchanted air. I leaned closer and it was like stepping, one more time, into the winds of another world. When I pressed my lips to the old scar over his throat I realized how cold I must've been, how warm he was by contrast. He breathed out and swallowed hard under my lips and it was

it was

My mind was never quiet. It was always full of words, always teeming with them, often the wrong ones and never silent even when I slept.

But when I pressed my lips to Ellery Finch's throat and felt his hand come up to cup my neck, to tangle in my hair, all the words fell away. And when I moved my mouth up to his, my mind was finally quiet.

I don't know how long we held each other. But I know the moment came when we let go. When he moved away from me, toward the door to the Night Country. All that impossible possibility. All that endless, devouring want. On this side the door looked waterlogged. I watched him press his hands to it, and closed my eyes.

I didn't think about dying. I couldn't think about how I might be leaving Ella behind. I dreamed instead of another world. A place that could reach out and catch the people I loved. The broken and the frail of them. The solid and the already gone.

I heard Finch curse, then a distant, submarine howling, and the creak of wood below his palms. I squeezed my eyes tighter.

There was a world where this could work. There was a world where all of it fell into place. There was a world. There was a world. There was a world.

~42~

On a cool, unnaturally still night in June, a piece of sky over Manhattan went white. What happened beneath it was stranger.

There was a circle of city — a true circle, like the eye of god had cast itself over a patch of about twelve city blocks — where a plague struck.

Birds fell from the sky, dead insects littered the ground like shotgun casings. Cars idled and ran down, or crashed, or hunkered down in rows along the sidewalks, eaten away with a powdery, pale kind of rust. Buildings within the plague site grew scoured and worn.

And the people within the circle fell asleep. In restaurants and houses and smashed-up cars. In bathrooms and cross-walks, across curbs and on sidewalks. For a day and a night, the crisis site spread like an inkblot and police barriers were put up then moved back, and people in hazmat suits waded around unconscious bodies like astronauts, till they, too, succumbed to the sleeping.

The sleepers dreamed of the soft black velvet of an unmade world. In their dreams they filled that world with the things they wished for and the things they feared, and in some heads you couldn't tell which was which. Some woke up screaming, and some were followed out of their dreams by longing, a silent gray shadow that would walk with them to the end of their days.

Parts of the borough were evacuated. A national emergency was called. Schools closed and flights were rerouted and the bridges all ran one way, clogged up with people trying to get out. The subway, I heard, was an absolute shitshow.

I didn't disappear when Ellery Finch killed off his night country. I didn't disintegrate or burn into ash. His world didn't die screaming, or in flames. After all the blood and dismemberment, the death and the waste, it whined and rolled over beneath his hands. It winked out.

The door did, at least. I had to trust him when he told me the world was gone.

I'd opened my eyes and found Finch standing in front of me, looking at me like I was a door, too. The kind he wanted to walk through.

Hand in hand, we'd made our way out into the city, to see how far the damage spread. We found a world rendered in gray scale, littered with sleepers. Near its edges were silent police cars whirling their carnival lights, officers slumped inside them. Beyond that, a press of camera crews and bystanders, too thick to walk through without being caught.

We stole a car — borrowed it. Its driver-side door was open, the keys still in the ignition. We drove it slowly through the crowd, who scrambled away from us like the car was infected, too. It took some tricky driving to get clear of the ones who tried to follow us. I wanted to take it all the way to Brooklyn, but Finch argued that overstretched the definition of *borrowed*.

My phone didn't work, neither of us had a watch, and we couldn't tell if it was dusk or dawn. The sidewalks were full, the city ground down to observe the arrival of some strange disaster. We couldn't get a cab to stop for us, didn't dare try the train. Later we learned more than twenty-four hours had passed while we were in the Night Country. The sun was rising over an altered world as we walked together over the bridge.

We didn't understood yet how big it all was. That even if we'd had a working phone between us, cell service was out around the city. We walked all the way home, Finch so weak by the end I worried I'd have to carry him. The keys still in my pocket were a miracle, but the apartment was empty when I let us in.

It was hours before she came home. Finch ate the ice cream from the freezer and all the pasta we had in the cabinet, with butter and pepper and Parmesan. I brewed him cups of coffee and watched him run his eyes over the surfaces of all the things he must've thought he'd never see again. We played every Beatles album we had. We took showers one at a time and stared at each other when we thought we might not get caught and it wasn't till I was in clean clothes and he was in a towel and Ella's biggest, oldest T-shirt that we kissed again, in the dark of the hall, because it's harder to be brave when you're not facing down the end of the world.

Her purse was gone, and her phone and her keys. That told me she'd gone out, that she'd be back, and I was too exhausted to believe anything else. I felt her imprint on the space, and I felt Sophia's, too. Finch didn't ask why I ducked my head out to check the fire escape, but he opened his arms when he saw I'd started to cry.

He let himself sleep, finally. I took the cushions off so we could both fit on the couch, Sam Cooke playing low and the pale sun dropping. All day we'd heard sirens come and go, like the whole city couldn't settle, but now it was quiet at last, that incomplete, city kind of quiet.

I was drowsing off, too, when she came in like a hurricane, feet pounding up the stairs and key a panicked jangle in the lock, because she'd seen the lights on from the street.

I didn't tell her much right then. Ella knew — she *knew* what had happened had something to do with me, and the Hinterland, and the hunch I'd been chasing. She'd been running around town looking for me, for other ex-Stories, anyone who could help her track me down.

She never found them. Neither did I. Whether they were lying low after what happened at the party, or had gotten wind of what Daphne really was and skipped town, or whether it was something else completely, they were unfindable. The hotel when I visited it a few days later was a ghost town, the lobby empty and the halls quiet. Half the keys were still behind the desk; Finch and I tried a few of the rooms, just to see. But the dust was already gathering. The whole place had a whiff of the condemned. And I wondered. What had really become of them, what manner of gone they were.

But first. There, in our apartment, hours after the cataclysm. Ella rushed me, so fierce I really thought she'd slap me this time, but she just pulled me in. Then she saw Finch, dead to the world, and pressed a hand to her mouth. I remembered then that I'd told her nothing about his letters.

"That's him, isn't it? That's the boy who saved you."

In the Hinterland, she meant. From my story. I didn't know how to tell her everything he'd done, everything he'd saved. I just kissed her cheek, and reminded her.

"You saved me first."

They liked each other. Once he'd woken up bleary-eyed and blinking, to the smell of the microwave burritos I'd run to the corner for. Of course they did. They had some very weird shit in common, and Finch was smart enough not to mention her mother.

Two days later I drove him to the Upper East Side. The city was a sluggish blend of empty and overrun, with an apocalyptic, carnival feel. We'd coast for a mile, treating red lights like stop signs, then spend twenty minutes crawling down a single block.

I sat on the hood of the car while he went up to see his dad. He was gone one hour, two. I jogged a couple of blocks to find a sandwich. After the third hour, I became paranoid: that his dad would try to keep him. Against his will, away from me. But when he finally came out, his father came with him. The man looked smaller than I'd imagined. Gray hair, shoulders bowed, hands gripping the back of his son's shirt as he held him. They held each other long enough that I knew to look away.

When Finch got to the car, he'd been crying. He still was, a little, and didn't try to hide it.

He still hasn't told me what they talked about, but he knows I'll listen if he does.

He did tell me about Iolanthe, the blood door, the string of worlds they walked through. That the air in Death's kingdom tastes like fennel seeds and somewhere there's a library in a dead land whose shelves are lined with doors. I told him about Sophia and Daphne and the Hinterland meetings. How his letters came to me, one by one. He laughed till he cried when I told him about the time a squirrel got into Edgar's bookshop, and Edgar went into battle with a broomstick and an atlas belted over his chest. We were sitting by the fountain at Grand Army Plaza, watching water refract itself over all the stone merfolk, when I told him about running into Janet and Ingrid in Manhattan so many months ago. How Janet had told me about his adventures, and I thought I'd never see him again.

"They were tourists," I told him. "World-hopping with their magical passports and their money belts."

"We could do that," he said offhandedly. When I looked at him, he was staring at a laughing merman.

"Do what?"

"Travel. We could look for them, even. I'm going to see them again." It was a little prayer, I think, spoken like a certainty.

I thought about it. Thought about my mother talking about getting a degree at last. Paging through those college catalogs still, but dreaming now for herself. I considered the way her dreams for me took different shapes, and how one of them might look like this: back on the road with someone else who knew me. *Knew* me. Who could love me, maybe, if I stuck around long enough to let him.

His palm was going sweaty on mine.

"Where do you want to go?"

"I mean. Montreal? LA? This world I went to that's basically one big garden, where everything's edible but it all gives you really weird dreams?" He looked at me. "Or we could just go to New Jersey. Eat pizza."

"That sounds good," I told him.

"Which part?"

"The part where you're with me."

Falling for someone makes you say shit that would've made you vomit, back before you were toast.

It's true that sometimes I think about the third Alice, the one the Spinner claimed I carry inside me. If I'm still here, she must be, too. And I wonder, again, *how* I'm still here. Whether it's by the grace of the slumbering Spinner or whether being loved by people who actually belong in this world made all the difference. Maybe Finch did something wrong when he ended his world. Or he did something right, and kept it a secret. If the Spinner's still alive somewhere, I hope she's sleeping in her golden cage. Hurting no one. Dreaming of fairy tales. And if she's gotten out, remade herself, I hope she doesn't come looking for us.

I don't think she will. We're something formidable now. I'm an ex-Story, the girl who got away. He's a Spinner who survived the rise and fall of his world. We're both survivors, the two of us. We're wanderers. We could make a home in any world.

ACKNOWLEDGMENTS

Hats off to the usual suspects: Faye Bender, my indispensable agent; and Sarah Barley, my tireless editor. Sarah, this book would be a blob floating in space without your patience, your faith in the story, and most of all your questions, which never failed to unlock doors I didn't know were there. To the whole Flatiron team, my eternal gratitude for the care you've taken with this book and its weird sister (or maybe this book is the weird sister). The Hinterland and I couldn't have found a better home.

Thank you also to two intimidatingly brilliant authors who helped make this book better: Emma Chastain, for your sharp, life-saving story notes; and Emily X. R. Pan, for turning your gimlet eye on the so-close draft.

Second books are hard, I've heard. Wouldn't know. (Hahahahaha!) Thank you, thank you to *all* those who generously shared their advice, a listening ear, and most of all their own stories of surviving the trials of the second book. You will go unnamed here, but you know who you are. Thank you also to Tara Sonin, for offering emotional text support; and to Josh Perilo, for patiently listening to a whoooole lot of angsting. Stephanie Garber, thank you for being a lighthouse of kindness. Bill Tipper, thank you for your practical support and understanding.

Thank you to my parents, my first readers and the best unpaid street team I could ever ask for. Thank you to Michael, for too many things to write down here without getting hot eye. And Miles, my Miles. Thank you.

ABOUT THE AUTHOR

Melissa Albert is the *New York Times* bestselling author of *The Hazel Wood*. She was the founding editor of the *Barnes & Noble Teen Blog* and has written for publications including *McSweeney's, Time Out Chicago,* and MTV. Melissa lives in Brooklyn with her family. *The Night Country* is her second novel.

The employees of Thorndike Press hope you have enjoyed this Large Print book. All our Thorndike, Wheeler, and Kennebec Large Print titles are designed for easy reading, and all our books are made to last. Other Thorndike Press Large Print books are available at your library, through selected bookstores, or directly from us.

For information about titles, please call:
(800) 223-1244

or visit our website at:
http://gale.cengage.com/thorndike

To share your comments, please write:
Publisher
Thorndike Press
10 Water St., Suite 310
Waterville, ME 04901